Jana Rieger

A COURSE IN DECEPTION

Tellwell Talent

www.tellwell.ca

ISBN

978-1-77302-530-8 (Paperback)

978-1-77302-529-2 (eBook)

Dedication:

For my loving mother, Rose, who was never without
a book by her side, a prayer in her heart, and a miracle
just around the corner.

Dear Brad,
May the truth always
find you at UA South!
Jana

A Course In Deception

Chapter 1

THE PHONE CALL

Two words, *DONT WALK*, flashed in red. It was one of those moments. Break the law or be late? I teetered on the curb before coming to a full stop. Too many rules already had been broken. I backed up out of the hot July sun, into the shade cast by a high rise, and caught my breath. In through the nose, out through the mouth. Ignore the research ethics building across the street. It's just concrete and glass. I closed my eyes and focused on my breathing. In through the nose, down to the solar plexus. When I peeked to check the traffic light, the ethics building was still looming. So were purple storm clouds in the distance. I squeezed my eyes shut. In through the nose, and – ping – down to the ringing phone in my pocket. There was no hello. Just Anbu's voice, an octave higher than usual. On the road beside me, the diesel clatter of an Edmonton city bus was drowning out Anbu's voice.

The light turned green. *WALK*.

I pressed the phone against my ear and asked Anbu to repeat while I stepped off the curb. He shouted, but the pressure burst from the bus's air brakes obscured his message. The last thing I heard was, well, I'm not sure what it was. The fact that I couldn't understand what seemed to be a simple message had nothing to do with Anbu's South Indian heritage. He was educated in British Schools and spoke the Queen's English. Even in light of that, the only words I could make out were 'save the rays'. Or maybe it was 'say a raise'. Whatever it was, I had to know. I asked him to repeat.

Static.

"Hello? Bu? You there?"

Silence.

I'd lost him.

The entrance doors of the ethics building slid open to let me step inside. I thought for a moment of Jonah in the whale's belly. I, too, needed to calm the storm that had risen around me. I dialed Anbu's cell and dashed up the stairs to the second floor. He should've been going into the meeting with me instead of driving from Edmonton to that conference in Calgary. Never mind the fact that his car was held together by duct tape and, earlier in the morning, there'd been a tornado watch issued for the province. Even a strong gust of wind would surely rip the bumpers from that car. Then all four doors would fall off, the tires would go rolling, and Anbu would be sitting there with only the steering wheel in his hands.

At the top of the stairs, all I got was his voice

recording saying that he was sorry to have missed my call, that I should leave a message. The beep to do so came just as I got to the reception area.

"Text me," I said and hung up.

Before I could say anything, the woman behind the reception desk stood and said, "Right this way, Dr. Smith. They've been waiting for you."

Dr. William Clement, the chair of the animal welfare committee, was sitting at the head of the table. In front of him, two file folders thick with accusations against me. He didn't look up when I entered the room. Drs Luke Hesuvius and Jerome Schlemmer, two of my colleagues from the sleep clinic, were seated on either side of him. Luke smiled and winked. Schlemmer, being Schlemmer, sat and scowled.

I took my place at the table. William lowered his head into his hands and sighed. His scalp shone through his thin grey hair. Was he ever going to acknowledge my presence?

The air conditioner shut off with a bang. The room was dead silent.

Schlemmer looked at his watch. "Can we get on with this?"

William leaned back in his chair and ran his hands down his face. Trying to close the curtain on the scene, perhaps. There would be hell to pay if anyone from *CAFÉ*, the *Citizens for Animal Freedom and Ethics*, ever found out about this.

"So, let me get this right." William looked at Schlemmer, the most senior of all of us. "You were trying to fatten your rats by force feeding."

Schlemmer pointed to me and said, "Mackenzie's rats."

William glared at him. "Are you saying you have nothing to do with this?"

Schlemmer sat plumb straight in his chair. "That's exactly what I'm saying."

"Well perhaps you could explain to me. Because there are so many layers in these files, I can't see straight."

"Luke and I run the clinic," Schlemmer said. "We don't babysit rodents."

Luke smiled and leaned forward. "Let me elaborate." He waited for William to look at him instead of Schlemmer. "Jerome and I started the sleep clinic." Luke said, still smiling. "We do clinical research. With patients. Mackenzie joined us to extend that. She's our animal branch. Unfortunately, Jerome and I are fairly uninformed when it comes to animals, but we certainly support Mackenzie's work."

"Yes." William nodded and mirrored Luke's smile. It wasn't sincere, though. "Your names are certainly on this ethics proposal. An animal ethics proposal."

"You know administrative structures around here," Luke smiled. "It was politically necessary."

William looked to me. Finally. "Do tell your version of the story, Mackenzie."

My version was fairly simple. There's a relationship between obesity and sleep apnea. I wanted to understand it better. We were force feeding rats a mixture of oil, dairy, and starch. A diet any rat would dream of. They didn't care how it got in there. All they knew was that they had a full warm belly. And all they had to do was open their mouth. If I were a rat, I'd be pretty happy about that.

"And, somehow," William said, "the tube was fed through their mouth and into their lungs, instead of their stomach."

"Yes."

"So, basically, they were drowned in food."

Drowned. That sounded so harsh. Did he really need to put it that way? We'd done hundreds of these feeds, always with the utmost care, and never with a problem. Something went wrong, though. The independent report of their deaths said they died of 'aspiration and eventual asphyxiation from a food substance'. So, what could I do? The evidence would suggest that the tube went down the wrong hole. Couldn't deny that.

"You're admitting, then," William said, "that you or your staff – outside of your colleagues here, of course – were incompetent?"

My phone vibrated. A text message had arrived. I wanted to look, but William was waiting for an answer. My only saving grace was to point out that Anbu's documentation in the lab book proved all four rats were fine, even two hours after their last feed. I reminded everyone that, if the tube really did go down the wrong hole, the rats would've been in distress immediately.

"Well, then," William said, "how do you explain their deaths?"

My phone vibrated again. I slid it out of my pocket and glanced down. It was my husband, Steven, asking if we needed eggs.

"Something more pressing?" William asked.

"No, of course not." I slipped the phone back into

my pocket. Their deaths. I'd been over and over it, in my head and with Anbu. I'd tossed and turned at night for the past month trying to figure it out. I thought of it when I ate my bran flakes in the morning. I thought of it when I wiped off my mascara at night. I even thought of it when Steven stood at the end of the bed, naked, and flexed his muscles.

"I'm sorry," I said, "but, there's no good explanation."

"You're going to have to do better than that," William said. "If there's nowhere to point a finger, it'll be pointing at you."

"Why Mackenzie?" Luke interjected. "She wasn't the only one working with the rats."

"You suggesting Anbu was responsible?" William asked.

Before Luke could say anything, Schlemmer jumped in. He said how conscientious and thorough Anbu was in everything he did. I nodded. Reluctantly. Not because I disagreed. Anbu was the best research associate I'd ever had. It just felt wrong to agree with Schlemmer.

"Here's the problem," William said, "an entry in a lab book is weak evidence."

"It's all we have," I said.

"Nothing more objective?" William asked.

"No."

"No video evidence?"

"The only video camera we have is on the main lab door. Not on the rats."

"Look," Luke said, "Mackenzie did everything by the book."

Schlemmer shook his head. "That won't help when

CAFÉ gets wind of this." He leaned back and mumbled, "Can't believe my name is on the ethics application."

"You were happy to have it there when you thought it'd be good for you," I said.

"Listen," Luke said, "Mackenzie had a spotless record. William, you even said so, before she got here."

My phone buzzed again. I slipped it out of my pocket and tried to look down without moving my head. A text had arrived from 888-888-8888. *'We know about your rats. Love CAFÉ'.*

Shit.

"Doesn't matter," William said. "We need an explanation."

I stuffed the phone back in my pocket. "I don't have one. However, I can tell you that I won't force feed. Ever again."

William laughed. "Well you're right about one thing. You will *never* force feed again. I had four people review this case. Two recommended shutting down your lab."

"But this —"

"Two were a bit more lenient." William's eyes pierced into me. "I get the deciding vote."

"Hold on," Luke said. "Mackenzie's research is vital. Shutting it down because a few rats died would be a mistake."

Schlemmer slapped his hand down on the table. "Neglecting our reputation would be a mistake. We sure as hell don't need to be on the receiving end of *CAFÉ*. Just because of some choking rodents."

"*CAFÉ* has no way of knowing," Luke said.

A sting ripped through my chest, down to my gut.

"Let's focus on the facts," Luke said. "Anbu was the one responsible for feeding the rats. Why isn't he here?"

Luke knew exactly why Anbu wasn't there. Luke was, after all, the one who insisted that Anbu go to the conference in Calgary that morning. Whatever Luke was up to, I'd learned long ago not to question. He always set up situations beautifully so that people said and did things he desired without it dawning on them until months or even years later.

William looked at me. "Well?"

"Let me check my email. Anbu was supposed to send a document for today's meeting."

The download indicator on my phone swirled, round and round.

"Anything?" Luke asked.

I shook my head.

Schlemmer mumbled something about a waste of time at the same moment that a flash of lightning turned the walls blue.

My email notification finally chimed and six messages downloaded, but not one was from Anbu. "Sorry. Nothing."

Thunder shook the room.

"So, what you are all telling me," William said as hail pellets ticked against the window, "is that Mackenzie never fed the rats, that Anbu was responsible, and that he had something to say, but isn't here. Things seem pretty clear to me."

"No," I said. "Anbu did not have anything to do with this."

"Are you saying, then, that you did?" William asked.

"No."

"Are you saying that your lab was compromised by someone else?"

"No."

"Then what are you saying?"

"I'm saying I don't know. We really need to hear from Anbu."

"Well, he should've been here today, and he's not. That says something." William scribbled down several points. The hail hit the window with more ferocity while he wrote. Finally, he put down his pen. "Here's how this will work. One, no force feeding. Two, animal research recertification for you and all lab staff. Except Anbu. He's suspended indefinitely from handling animals, and I strongly recommend he be dismissed. Three, random audits for a period of at least one year. Four, any future incidents and you're shut down. Five, pray this doesn't get out."

Schlemmer blew a puff of air through his nose. "I'll be the first one kneeling." He stood to leave and pulled hard on the handle of the glass door. It didn't budge. He pulled again, so hard that the glass vibrated inside the metal frame. He huffed and must've finally noticed the arrow on the glass. He slid the handle to the side. The door glided open in the track.

"He was trying to bury me," I said, while Luke and I walked back to our faculty building.

"No. He was just being Schlemmer."

"Like I said." I kicked a small pebble. "Why does he despise me so much?"

"He doesn't."

"No? Did you see the looks he was throwing me? I should check for puncture wounds."

Luke laughed.

"From day one, he's despised me. I'm only a *lowly* PhD. He's an MD."

"I'm an MD. I certainly don't despise you." Luke flicked his eyebrows at me.

I shook my head and tried not to smile. We had reached Luke's office door. He was about to ask me something when a young woman with flaming red hair bumped him. A wide open corridor and she managed to run into him. She smiled and put her hand over her heart. "I'm so sorry, Dr. Hesuvius." He smiled back and told her not to worry.

Luke watched her walk away. "Anyway. Why are you worried about what Schlemmer did or didn't say? The result was much better than we could have imagined."

"Are you kidding? I am so under the gun now, and I feel horrible about Anbu."

"I'm sorry if it seemed like I was being hard on him. I just didn't like the way things were turning against you. Better him suspended than you. He'll come forward with information that helps his case."

"What if he doesn't?"

"He will."

"He was trying to tell me something just before the meeting, but his phone died. I still haven't heard back from him."

"He's fine. As fine as when I saw him at Tim Hortons this morning."

"You saw him? Did he say anything?"

"Just that he needed some caffeine, because it was early and he was tired."

I looked at my watch. "He should be in Calgary by now."

"Don't forget, that thing he calls a car has a top speed of ninety kilometers."

"Be nice. He's got a wife and child to support. Speaking of which, I won't be able to join you for drinks after work."

Luke pretended to pout.

"Anbu asked me to check in on them. You know how he worries about Rubee, since she had the baby. I told him I'd bring her dinner."

Luke gave me a hug and told me how relieved he was that this situation was over. While he walked away, the text from *CAFÉ* flashed in my mind. I needed to talk to Anbu before they got in touch with William. Or worse, the media.

Chapter 2

DEADLY NEWS

I stooped under the front door's overhang and rang the bell. The bag of Chinese takeout was getting heavy, and I was getting soaked. If Rubee didn't hurry, I'd sit down on the wet steps and eat it all. Rain or no rain. It'd been a long day, and my stomach was aching. Hard to tell if it was from skipping lunch or from worrying about *CAFÉ*, not to mention Anbu. I still hadn't heard from him.

The lock clicked and the door opened, just enough to let in a beetle.

"Hello?" I said.

Rubee peeked through the crack. It had taken several years for her to feel at ease with me, seeing as how I was Anbu's supervisor. She and I had come a long way and enjoyed each other's company immensely, yet there was still this shyness about her. Even when I had said I'd like to call her Bee, just like Anbu did, and she could call me Mack, she had shaken her head no and said she couldn't possibly. Anbu reassured me that it was just how things were done at home in India.

"Hi Bee."

She smiled, like she always did when I called her that, and whispered for me to come in.

I pushed the door gently and poked my head around it. Her cocoa-colored eyes met me on the other side. They were sunk deep and her brown skin looked sallow. Three-month-old Emily was sleeping on her shoulder.

Rubee stepped back to let me enter. "I wasn't expecting you." She looked down at the bunny rabbit slippers on her feet and then back to me. "I'm sorry. Anbu bought them for me. I feel like I must wear them." She smiled softly.

"They're perfect." I set down the bag of food and removed my wet jacket. "Didn't Bu tell you I was going to bring dinner?"

She sighed. "No. He's been too busy."

I put my hand on Emily's warm back. "Looks like you've been busy too."

"Yes. Come." She turned and waved her hand for me to follow. Her slippers scuffed across the hardwood floor. She was heading towards the kitchen.

"Bee, you just sit. I'll get this ready."

"No, no."

"I insist."

She nodded. "Thank you." She went to the couch and sat gently. Emily didn't flinch.

"Have you heard from Anbu?" I said.

"No." She rested her head against the couch pillow.

"But he never calls until Emily's bedtime."

I checked my watch. Didn't all babies go to bed around this time?

Rubee and her bunnies stared up at the ceiling. I told her to stay there. In the kitchen, both sinks were piled with bowls and plates. The counter was buried under rubber nipples and plastic baby bottles. One nipple had fallen to the floor. I picked it up and unravelled a long black hair from the tip. This was not the way Rubee and Anbu kept things. Anbu was a clean freak. Rubee did the cooking. He did the cleaning. I knew he had been preoccupied with the rat issue, but I didn't think it was this bad.

"Sorry about the mess," Rubee called from the living room. I peeked around the corner. She was still staring at the ceiling.

"Don't apologize. I can't even begin to imagine." Nor did I want to. A sixty-pound dog was enough for Steven and me.

When I set the plates of food on the coffee table, Rubee sat forward. I offered to take Emily, who squirmed while she sank into my arms. Her head was warm and smelled sweet. I asked if I could put her to bed.

"Oh yes, Dr. Mackenzie. She is so very tired." Rubee sighed. "And so am I." She smiled. "I appreciate your kind gesture."

I rocked Emily on the way to her bedroom and didn't lay her in the crib until her eyes were closing. It didn't take long.

Back in the living room, Rubee was using chopsticks

to scoop the food into her mouth.

"Glad you like it," I said.

She smiled and swallowed. "It tastes better when you don't have to cook."

"Bu should cook you some meals."

She nodded and took another bite of food.

"It's been a tough time," I said.

Rubee stopped chewing and stared.

"I'm just guessing," I said, "with the rat issue and all."

She wiped her lips with a napkin. "Did he talk to you?"

"We got cut off today. Why?"

"No reason."

"Sounded like he wanted to tell me something about work. Do you know what it might be?"

"He does not share details of his work." Rubee switched the topic to how she and Anbu would like to go back to Kerala, their state in South India, to have Emily baptized with their families. Anbu was a devout Catholic, as was Rubee. This had surprised me when I first met them. Bu was so pleased to educate me on how many people in Kerala were Catholic. And, even though he didn't say so, it seemed like he found comfort knowing that I, too, had been raised Catholic. The difference between him and me was that it had been years since I'd been in a church.

"Dr. Mackenzie, I hate to ask this, but would you mind terribly if I took a shower while you are here. It is just so hard with Emily."

"Go right ahead."

I took the plates to the kitchen, while she slipped

down the hall. Anbu's office was next to the bathroom. Maybe there was something in there. Just laying on top of his desk, waiting for me to find it. I started clearing dishes from one sink while I waited for the shower to start. Just as it did, the doorbell rang. I ignored it and made my way towards Anbu's office.

Whoever was at the door started pounding, so loudly that they were going to wake Emily.

I tiptoed back to the front entrance and looked through the peephole. Two police officers stood with stone faces. I opened the door. They didn't move. Fat drops of rain beaded on the plastic brim of their caps. A Royal Canadian Mounted Police badge was fixed right above each of their brims, on top a yellow band. The bumble bee color of the band matched the stripe that ran down the outside of each of their pant legs.

"Good evening, ma'am," the taller one said. "I'm Constable Thickett and this is Constable Chung. Are you Mrs. Mathew?"

"No."

"Is she home?"

"Yes."

"May we speak with her?"

"She's in the shower."

A crack of thunder shook the house. Emily started to cry.

"May we come in and wait?"

"Yes. Of course."

They both stepped inside and removed their hats. "Are you family?"

"No. I work with her husband."

"Anbu Mathew?"

Emily was now in a fit.

"Yes. Why?"

"We need to talk to Mrs. Mathew."

I told them they were welcome to wait on the couch. One constable sat where Rubee had been staring up at the ceiling just an hour before. The other remained standing.

"Did something happen?" I said.

"Perhaps you want to get the baby."

Emily's crying had become a buzz. All I could think of was Anbu not calling back. I rushed to her room and flicked on the light. Diarrhea had escaped out of her diaper and down her bare leg. I searched for baby wipes and, while I did, Emily kicked her feet against the crib mattress and cried even harder. The shower shut off just as I was getting her into a clean sleeper. I closed the snaps quickly and stuck my head out the door. The two constables were now both sitting silently and looking at the floor.

With Emily in my arms, I slipped down the hallway to the bathroom and tapped on the door.

"Yes?" Rubee said.

"Bee," I said quietly, "Open the door."

"I am not proper."

"Please, Rubee."

There was shuffling and, finally, the door opened. "Is it Emily?" Rubee held her robe together at the chest.

"The police are here."

She stared.

"They're in the front room."

"Why?"

"They wouldn't say."

"Why are they here?"

"I don't know, Bee."

"Anbu. Oh no. Is it Anbu?"

She lowered her hands to push past me. Her robe fell open.

"Rubee! Wait!"

Her robe was flying out to each side as she ran into the front room.

The constables stood up and avoided looking directly at her.

Rubee stopped, her robe now hanging limp. I ran around to her front and used my free arm to pull one side across. She pulled the other and tied it shut.

"Mrs. Mathew?" Constable Thickett removed his cap and held it over his chest.

"Yes." Rubee's voice was shaking.

"This is never easy to say, but I'm afraid we have bad news for you."

"Bad news?"

"Your husband, Anbu —"

"Yes, Anbu!" Rubee stepped toward the constable.

"He was involved in a vehicle accident on highway 795 today."

"Oh no. Is he okay? Is he in the hospital?" Rubee grabbed his arms. Constable Thickett bent his arms under hers for support.

"We're sorry to tell you —"

"No!" She screamed in his face.

"I'm sorry." He dropped his head for a moment.

"He died as a result of his injuries."

"No, no, no," Rubee's cry turned into a whisper. She crumpled in Constable Thickett's arms. He put one arm around her rib cage and walked her to the couch. She was trying to say something. Her voice sounded like a child's.

Emily was suddenly heavy in my arms. I wasn't sure I could hang on. The other constable approached me and took her. She looked so tiny against his navy blue uniform. He placed her in the infant carrier that was beside the couch and gently brushed a tuft of hair from her forehead. He came back to me and asked if Rubee had any family close by.

I was stunned and couldn't think.

"It's okay. Take your time," the constable said.

"She and Anbu are from India. Anbu has an aunt here in Edmonton that they're close to."

The constable looked over to Rubee and then back to me. "Could you help me find that aunt's phone number?"

We walked to the kitchen and found the phone. He scrolled through recent callers and frowned. "Is this it?"

Ammaayi was displayed on the screen. I nodded. I had heard Anbu use that word when he talked about her, which was always with fondness. She lived clear across the city and so they didn't get to see each as much as they'd like, but I had the impression that they spoke by phone often.

The constable wrote the number on his notepad and called. While he talked to her, I stared at the cartons of uneaten Chinese food. I thought of how much Anbu would've loved the chop suey and how he would've eaten all the egg rolls.

Rubee's sobs echoed from the front room.

The constable who was with me in the kitchen hung up the phone and made another short call to the station to ask for a car to be dispatched to pick up Anbu's aunt and bring her to the house. When he was finished, he turned to me. "His aunt will be here as soon as possible." He studied my face. "You okay?"

"What happened?" I asked.

"Mr. Mathew's car went off the road. Poor conditions today with all the rain. The storm hit quick. Looks like he lost control." The constable stopped for a moment. "His car went down a small embankment and rolled."

"When?"

"Hard to tell. The place that his car came to rest wasn't visible from the road. So he could've been there for a while. A cattle rancher spotted it. We got to the scene around noon."

"Where?"

"About 120 kilometers out of the city."

"That's it?"

"Yes. Why?"

"He should've been farther than that by noon."

The constable frowned.

"I talked to him much earlier in the morning," I said. "He was already on the road to Calgary. He was supposed to be there by mid-day."

"He was talking to you on his phone while he was driving?"

"Pardon?"

"You just said he was already on the road when you were talking to him."

"Sorry. I'm not thinking straight."

The constable asked for my contact information. He scribbled it on his notepad and left me standing in the kitchen staring at cold egg rolls.

The next day I was summoned to RCMP head-quarters. I don't remember driving there. Or parking. Or walking in and proceeding to the counter.

"I.D." The male attendant's voice came from behind a wall of glass.

I slipped my driver's license through the metal slot in the glass.

"Who you here for?" He looked back and forth between his screen and my identification.

"Corporal Armstrong."

"Look into the camera." He pointed to his right.

Less than a minute later, he slid me my ID and a visitor pass with my mug shot on it.

"Have a seat." He nodded to the chairs against the wall without looking at me.

I sat in a chair at the far end of the waiting area. A few minutes later, the door beside me buzzed and a middle-aged man stepped out. He was wearing khakis and a plaid shirt.

"Ms. Smith?" he asked.

I stood. "Call me Mack."

"Mack. Good name. Follow me." He took me to his

office and offered me a Nescafé. I shook my head no.

"First, let me say I'm sorry about the death of your colleague, Anbu."

I couldn't look at him.

"The constables who were at the house last night said you might have some important information to share."

I looked over. Armstrong's eyes were piercing blue, and when he held my gaze, it felt like they were searching around inside my head.

"You talked to Anbu in the morning?" he asked. "By phone?"

"Yes."

"Was he driving?"

"Probably not. Not if he was on the phone. He was against that."

"Did he say where he was?"

"No."

"What did he say?"

"It was a short conversation."

"Do you mind if I see the incoming on your phone?"

"Of course not."

He scrolled through my calls. "Anbu Mathew. Incoming. Twenty-five seconds." He handed back my phone. "Tell me everything you remember of it."

"It was garbled. I think he was saying something about a document he needed to send me."

"How did he sound?"

"Sound?"

"Yeah. Was he calm? Excited?"

"He sounded in a hurry. He needed to be in Calgary before noon."

"Did he send you what he said he would?"

"No."

"How was Anbu otherwise?"

"What do you mean?"

"Was he depressed?"

"No. Why?"

Armstrong paused for a long time and then said, "Maybe he was feeling overwhelmed."

"You think he did this on purpose?" I said.

"I have to ask."

"No way. Not with his little girl. He'd never leave her."

"Did he say anything about car problems, when he was on the phone?"

"Don't think so."

"You don't think so?"

"Well, not that I could hear."

"Were you having trouble hearing him?"

"Yes."

"Car noise?"

"No. Static."

"How did the conversation end?"

"We got cut off."

"Did you try to call him back?"

"Yes. There was no answer. I left a message."

"What time was that?"

"Just before a meeting. Around nine o'clock, I guess."

"His wife said he left the house just after seven." Armstrong started scribbling numbers on a notepad and mumbled. "He drives through the city. Thirty minutes. Maybe stops for gas. Fifteen. Maybe drives a little slow.

One hour." He set down his pencil and looked at me. "Puts him near the scene of the accident about the time you got cut off."

"He never talked and drove, if that's what you're thinking."

"Just a theory. There are alternates."

I sat quietly while he tapped his pencil.

He stopped and said, "Maybe he was driving too fast, trying to make up time."

"He never drove fast. Couldn't, really, with that car."

"Maybe he stopped somewhere in the city for a couple hours before heading out. He calls you when he gets the chance, someone walks in, he hangs up."

"Someone like who?"

"How was his marriage?"

"His marriage?"

"Were they happy? Having a child can be hard on a couple."

"I don't understand."

"It's not uncommon. A child comes along. The woman spends all her time doting on the little one. The man feels left out and maybe seeks attention elsewhere."

"No way. Not Anbu. He'd never do that to Rubee. Those two were in love like I've never seen."

Armstrong looked up at me out of the corner of his eyes. "Of course," he said and looked back down to his notepad. After scribbling a few more lines, he stood and thanked me for my time. He held out his hand, and as I extended mine to his, I noticed the last thing he scribbled – *get Mathew's cell.*

Chapter 3

THE FUNERAL

In a rather large picture on the front page of the *Edmonton Sun*, the underbelly of Anbu's car was exposed. Thick weeds were all around trying to consume it. A yellow tarp had been stretched over the driver's side and a fireman was looking underneath. The newspaper article appeared the same day as Anbu's funeral. The caption under the picture read, 'Anbu Mathew was under investigation for the mistreatment of laboratory animals at the time of his death'. The main article appeared on page three. The first sentence described the accident. The rest of the story was dedicated to an interview with an anonymous *CAFÉ* member, who somehow knew about the meeting at the animal ethics office and that the decision there was to suspend Anbu from his duties at work. The reporter closed the article by saying, 'Mr. Mathew was scheduled to attend the ethics meeting on the morning of his accident, but never showed. There is speculation that he was fleeing Edmonton at the time of his death'. I barely closed the paper when my phone rang. It was Corporal Armstrong.

His office seemed brighter and like it had more pictures on the walls than it did the other day. His eyes hadn't changed.

"I need some clarification," Armstrong said from behind his desk. "Things aren't adding up. For example, why didn't you tell me about the rats?"

"You didn't ask."

Armstrong laughed and shook his head. "How, exactly, would I know to ask about rats?" He held my gaze. "You could've mentioned that there were some stresses at work."

"Sorry. Didn't think it was relevant."

"In my world, when a man drives his car off the road, it's relevant."

"*Drives his car off the road*?"

"We're not convinced it was a slick road – if he was driving as early as you say he was."

"Why not?"

"The rain hadn't hit there yet. The farmer who found him said it didn't start until eleven." Armstrong tapped the eraser of his pencil on his lip. "Then again, if it did happen that early, maybe he was distracted." Armstrong stared. "But you said he doesn't talk and drive."

"He doesn't. When people first started talking about a distracted driving law, Anbu was the one running around with a petition."

"So, maybe it *was* a slick road. But that means he got there later." Armstrong tapped his pencil on the desk. "Makes me wonder what he was doing in Edmonton for a good part of the morning."

I explained to Armstrong that, if Anbu was in Edmonton, he would've been at the meeting with me.

Armstrong pondered for a bit and finished making notes. "Here's the other problem. We can't find his phone. It wasn't with his personal belongings from the scene. We figured it might've flown out into the ditch. Had the dogs down there. Didn't find a thing. Searched every inch of his car. Nothing."

"That doesn't make sense."

"It does, if you consider my theory about him being somewhere else and accidentally leaving his phone there."

"What about location services?"

"Working on it. I need an ID and password. His wife has no clue." He reached forward and put his hands on the desk, a safe distance from mine. "Can you see why I need you to tell me *everything?*"

And so I did. I explained the rat story the best I could and reluctantly showed him the text from *CAFÉ*. I had to explain who they were.

"They vandalize labs?" he asked with a genuine sense of wonder rather than criticism. "To what end?"

"To make the lab non-functional. Costly to repair, challenging to restock."

"Do you like animals?' he asked.

"Yes."

"Did Anbu?"

"He loved them."

"Tell me about his phone call again."

I told him every detail.

"So, what did he say at the end? *Say a raise? Save the rays?*"

"Something like that. Neither makes sense."

Armstrong scribbled more notes.

I waited with a knot in my stomach. I couldn't take it anymore. "Anything else, Corporal?"

"You in a hurry?"

"Anbu's funeral is today."

He set down his pencil, said how sorry he was, and reassured me that he would do everything he could to put Anbu's case to rest.

On the way to the church, I passed the funeral home where Rubee and I had picked out Anbu's coffin just a few days before. None of her family members were able to travel from India to help, nor were any of Anbu's. His aunt, *Ammaayi,* could only get time off work to travel with his body back to Kerala the following week. They would hold a proper burial there. Luke graciously offered to buy a plane ticket for Rubee, so she and Emily could go along. She accepted but insisted that Anbu would've wanted a proper send off in Canada in the church he had grown to love. Seeing how distraught she was, I offered to arrange the service. The planning was awful. I could barely think of Anbu without my eyes welling up and my throat constricting. When I thought about getting up to speak at the funeral, it only got worse. So, I asked Schlemmer to do the reading and Luke to do the eulogy.

Inside the St. Andrew Catholic Church anteroom, Rubee stood closest to the casket. Emily had fallen asleep on her shoulder. Rubee spread her hand across the back of Emily's head and stared at the closed coffin. People filed past and gave their respects to her. Luke stood off to the side, reviewing his notes for the eulogy. When Anbu's aunt tapped him on the shoulder, he startled. Luke grasped both of her hands, looked down, and shook his head. She did the same. Rubee lifted her eyes to them for a moment.

Father MacIntyre approached me. He and I had spoken by phone a couple of times over the past week. I'd known him when I was a child and accompanied my mom to mass. Even though I hadn't been to church in years, he recognized me immediately. He took my hand and told me how nice it was, before this horrible event, to see Anbu in church every single day.

"Anbu?" I asked.

"Yes. Well, you know he and Rubee came every Sunday. But over the last few weeks, I found him here daily." He paused and placed his hand on my shoulder. "Sometimes, my child, the soul knows where it's going before we do."

I nodded, not so much because I agreed, but simply because I didn't know what else to do or say. Father MacIntyre smiled and handed me a copy of the reading for Schlemmer, who I finally found in a small room, by himself, standing beside a rack of altar boy garments. The back of his shoulders were hunched and he was fiddling with something in his hands.

I cleared my throat.

Schlemmer spun round and shoved his hand into his pocket. The tail end of a hankie hung out. His eyes were red.

"This is for you," I said.

He nodded, took it, and turned back around. I didn't see him again until we were all seated inside the church.

I sat in a pew near the front. Steven came in and joined me just before the entrance hymn. He squeezed my hand, when the pall bearers rolled the coffin down the aisle, and again when Luke got up to deliver the eulogy. Luke's voice was warm and steady, while he said how honored he was to be able to share some thoughts about Anbu.

"Many of you might not know this," Luke said from behind the golden podium, "but Anbu arrived in Canada when he was only eighteen. He came without a cent in his pocket." Luke paused and scanned the crowd. "He shared a story with me that I don't think he'd mind me telling you today." Luke paused again and, in a quieter voice, continued. "He was hungry and cold. Crazy guy came here in February. From a tropical land. He thought the snow was white sand when he first saw it from the plane window."

A few people in the congregation chuckled.

"Anbu found himself in the *Superstore*, walking down the bulk aisle. He hadn't eaten for a couple of days and had no money. He picked up a plastic bag and filled it with peanuts. For the first and only time in his life, he took something without paying for it. After checking over his shoulder, he stuffed the bag in his coat and left the store. But, this was Anbu." Luke's voice cracked. "No sooner was he out the door, than he went back in and asked to speak to the manager."

Luke stopped, apologized, and asked the congregation for a moment. He cleared his throat and continued.

"When the manager came over, Anbu pulled the bag of peanuts from his coat and admitted that he had taken them. He then told the manager that, even though he was starving, he just couldn't bear to eat them."

Amidst sobs from the congregation, Luke told how the manager put his arm around Anbu, took him up to the staff room, and fed him. He also gave Anbu his first job in Edmonton. With that first paycheque, Luke said, Anbu bought his first ever winter boots and retired the leather shoes that he'd been freezing his feet in. Luke took a handkerchief from his pocket and wiped his tears. After a moment, he continued to talk about Anbu's unfailing work ethic and love for his family.

I swallowed hard and looked anywhere but at Luke in an effort to prevent myself from weeping uncontrollably. Off to Luke's left, illuminated in a candle-lit niche, Joseph held baby Jesus and stood guard over Mary. On the other side of the altar stood St. Therese. She smiled gently. If Anbu were beside me, he'd have been giving me details about her life as a saint. The how, where, and why. In fact, I knew he prayed to her for miracles. He used to say how he *knew* his prayers were answered when a rose showed up. Heck, it didn't even have to be a real rose. It could be an emoji of a rose, or he could drive by a rose bush or, at the very least, swear that he walked into a room and it was filled with the scent of roses. That was his miracle.

When I tuned back in, Luke had become silent. His head was bowed. He glanced up at Anbu's coffin and then to the first pew where Rubee was sitting with Emily. "Rubee, our hearts are with you. And Emily. We have lost a great man. I have lost a great friend." Rubee did not look at Luke. She was weeping uncontrollably in *Ammaayi's* arms.

At the end of the service, Father MacIntyre circled Anbu's coffin three times with a brass thurible of burning incense. The container clanged against its thick chain as he swung it back and forth. Smoke curled out and filled the air with the scent of frankincense. Father MacIntyre concluded the funeral service by sprinkling holy water over the coffin with an aspergillum and pronouncing, "Rest in peace."

The Anbu I knew wouldn't be able to find a stitch of rest, if there was any chance his sweet little Emily might be told he left on purpose. He wouldn't rest, until it was fixed. Neither would I.

Between the stale slices of Wonder bread, the church ladies had carefully arranged processed ham, Velveeta cheese, and iceberg lettuce that had become translucent. Little triangles with no crusts. Conner Bigley was in front of me in the food line-up. He had befriended

Anbu years ago, when they worked together at the *Superstore*. Anbu often talked about Conner's many kindnesses, while Anbu was trying to adjust to life in Canada. "Such kindness!" Anbu would say emphatically.

Conner piled six mini sandwiches on one side of his plate and about the same number of Nanaimo bars on the other.

"Hey, Conner," I said.

He turned and pushed his thick black glasses up on his nose. "Hey, Dr. Smith."

"Mack. Remember?"

"Oh yeah," he smiled.

"This must be very hard for you." I touched his arm. "Anbu was a good friend."

"Yeah."

Conner agreed to join me for lunch. It was nice to have his company, since Steven had been called back to work. We sat across from each other at one end of a long wooden table.

"I liked Luke's speech," he said.

"Me too."

Conner bit into one of the sandwiches and started talking. "Luke must feel kinda bad, huh?"

"We all do."

He washed the sandwich down with a mouthful of raspberry punch and stared at his plate. "Did he tell you about it?"

"Did who tell me about what?"

"Luke." Conner's eyes flicked up to me and back to his plate. "We stopped for coffee at Tim Hortons. That morning."

"Luke said he saw Anbu. Were you there too?"

He nodded.

"What were you doing with Anbu?"

"He was dropping me off at the airport. It was on his way out. I was going to see my grandma." Conner bit into a Nanaimo bar. "Anbu was acting kinda weird."

"How so?"

Conner shrugged.

"Was he upset?" I asked.

"We stopped at your lab."

"Why?"

"Anbu needed a computer file."

"Did he say what it was?"

"No. Just that he had to send it to you."

"I didn't get anything."

Conner thought about this for a moment. "That's probably because he didn't get it."

"Why not?"

"Network was down." Conner licked Nanaimo filling off his fingers. "But he had one of those SecurID fobs. Never used it before. Can you believe it?"

I could believe it.

"I showed him how," Conner said.

Of course he did. Even though Conner dropped out of university, he did pretty well for himself doing this and that with computers.

"What does all this have to do with Luke?" I asked.

"Anbu got really mad at Luke's friend in Tims."

"Luke's friend?"

Conner shrugged. "Anbu just said he knew why they were together. She was pretty."

"Anbu talked to them?"

Conner nodded. "Didn't look good."

"What did they say?"

"Don't know. I was getting coffee. But Anbu was waving his hands in her face. I figured he should be careful or his phone would go flying. Then she stormed out."

"And Luke?"

"He talked to Anbu. Only for a bit. Then left, too."

"What did Anbu say about the whole thing?"

"Just something about a 'stupid conference'. He was kinda mad when we got to the airport, though."

"Why?"

"He tried the fob before I got out, but the network was still down. Said he'd try again further down the road."

Two women stopped near our table to say hello to one another. I waited until they left. "Conner, I need to know what Anbu wanted to send me. Do you think you could help me get onto his network drive at the hospital?"

He put a whole Nanaimo bar into his mouth. "Piece of cake."

Chapter 4

INFORMED CONSENT

The sleep clinic receptionist, Genie, greeted me with a semi-enthusiastic, '*Good afternoon, Dr. Smith*'. She handed me a file and pointed to a young woman in the corner of the waiting room. Angela Ashbury. A bright orange sticker on Angela's file said *Guarafit* – the name of the herbal weight loss drug that Luke and Schlemmer were testing. I'd stepped in where Anbu left off to help them enrol patients. I called out Angela's name. She stuffed a dog-eared copy of Vogue magazine under her arm, rocked back and pushed herself up. By the time she had shuffled to the consultation room and taken her seat, she was wheezing. Her flushed cheeks made her green eyes seem even brighter than they had when she was seated in the waiting area.

I opened her file and reviewed the summary page. Married. Thirty-one years old. Three hundred and twenty two pounds. Saw Luke two years ago for sleep apnea.

"Okay, Angela, let's review a few details."

"Where's Dr. Hesuvius?"

"I need a moment with you. Then you'll see him. Can't have you feeling any pressure to participate."

"Don't worry. I'm a keener."

I read aloud a number of points of information.

She squished her body against the table when I got to the part about how losing weight might alleviate her sleep apnea. At the end of the first page, when I paused to check in, her face was only inches from mine. Her wide, unblinking eyes finally blinked.

"How long 'til I fit into a size six?" Before I could say anything, she flipped to the dog-eared *Vogue* page and pushed it towards me. "Like this one," she said poking the page repeatedly. A model in a fitted pink dress was splayed out on a chaise lounge. A size two might have been generous.

"That's gonna be me." She nodded with unabashed certainty. "By Christmas." She pulled the magazine back over to her and stared. "I'm going to hang this picture on my fridge."

"Our primary concern is your sleep apnea. Not weight loss."

She closed the magazine, laid her hands on top, and locked her eyes on mine. "Not to be rude or anything, but look at you."

I looked down to my outfit. Steven had made a comment about my skirt that morning. About how it showed off my 'assets'.

Angela smiled stiffly. "You probably always looked

this way. Skinny enough to see your muscles. Pretty with all that red hair."

I felt my cheeks flush.

"You have no idea what it's like," she said. "People don't take me seriously. Just 'cause I'm fat." She sat back in her chair. "So, yes, I hate sleep apnea. But I hate being fat even worse."

The three seconds of silence that followed felt like sixty.

"Just a few more things," I said. Like the dose, time frame, and monitoring. Details that patients had to understand and accept. I made sure to emphasize how we couldn't promise any results, but there was no acknowledgement from her, head nod or otherwise, to suggest that the message had sunk in. The only indication that she was still with me was the pen clicking that started every time I stopped to take a breath. I barely finished the section on 'quitting with no consequences' when she leaned forward, grabbed the clipboard, and scribbled her signature on the consent form.

"There!" She pushed it across the table. Her eyes were brimming with excitement.

Before signing as a witness, I paused for a moment. Then when my pen completed its last stroke on the paper, Angela beamed.

The two of us walked over to the treatment room, where Luke looked up from Angela's medical file. "Well," he stood and cracked a huge smile. "I see my favorite patient is here."

She laughed and waved off his compliment.

I handed her research folder to Luke. "All the forms

you need should be here."

"Thank you, Dr. Smith." He turned to Angela. "Ready to get started?"

"Never more ready in my life."

On my way back toward the consultation room, I heard Angela giggle repeatedly. Par for the course, when women were with Luke. I sat down and added Angela's signature page to the consent folder with all of the other patients' pages. Anbu's hand writing was on most of them. It made me miss him. As I was closing the folder, it slid off my lap and the consent forms fanned out all over the floor. Out of any recognizable sequence. Not good. Luke was meticulous. I got down on my knees and scraped them together.

I pulled out the master list to cross-reference the participant numbers and restore order. Three consent forms were missing. They weren't under the table, the file cabinet, or anywhere else in the room. According to the master list, numbers F007, F015, and F020 had vanished. I checked and re-checked. My guess? They probably got mixed in with the patients' medical records, accidentally, instead of their research records. I went back to the master list and wrote down the three medical record numbers. Then, in the electronic medical database, matched those to names. I shouldn't have done it, but if it came to light, surely the ethics board would understand. Breaking confidentiality rules to find lost study forms was better than potentially allowing patients' private information to circulate where it shouldn't. And who knew where it was?

Genie wasn't at reception. I slipped round her

cluttered desk to the file room. The patient files were packed in so tightly that it was impossible to search through them without slicing my cuticles. How did they ever find anything in there? The first patient's medical folder was filed on the top shelf. I stretched; the tips of my fingers barely reached the edge. I grasped the corner and pulled.

"What 'cha doing?"

I jumped back. The file came with me.

Genie snapped her gum.

"I'm just checking a few things, Genie."

She raised her eyebrows. "Not sure Dr. Hesuvius would like that. Didn't want Anbu back here. Dr. Hesuvius said specifically these were medical files and Anbu didn't need to see them."

"Dr. Hesuvius will be just fine with this. Don't worry."

She shrugged her shoulders and walked away.

I searched through all three files, careful not to let my eyes wander over personal medical details, but found no consent forms for the research protocol. There was one last place to look.

In the back corner of the room, behind the rows of medical charts, sat a filing cabinet with a bright orange *Guarafit* sticker on the top drawer. Perhaps the consents accidentally got filed in the individual research folders. I pulled on the drawer handle, but it didn't budge. A panel with multiple key hooks was a few steps away. An orange tag hung from one of the keys. It shone like a beacon.

Genie was nowhere in sight. The key slipped off the hook with ease and fit perfectly into the cabinet lock. In the top drawer, the research files were neatly in order, from F001 to F099. Except for the three in question. They were gone. Before I locked the cabinet, I double-checked, replaced the key, and went back to reception. Only two other people might be able to help.

"Genie, can you let me know when Dr. Hesuvius is done with Angela?"

She turned in her chair and smiled. "Too late. He's already done. Speedy, huh?"

"Could you page him, then?"

"No. You missed him, when you were back there. He left."

"He did?"

"He's taking his wife and kids on a surprise trip to the mountains. Isn't that sweet? You know, with the stress around Anbu and everything over the past month, he just needed to get away. But, if it's urgent—"

"No. Is Dr. Schlemmer around?"

"Nope. Anyone else?"

I shook my head and started to walk away.

"And, don't worry," Genie said, "I won't say anything about you being back there."

First thing on Monday morning, a student with long, Clairol-red hair was perched outside Luke's open office door. One hand rested casually on her hip, the other stretched up his door frame. Her outline was a perfect 's'. She threw her head back and laughed. Luke's eyes met mine as I came up from behind. I raised my eyebrows. He smiled and said hi to me.

The student turned. She was the same one who'd bumped him in the hallway a few weeks ago. She scrutinized me, from my shoes to the waist of my skirt.

I checked my belt buckle to be sure it was done up.

"Hi." She hooked her thumbs through her belt loops and drew back her elbows. Her chest, prominent before, had now taken on a life of its own.

"Hello," I said.

She turned back to Luke and told him she'd be in touch. As she passed me, she said, "By the way, I love the color of your hair. Red heads should stick together."

What was that supposed to mean?

The fact that she was pretty and seemed so friendly with Luke made me think of my conversation with Conner Bigley at Anbu's funeral. I waited until she was out of range. "Is that the woman you were with at Tim Hortons?"

"Pardon?"

"The morning of Anbu's accident."

Luke repeated this to himself, keeping his voice neutral, until the veil lifted. "No. Why?"

"Conner mentioned you were with someone and that Anbu seemed mad at her and vice versa."

"I was with a new resident. We got carried away talking. When Anbu came over, she realized she was late. She left in a hurry, but she wasn't mad."

Before I could say anything else, Luke held up a copy of *Folio*, the university newspaper. There he was, on the front page, with Schlemmer. Each had one arm stretched toward the camera. It made their hands look bigger than their heads, and the *Guarafit* pill in each palm the size of a navel orange.

I smiled. "You look good."

"Not bad." Luke grinned.

"Not bad. Come on. It's not every day you get that kind of recognition."

He set the paper down. The corners of his lips flattened "It's just hard to be happy about it, you know?"

"Anbu?"

"Yeah."

"He'd be happy for you."

Luke dropped his head. "I wish I hadn't insisted about the conference. Shit. I thought it'd be a good experience for him."

"I'm sure he did, too."

"He wasn't happy about it. Didn't want to leave Rubee."

"Still, it's not your fault."

"If I hadn't suggested it, he'd be here."

"There's been a lot of that," I said. "If it hadn't been raining. If he hadn't been on a crappy road. If he hadn't been on his phone. Don't do this to yourself."

"Fine. Sure. Whatever." Luke forced a smile. "Now, what can I do for you?"

"We need to talk about a little problem. Something I found after I enrolled Angela."

He moved his hands in circles as if to say '*get on with it*'.

His eyebrows shot up when he heard about the consents. The tips of his fingers grasped the edge of his desk and progressively lost color during my rendition of events. I admitted that I checked the medical files, half expecting him to explode. He and Schlemmer were, in essence, the only ones who should have access to those files. But in his usual Luke way, he reassured me, and said there was no one he'd trust more.

I wasn't certain if I should tell him that I looked in the *Guarafit* filing cabinet, but he asked. When I told him that the three research folders were missing from there, his face went ashen. He probably was having visions of the poor guy who, about a year ago, left a research file with patient identifiers in a coffee shop, only to have someone find it and take it to the media.

An alarm sounded on his phone. "Dammit." He picked it up, looked at the notification, and threw it in his briefcase. "I don't have time to deal with this." He stood and struggled to put on his suit coat. He looked like a bear ready to rage.

"Easy does it," I said. "You go see patients. I still have one last place to look."

On my way from Luke's office to the clinic, I picked up a *Folio* from a newsstand. The picture was good, but I wanted to read the article. The first two lines were about how Schlemmer landed a half-million dollar grant from the national funding agency to study *Guarafit* and how results were to be published later this month in one of the leading physiology journals. This set him up nicely for a renewal of another half million dollars to roll out a Phase III clinical trial. I wondered how Luke felt about all this. Even though he was in the picture, there was no mention of him in the article. I guess because it was Schlemmer who got the grant. Yet, as far as I could tell, Luke was working just as hard on the trial as Schlemmer.

Schlemmer's office door in the sleep clinic was open a crack. Only the back of his shoulder and arm were visible. When I knocked, he didn't budge. I knocked again, this time with more force. Still, no movement. I pushed on the door. He was leaning back in his chair with his feet up on the desk. Large earphones, with at least an inch of padding, jutted out from each side of his head. Deepak Chopra and Oprah Winfrey smiled at me from his 27" widescreen monitor. Underneath them, in luminescent letters, were the words *Meditation Challenge* and a picture of a monarch butterfly perched on the edge of a pink daisy. I walked in and tapped him on the shoulder. His feet flew off the desk and his chair tipped forward. He ripped off the headphones as if they were on fire.

"Jesus!" He snapped shut the computer window. "You'd think when someone's door was closed, they could have some privacy."

"It was open."

Schlemmer glared.

"Three *Guarafit* research folders are missing," I said. "Have any idea where they might be?"

"No."

The bottom drawer of the filing cabinet beside his desk was open. At one end, there was a folder with what appeared to be an orange sticker on it.

"They wouldn't happen to have gotten in there by mistake?" I pointed to the drawer.

He reached down and gave it a push. "No."

"Fine. Happy meditating. Want me to shut your door?"

"Yeah, and don't let it hit you on the way out."

I closed the door. Oprah and Deepak could do nothing for a man who could tell a lie while meditating.

I left Schlemmer's office to find Luke. Genie informed me that he was in a treatment room with a patient. Considering the circumstances, I thought it best to interrupt. Luke excused himself immediately and stepped out. His face was still pale and drawn.

"You might want to talk to your friend, Schlemmer," I said. "I think you'll find what you're looking for."

Chapter 5

FAVORS FOR THE CHAIR

My lab was in the basement of the hospital, close to the morgue. There were no windows, no signs of life, only the odd cast-off skin left behind by a silverfish. In fact, the brightest thing down there was my lab door. It was sky blue, except for a gash in the paint at eye level. A note had once been tacked there with a pocket knife. In it, a message spelled out with block letters that had been clipped from a glossy magazine. *Free the rats or face the consequences*. It was signed *CAFÉ*. Hospital security installed a video camera above the door after that, but nothing ever came of it, making the whole thing easy to ignore. Until now.

I opened the lab door. An earthy scent was overlaid on the usual antiseptic smell. The new smell came from an orchid that had been placed in the middle of the lab table. White flowers with purple veins and bright yellow lips bloomed abundantly along its spike. A florist's card rested against the glazed pot.

Dearest M,

Couldn't have finished the trial without you.
Thanks for your unfailing support.

Yours,
L

The plant would have to go to my office; it'd never survive in the lab. The card, well, it wasn't the kind of thing I could prop up on the mantle at home. I slipped it into my brief case. It would go to my office, as well.

At the back of the lab, behind a heavy metal door with a small window, was the dimmed rat room. I turned the door handle and leaned my body into the cold steel. The hinges squeaked. In an instant, all scurrying ceased. The rats waited. When would it be safe to move again? A stray kibble of food had fallen to the floor, just in front of the cage that housed Anbu's three favorite rats. Huey, Dewey and Luey. Fully grown now, they were just babies, really, when Anbu started in the lab. He bet me he could teach them to do tricks. And he did. They jumped through hoops, retrieved pennies and put them in medicine cups, and stood on their hind legs and twirled. All for a treat or two. They had somehow escaped the recent fate of the others.

I picked up the kibble and snapped it in two. Huey, white as snow except for a grey fringe around his nose, peered over a pile of shredded paper. Dewey, spotted like a Holstein, got up on his hind legs and swept the air with his whiskers. Luey, with teeth as big as tree stumps, didn't seem to notice at all. I dropped the kibble through the wire hatch. Huey and Dewey tunneled through the paper bedding to find it. Luey just sat and watched and only dove under when the lab phone rang.

MontgomE was scrolling across the call display. Dr. Elizabeth Montgomery, my department chair. It was 7:30 am.

"Hello, Mackenzie Smith speaking," I said, as if her identity was a mystery.

"So glad I caught you." She sounded cheery, which was unusual. "I'm calling about one of our new students. Fennel Gutterson."

Fennel was the daughter of one of Elizabeth's colleagues from medical school. A very wealthy colleague. Apparently, he'd called her and said that Fennel was interested in working in my lab.

"I owe him a favor," Elizabeth said. "I told him it'd be no problem."

The pressure of my fingers against my eyelids felt good, like it could push Elizabeth out of my head and make her disappear. I wanted to tell her no; I had no time or money to support a grad student. Especially one that I didn't choose. But, I was up for tenure and promotion. I needed Elizabeth to provide a positive recommendation to the dean. She'd been known not to, if you didn't play along. To make things worse, she emphasized the jeopardy that we'd be in without the generous donation from Fennel's father. With all the government budget cuts, department members would lose their jobs. Especially those without tenure.

"It's the least we can do," she said. "She's a good

student, I'm sure."

Pain shot up the left side of my face, from my jaw to my temple.

"By the way," Elizabeth continued, "I've taken care of that pesky little *CAFÉ* problem for you."

I almost choked on my saliva. "Pardon me?"

"Yes. Not to worry." She let out a satisfied 'hmph'. "I'll send Fennel your way."

The afternoon sun streamed through my office window and lit up the petals of Luke's purple-veined orchid. I closed my eyes. Thoughts of how time and circumstance positioned the two of us together were eventually replaced by those of my rats. Their motivation. Their weight. Their scent. So vivid, even the room seemed to fill with it. Or was it? I spun in my chair. Miss Clairol, the student from Luke's doorway, was now standing in mine. Her musk perfume floated like a thick cloud into my office.

"Can I help you?" I asked.

"I'm Fennel."

"*You're* Fennel?"

"Yeah. What were you expecting?"

I invited her to have a seat, but needn't have. She was already on her way. The green geometric patterns on her shirt reminded me of our bathroom wallpaper when I was in grade school. And like that wallpaper, her top was glued on. Once she'd settled into the chair, I started with the one fact I knew.

"I hear Dr. Montgomery knows your father."

She rolled her eyes. "You know fathers. They can be a pain sometimes." She smiled. "He wanted me to be a doctor, just like him. Finally agreed on second best."

"Which is?"

"A PhD." She laughed.

He'd warned her that she'd be making a fraction of his salary, and that she'd have to do a masters first. She didn't care. As long as, in the end, she wasn't on-call 24 hours a day like him. Besides, she added, he was paying for her education, so why should she worry? Plus, she'd get to work with people like me. You know, PhDs who work in a clinical setting with patients, she said.

Here was my out, with no explanation necessary to Elizabeth. If Fennel was interested in clinical work, my lab wouldn't be right for her. My focus, now, was animals, so I explained that to her in great detail.

Fennel laughed. "Wait 'til my father hears that."

"He doesn't like rats?"

"Who cares? I love rats."

Of course she loved them. Had them as pets, she said. But lab rats were different from pet rats, I told her. And that she'd need to learn to deal with it. She was about to respond when my phone rang. It was Luke. He launched into a story before I could even say hello. I glanced over to Fennel. She was staring intensely at the string of pearls around my neck. They were my only keepsake from my mom. I missed her and wore them on days when I woke up with an ache in my heart.

With the click of the phone in the cradle, Fennel's eyes flashed away from me and to a picture on the bookshelf. "Are these some of your rats?"

"Yes. Huey, Dewey, and Luey."

"You named them?"

"No. Someone else did."

Fennel went over to the picture and brought it to her face as if she needed glasses. "They're cute!" She put it back and sat down.

"They're food-motivated."

"Are they part of your obesity research?"

"Yes." Good for her. She knew about my research. But how much? As we delved deeper into the topic, her comments and questions became increasingly intelligent. Perhaps she wasn't just regurgitating a briefing from her father.

"One more question?" she said.

"Sure."

"Where did the name come from?"

"The name?"

"For the sleep clinic."

"Ninsun? It relates to dreaming. You know, Gilgamesh."

Her eyes looked vacant. I explained that he was an ancient ruler and that his mother, Ninsun, would interpret his dreams to predict the future.

"My mom used to love interpreting dreams," she said. "My father thought it bordered on black magic. Being Baptist and all." She moved to the edge of her chair. "One last question?"

I glanced at my watch. "A quick one."

"Will I get to work with Dr. Hesuvius, too? On his research?"

"We help each other out."

"So, yes?"

"You'll need to talk to him."

"For sure."

After she left, there was only one thing of which I was certain. Luke would be getting a visit soon.

Chapter 6

RUBEE'S REVEAL

I rang Rubee's doorbell and waited. She hadn't been returning calls and didn't know I was coming. I was concerned for her and, of course, for Emily. They were essentially alone, and I knew that she must be making the hard decision of whether to stay in Edmonton and raise Emily as a Canadian, as Anbu would've wished, or if she'd go back home to the comfort of Kerala. Checking on them was the least I could do for Bu. Besides, there were things I needed to know. It was time to just make an appearance. A mounting sense of unease stirred beneath my rib cage, however, when Rubee didn't answer. Should I try the door? Break in through a window? I rang the bell again.

The door inched open. Rubee peeked out at me. Her knuckles stuck out like waxy knobs. "Doctor Mackenzie," she smiled. "I was wondering when I would see you again."

"I've been worried."

From behind Rubee came the sound of pebbles sifting onto the floor. I peeked over her shoulder. Emily was sitting beside a spiked plant, about to stuff a fistful of dirt in her mouth. Rubee ran to her. I stepped inside, onto the welcome mat.

Rubee turned to me with Emily in her arms. "Please. Come in. We can have tea."

I walked over to her and asked if I could hold Emily. She handed her to me and walked to the kitchen. I followed and brushed bits of dirt from between Emily's pudgy fingers.

Rubee's jeans slipped past her hip bones when she reached for a box of tea. I asked how she was doing. She softly said okay. Her eyes were glassy when she turned to fill the teapot with water. As she did, Emily patted my face and cooed. I shifted her to my other hip and asked Rubee if she'd heard from Corporal Armstrong.

She sighed. "He called. They ruled it an accident. I guess I can get the insurance money, now that they don't think it was suicide."

"I'm so sorry, Bee."

"Everyone in India believes the newspapers. It is disgraceful. How can I take Emily back there?"

We all stared, even Emily, as the steam squealed out of the teapot.

"Did they find his phone?" I asked.

"No. They kept asking me about passwords, and I kept telling them that I did not know. I do not think they believed me."

Rubee poured the hot water into cups and dropped

a teabag into each.

"Milk?" Rubee asked.

"No thanks."

"Thank goodness, because we do not have any."

We both giggled.

I sat down. Emily felt solid on my lap. At least she was eating. Rubee dropped four cubes of sugar into her tea and stirred.

"I'm sorry," I said.

She grabbed two more sugar cubes. "For what, Doctor Mackenzie?"

"What you're going through."

She swallowed hard and kept stirring her tea.

"I talked to him that morning," I said. "We got cut off. He wanted to tell me something about the rats."

"Which ones?"

"The ones who died in my lab."

"Oh, the four-legged ones." Rubee dropped her eyes to the tea again.

"What do you mean, Bee?"

Emily banged on the table with both fists and screeched. Rubee reached behind to the counter and grabbed a biscuit. "He did not deserve this. He would never harm a fly."

My throat constricted. "That's why I need answers."

"That newspaper article was disgusting." I'd never seen fire in Rubee's eyes before. "A rat killer. As if that could ever be true."

"I know."

"The university did not even respond."

"They want it to be over."

Deep in thought, she took a sip of tea. "Tell me something. If Anbu were still here, would it be over?"

"Truthfully?"

She tilted her head and locked her eyes on me. "Doctor Mackenzie, I would expect nothing less of you."

"They were going to go after him."

"I thought so."

"I don't want Anbu to be remembered this way. And I know you don't."

"It will be terrible for Emily. How will I explain, if she ever sees those newspaper articles?"

"I can't stop thinking about what he wanted to tell me. Bee, if you can remember anything, it could be really important."

"There is nothing."

I smoothed my hand over a tuft of Emily's hair. "What did you mean by the rat comment?"

"Please. Never mind that. I should not have expressed it." She looked down and sipped her tea. I didn't take my eyes from her until she looked back to me.

"All I know," she said, "is that he was in a hurry to get to that conference. I started asking questions. He got mad."

"Did he say anything?"

"Just for me not to worry. That it would all be over soon and that he found what he needed."

"Did he say anything about what he found?"

"Just that it was big."

"Did he say anything about consenting patients?"

"Patients?" She shook her head. "That was very

confidential to him. He never shared."

I asked if maybe there might be some clues at home. In his den.

"If there were any, they are gone now. I am sorry, Doctor Mackenzie. I shredded it all."

"Oh no. Why?"

"I just could not look at it anymore. And, well," tears welled in her eyes, "I know Anbu wanted Emily to be raised as a Canadian, but I am so homesick. I am getting ready to move back."

I felt like I'd just been kicked in the gut. It wasn't like I saw her all the time. But, somehow, if she left, then all of Anbu would be gone.

"Did I do the wrong thing?" she asked.

"Oh, Bee. No. It's just that there could've been something in there to clear his name. Are you sure you destroyed it all?"

"I think so. But let us have a look."

We walked together down the hall towards his office. When we got to the door, she took Emily.

"I do not think it is good for her to be in here." She continued down the hall to Emily's bedroom.

The office was pristine. Either because Anbu kept it that way or because Rubee did an absolutely thorough job cleansing it. The drawer of his metal filing cabinet sounded hollow and tinny when it rolled open. It was completely empty. Every other drawer was the same, except for the last. On the bottom was a flyer for the conference in Calgary.

"It is silly," Rubee said from behind, "but I thought I would keep that as a reminder. Anbu did not want to go. He was mad at Luke."

"Rubee, tell me something honestly. And don't worry about what I will think. Are you mad at Luke?"

"Yes," she said in a quiet voice.

I stepped toward her and put my hand on her shoulder. "Luke had no control over what happened that day. You know that, right?"

"I know. But he seemed to have control over other things."

"Like what?"

She shrugged. "I just felt sorry for Anbu. He worked so hard. And, please do not say anything, but I do not think Luke appreciated it."

I knew that Luke appreciated Anbu. I certainly couldn't have afforded to keep him in my lab without Luke paying half his salary from his clinic budget. Never mind the fact that Luke lobbied human resources to give Anbu a raise beyond his pay grade and to give him full benefits. On top of it all was the life insurance package she was about to get. That was Luke. I knew that Bee was just hurting. I couldn't blame her for trying to make sense of it all somehow, and if that meant blaming someone, then so be it.

"Luke loved Bu like a son," I said.

She nodded.

In silence, we checked the drawers in Anbu's desk. There was nothing.

At the front door, I promised her that I wouldn't stop until I found out what happened so that Anbu could rest in peace.

Chapter 7

DECK SEX

Overripe crab apples had fallen from the sprawling tree next door. They lined our back fence like a ribbon of red. Their scent rose up in the heat of the Indian summer, heady and full. Diesel, our 8-year-old dog, turned his head, caught sight of me coming from the garage, and inched to the edge of the hammock. His bearded muzzle was flattened from sleep, but his bushy eyebrows stood erect. He was a black version of Snowy from the comic strip *Tintin*. I crossed the deck to him. His stub tail flicked back and forth like the arm on a metronome.

Steven came onto the deck through the back door of the house with two bottles of beer. Beads of condensation ran down the sides. He kissed me. It was intense. Hadn't felt that for a while. Made me catch my breath. He pressed a bottle into my hand and, one after the other, we slipped onto the hammock without displacing

Diesel. We balanced each other, Steven and I. My drive to get things done, with its sometimes sharp edge; his ability to relax and just let things roll out as they should.

Diesel, unfazed by the sway of the hammock, poked at a pink fuchsia that was hanging from a basket in the tree overhead. The bloom swung out and came back to rest at his nose. He tilted his head, waited, and repeated the cycle. His persistence made me smile. It was a characteristic I admired, in anyone. Steven was telling me about his latest multi-million dollar deal as if it was nothing, just another big takeover. He asked me to keep it confidential. Wouldn't be difficult. I wasn't really listening. I was admiring his full lips and the five 'o'clock shadow that made his lips seem even more red. The breeze was playing with a lock of his dark hair. Just like the day we got married, under a trellis of white oleander and blue forget-me-nots.

Steven stretched his arms over his head and said he needed a holiday. I reminded him about the conference in Banff. It would be a short, but good, break. Time where we could simply wrap ourselves around each other.

Diesel bumped Steven's elbow with his nose.

"What are we going to do with him when we go?" he asked.

Diesel stared as if he was curious to hear my answer.

"Hate leaving him at a kennel," I said. "Especially after last time."

"What about Brittany?"

"No. She's got allergies to everything. Maybe I could ask Luke about their dog sitter."

Steven looked off to the poplar trees. "I'm sure he'd be *happy* to help."

"Oh man." I took a sip of beer. "Not this again."

"What again?"

"Luke."

"Did I say anything?"

"Never mind."

The boy next door shouted at his brother for hitting him with a soccer ball, and a squirrel on the peak of the garage scolded the birds in the mountain ash. Steven didn't utter another word. He sat there, miffed, as he always did, when we got onto the topic of Luke. I touched his shoulder, told him we'd figure out the dog-sitting. Eventually, after my rambling about the mundane – the computer that crashed, the new grant deadline, and how much the rats were eating these days – the lines on his face softened.

"How are things with that new student?" he said. "What's her name again? Dill?"

I rolled my eyes. "Fennel. She's working out better than I thought. A real go-getter. Maybe a little too much."

Steven cocked his head to the side and squinted. "How so?"

Now was definitely not the time to bring up Fennel's flirtation at Luke's office door or a similar interaction I witnessed between them in the sleep clinic. I shrugged and said that her eagerness would probably fade when the semester ramped up.

Diesel repositioned himself onto his side, sighed and closed his eyes. His ear extended from his head like a bat wing and, with each breath he took, my heart expanded. So carefree and innocent. Was this how Anbu had felt when he watched Emily sleeping?

Steven spun an autumn-gold leaf by the stem. "And Schlemmer? Any new antics?"

"None since the missing consents."

"Were they in his desk?"

"Guess so." I hoped Steven would drop it. But he was staring, waiting. "Luke said he figured it out."

"Ah, of course he did." Steven pulled his thumb and fore finger across his eyelids. "That's his specialty, isn't it?"

This time I looked off to the trees and contemplated going inside.

"And Brittany, how's she doing?" he asked, as if everything were normal.

"Great." The last sip of beer slid down without much fizz.

"Well she does have a big brain." He turned onto his side. The boys next door were still fighting. The squirrel was nowhere to be seen. "Maybe even bigger than her beautiful aunt's."

I felt his stare boring into the side of my head. And that's exactly where it could stay.

"Maaack." He ran his finger down my arm. I tried not to smile, held out for as long as possible, but eventually turned towards him. He grinned and flicked his eyebrows.

I thumped his chest. A tussle started that sent our empty beer bottles rolling. In the chaos, Diesel hopped off. The hammock swung and I hit the deck first. Steven landed on top and crushed the wind out of me. It sent me into a moment of panic, until he lifted his body and air flowed back in to my lungs.

He smiled, lowered his body, and put his lips on that spot, the one in the crook of my neck. "Mmm, Red. What do you think?"

"I think there are kids playing next door."

"Who cares?" His breath was warm on my ear. He shifted the front of my skirt and pushed his hips between my legs. "Come on. Please." The low tones of his voice and the faint scent of cologne on his neck, never mind the fact that, recently, we seemed to be slipping into longer and longer periods of celibacy, made me lose all common sense. His fingers slipped into my hair and just as his lips were about to touch mine, a wet nose brushed my ear and sniffed. Diesel looked at us as if to say '*not this*', and promptly left.

Steven swept my jaw with the back of his fingers. Before I knew it, my blouse was unbuttoned and he was unfastening the clasp at the back of my bra. He pulled one strap down while, on my lower lip, he twirled his tongue tip, slow and deliberate. He asked if I might want more. I pushed his hips away and grabbed his belt.

With his shorts crumpled at his knees, we moved together, slow and hard, rocking and kissing, fingers intertwined, until I was breathless, pulsing and grinding against him, and trying not to make a sound while my brains fell out. Steven began to thrust and, as he gained momentum, I reached for a pillow to put under my head. That's when I noticed the fence. And the silence. And the four eyes. Peeking through two spaces between the fence boards. Wide and blinking.

"Steven! The eyes."

He opened his, looked at me, and thrust harder. "Oh yeah, baby? You like watching, huh?"

"No! Steven!" I pushed him off.

One of the boys started rotating his skinny ten-year-old hips in wide circles. His brother began bumping against him, saying, "Oooh baby", over and over.

"Hey!" Steven yelled at the boys. He pulled up his shorts while stumbling to his feet. The kids burst into laughter and ran away. Diesel barked and scratched on our back door to get in. I couldn't help but break into hysterics.

"What's so funny?" Steven snapped.

Still laughing, I couldn't respond.

He stomped to the door. "Get in!" Diesel ran past him into the house. The door slammed shut.

With my skirt pulled back down and my top buttoned up, I grabbed my underwear and flicked off a ladybug. All was quiet and still around me, except for the flash of red that retreated from the second-story window next door when I stood up.

Chapter 8

PUMPKIN-SPICED PRESENTATIONS

Steven said a total of fifty-four words to me in the two days following the deck event. I counted. On the third morning, I got up early, made him French toast with strawberries and a cappuccino on the side and served him in bed. The freeze thawed. He confessed that my fatal mistake on the deck was laughing, which he assumed was at him. I rolled out of bed, slid my fingers down the straps of my negligee, and told him to watch. I moved slowly at first, swinging my hips just a little, before flying into a full blown re-enactment of the boys next door. He laughed so hard he nearly spilled the tray of food. We kissed goodbye that morning. The world seem lighter even though the tasks at work, piled high and deep, were daunting. But I had help. Fennel. Pro bono, she'd said about the extra work. She just wanted to be involved. Her latest assignment was to lay out a presentation for Luke and me. It was going to save hours of work. I was on my way to meet them about it.

In Ninsun reception, the morning paper was spread over Genie's desk. The waiting room was empty, and she was nowhere in sight. Okay with me. Ever since our meeting in the patient file room, she'd become like a hawk.

I rounded the corner to the conference room. The soles of Luke's dress shoes, new and barely scuffed, were sticking out of the doorway. He was on all fours under the computer table, with his head squeezed between the wall and the CPU tower.

"What's up?" I got down on my haunches beside him. He smelled good, like bergamot and leather.

He was fiddling with a mess of cables. "Friggin' projector."

I shuffled in a little closer, watched for a moment and asked if I could help. He dropped one of the cables. I reached around him to pick it up.

"Whoa!" A voice came from behind. "What's going on *here*?" It was Genie.

Luke glanced at me and smirked.

Genie stepped in so close, her foot was between Luke's legs. "Did you hear that Brenda Deswicki died?"

Luke raised his head, drove it straight into the keyboard tray. "Fuck." He fell onto his elbows and closed his eyes. "Who?"

"Your patient," she said.

He rubbed his skull.

"Well," she said, "I guess she was Dr. Schlemmer's.

I never know who they belong to in that research project of yours."

"She was Schlemmer's," he said quietly and inspected his fingertips, for blood I presumed. There was none.

"Might've been her heart," Genie said. "Obit in today's paper says to donate to the Heart and Stroke Foundation."

I watched Luke to make sure he was okay. He had driven his head into the table so hard that his face was grey.

Genie shook her head. "So sad. Just when she'd lost a bunch of weight. What's her husband going to do? He followed her around like a puppy. Came to every single appointment. We should send him a card."

Luke rubbed his head again. "Of course. Please let me sign it, though."

Genie left, and without either of us touching a thing, light suddenly streamed from the projector to the screen. Luke shook his head, stood, and brushed specks of dirt from his knees. Just as I was going to ask him about the patient who died, Fennel appeared at the door.

"I got some pumpkin spiced lattes." She smiled at Luke. "I asked for yours to be extra spicy. Just the way you like it."

His face warmed to pink. He thanked her politely and sat at the table.

As she passed me my cup, I told her she was going to go broke. It was the fourth one she'd brought me in the same number of days. She smiled and, after a moment of contemplation, declared that she couldn't think of anything better on which to blow her new stepmother's potential inheritance. "Plus, I owe you for the extra time you've been spending with me outside of class. That anatomy stuff just doesn't stick."

"No debt for that."

"All I know is that, because of you, I'm going to pass the exam next week."

"No. Because of you, you're going to pass it."

"Of course." She flapped her hand at me.

I pointed to the empty coffee tray. "Where's yours?"

"I can't. I'm training. For a marathon. Like you did."

Luke spun his chair towards me. "You did a marathon? I didn't know that."

"There are lots of things you don't know about me." I smiled at him and looked to Fennel. "How did you know?"

"Your next-door neighbor."

"My neighbor?"

"Yeah, Dr. Roland. The ER doc. He worked with my dad in Idaho. Edmonton is such a small city." She laughed and shook her head. "They had me over for dinner a few days ago."

My stomach dropped.

"We got to talking," she said. "I couldn't believe it when we figured out you lived next door."

"When did you say you were there?"

"Just the other day. They've got such a beautiful house. Showed me all around. Even upstairs. You've got a beautiful back yard, by the way."

My face got hot.

"Guess I should've come over to say hi," she said, "but

I didn't want to interrupt you when you were *relaxing*."

Was it my imagination, or did she wink?

Luke looked back and forth between the two of us. His lips parted to say something.

"Better get moving," I said.

Fennel agreed and, while she loaded her presentation onto the computer, added that perhaps we could all have dinner together sometime with the good doctor next door. Luke included.

Luke locked his eyes on me. I pretended not to notice.

"I did something special." Fennel looked up from the computer and beamed. "I think you're going to like it." She maximized the PowerPoint window and there, taking up more than half the title page, was a head shot of me, probably from a web page.

"That's gotta go," I said.

Fennel scrunched her eyebrows together. "Why? It's a great picture."

Luke smirked.

"You look like that actress," she said, "you know, what's her name?"

"Julianne Moore?" Luke offered, knowing this would make me uncomfortable. I didn't look like her at all. Luke insisted I did and, when we'd travel together, he'd bet me that at least one person would come up to me and say so. He always won.

"Yes!" she said. "Has anyone ever told you that?"

Luke could hardly contain himself, laughing and dragging his hands over his face as he leaned back in his chair. I shot him a look.

"It's not appropriate," I said to her.

"Why not?"

"Trust me."

She snapped her finger on the mouse, highlighted the picture, and pressed delete. The next slide had a picture of Luke, standing casually with a sport coat slung over one shoulder. "I'm sure this'll have to go, too," she said.

Luke leaned forward and wiped his eyes while he composed himself. "Yes, please."

She flipped through each slide and, while she had made some excellent graphs that clearly outlined our findings, the slide background was deep purple and the text bright pink. Like one big fuchsia blossom. No problem. Easy to change. But then came the discussion slides. On the first one, she'd inserted an animated rat that ran back and forth across a tightrope as if he'd overdosed on caffeine. He stopped on each end only long enough to bite the corner off a piece of cheese. There were stick men with oversized heads and thought bubbles everywhere. The clincher, the point at which Luke finally muttered an 'oh', was the last slide. Fennel had inserted a cartoon of an obese woman in a bikini: she shrunk down to size zero, lost her suit, and frantically covered her female assets with her arms and hands.

Neither Luke nor I said a word.

She looked at Luke, then me. "You don't like it." She leaned back and folded her arms. "I'm sorry. I tried my best."

"Fennel," Luke said, "You laid it out perfectly."

"Doesn't seem like it." She stared straight ahead at

the screen.

"It just needs some minor adjustments," he said.

She sighed. "Okay, well I've no idea what."

"Well, take the colors. Black and white might look slicker."

She remained stiff and stone-faced until he said that her rat idea was great. Her posture softened and, when he suggested a picture of a real rat, she concurred. She could do that. No problem.

"I know you'll get rid of the stick men, too," he said.

"Of course. Slick, no stick." She jotted down a note.

And this was why students loved Luke. Why so many people loved him. The hammer he wielded was always velvet. Fennel left the conference room without realizing she'd even been hit with it.

"You are something else," I said, once we were alone.

He smiled and said he felt bad for her. She'd obviously worked hard and got some things right. I agreed. She had a wealth of tenacity. I just hoped that she had as much discretion, when it came to my *relaxing* the other day.

Before we parted, I told Luke that I was sorry to hear about their patient. He nodded. Said he regretted that he couldn't have intervened sooner, before the stress of obesity and apnea took their toll. He reflected for a moment and shook his head as if he were trying to shake the image of her out of it.

"Onto brighter topics," he said. "What was all that with Fennel and the next door neighbor?"

I just shrugged and said that he could forget being invited. The probability of having a civil dinner with him and Steven at the same table was close to zero. He laughed.

On my way out, I stopped to check for mail. Genie was at her desk. "Pretty sad about Brenda, huh?" she said.

A patient in the waiting room, engrossed in a game on her mobile device, stopped and looked up.

"Have a good day, Genie," I said and walked out the door.

Chapter 9

CONNER BIGLEY TO THE RESCUE

Conner Bigley pulled up beside me in the hospital parking lot. Bass from Marky Mark's *Good Vibrations* thumped from his stereo into the cool evening air. Wasn't he cold? And was he even born when that song came out? He powered up the window and, while he collected his belongings, the music vibrated the lime green doors of his new Mustang GT350R. After a few moments, the pulsing bass and engine rumble ceased. Conner exited his car with the grace of a beetle trying to get off its back. As he approached me, he looked up once, like a swimmer checking his mark.

"Hey, Conner. Nice car!"

His cheeks flushed as he smiled and explained that its 5 litre V-8 had 526 horse power and could do the quarter mile in 10 seconds.

While we walked through the hospital corridors, he told me, in bits and pieces, about the extended vacation from which he had just returned. "Wasn't long enough," he said. For me, it was too long; it felt like forever to get him to the lab.

When Conner sat down in front of Anbu's workstation, it was as if a switch flipped. I'd never seen this side of him. Fully in charge. He inserted a memory stick into Anbu's computer, tapped on an icon, and waited. A black box popped up. His fingers flew across the keys. The next thing I knew, every folder and file on Anbu's computer was available to be explored. There were all kinds of word documents – grants that we'd written, papers to be published, and excel files filled with data. Nothing out of the ordinary, though. Even the folder he had labelled 'rat inquisition' had nothing in it that I hadn't seen before.

Conner opened Anbu's web browser. The history had links to sites about weight loss, Ferraris, and batibats.

"Batibats?" Conner asked.

I shrugged.

He clicked on the link. "Demons?"

Yes, demons. Apparently disguised as fat old women who live in trees. I could only imagine where Anbu was going with that one.

Conner mumbled something about videos. He opened the movie maker program. There was one recent project named *HDL82much*. I studied the name for a minute.

Conner jumped, when I laughed out loud.

"What's so funny?" he asked.

"HDL. Huey, Dewey and Luey. His favorite rats. Ate too much."

Conner giggled like a school boy and clicked on the file. A message appeared: *The file "HDL82much. mov" is missing.*

"That's strange," I said.

"Not really. Probably just moved." An option to find the file took us to the 'rat inquisition' folder, where we got the message: *No items match your search.*

"Okay, now that's strange," I said.

"Yup." Conner pilfered through every other folder, including the trash, on both the network and the computer's local drive. *HDL82much.mov* had vanished.

"Maybe on a memory stick?" he asked.

I opened the drawer beside Anbu's computer. Pens without caps, wood-stubbed pencils, paper scraps, binder rings, and lanyards, all in a tangled mess. But no memory stick.

"Look underneath," he said.

"Pardon?"

"He liked to hide things."

We lifted the keyboard, the monitor, and scanned the bottom of the chair. Nothing. I opened the drawer again and slipped my arm back as far as possible. I turned my palm up and patted back and forth. The underside of the counter top was rough. Then, about halfway in, the wood felt slick. Scotch tape. And just a little further to the left, the pressed cotton bond of paper. I got down on my knees and peered in. An 8x11 manila Ninsun envelope had been taped there. I slipped my finger under a corner and eased it away.

"Holy shit!" Conner said, when he saw it.

The tab on the envelope had been licked and glued shut and secured with an extra layer of tape and four staples. I ripped it open and peeked inside. There were three sheets of paper.

"What the hell?" I recognized the looping witness signature on the top sheet immediately. Without pulling the documents out, I thumbed through them. The three code numbers, F007, F015, and F020, were there, one on each sheet.

"What's wrong?" Conner said.

I was too stunned to answer.

"Memory stick?" he asked.

"No, far from it." I tucked the envelope into my bag and, as I did, the alarm keypad outside the door beeped. Conner's eyes opened wide.

"Don't worry."

Brittany busted in. She stopped on the balls of her feet and put her hand over her heart. "Whoa!"

"Sorry, Brit," I said. "Didn't mean to scare you."

"No prob. I wasn't expecting anyone so late." She smiled and fluffed her fingers through her short blonde hair. "Just came to check on the rats."

"Conner, you know Brittany."

He raised his hand to say hi.

"That's a popular computer." Brittany set down her backpack.

"What do you mean?" I asked.

"Dr. Schlemmer was on it."

"He was? When?"

"Last week? No, the week before that."

"What was he doing?"

"He was with some IT guy. They were looking for files."

"Which ones?"

"Don't know," she said.

I bet I knew. And I bet they found what they were looking for. There was no doubt in my mind that *HDL82much.mov* was what Anbu had intended to get to me the morning he died. The consents were another story. Why Anbu hid them was unclear. One thing was for certain, though. Something reeked of Schlemmer.

Chapter 10

LUCKY LUKE

Luke stepped out of the parking garage stairwell into the cool autumn air. Navy overcoat, red silk scarf. Could've been going to a photo shoot. He glanced over his shoulder while repositioning the strap of his brief case and caught sight of me. He stopped. Smiled.

"Mackenzie! Going to the hospital?"

"You bet."

"Have time for a coffee?"

"For you? Always. Besides, I want to talk to you about something."

"Funny. I want to talk to you about something as well."

He didn't tell me what that was during our walk there. Nor while we were winding our way through the corridors, nor while we stood in front of the cafeteria pastry display. He loitered for an impossibly long time and finally picked a chocolate-covered donut. What he would have picked anyhow.

"Like one?" he asked.

"Not hungry."

"That's what you always say."

We found a quiet table, away from the hubbub of nurses and doctors who seemed to either be flirting or fighting. Luke slipped off his scarf, hung his coat on the chair beside him, and ran his hand through his thick blond hair. He offered me half his donut. I took it. He laughed and took a bite of his, still smiling while he chewed it.

"Before I forget," I said. "Did you hear any more about Brenda Deswicki?"

"Such as?" he said with his mouth still full.

"What happened."

He wiped his lips with a napkin. "Heart attack. You knew that."

"She was just so young."

"Young people have heart attacks."

"I know. It just seems wrong."

"What does?"

"She was getting fit. That should've lowered her risk."

"Theoretically. But think. People who stop smoking still get lung cancer. There are no hard and fast rules in this thing we call life, especially if the body has already taken a beating."

"I guess."

"Topic change?"

I nodded.

"I've got good news." He looked around to see who was within earshot and leaned in. "I found the missing documents."

A briny wave of cold swept from the top of my head to the pit of my stomach. "You found them?"

"Yes. Why so surprised?"

Because they were in my briefcase, beside my feet. "No reason."

"Truth is," he took a gulp of coffee, "I found the research folders. Still haven't found the consents. Bad comes to worse, I'll call up the three and ask them to sign a new one."

And just like that, I felt like I could breathe again.

"Anyway," he leaned back in his chair, "you said you had something to talk to me about?"

"Schlemmer."

"Uh oh. What now?"

"He was in my lab, on Anbu's computer. I had no idea."

Luke slid both hands into his hair. "Schlemmer. Jesus. What's wrong with him? I told him to clear it with you."

"You knew about it?"

His hands dropped to the table. His hair was sticking out in a multitude of directions. "Yes."

"You didn't think about talking to me first?"

"We needed the files. That day."

"What files?"

"Things like the log of patients in the study, the ethics proposal. All the study files basically."

"I'm a phone call away."

"Didn't think you'd mind." He smiled. "You know I've got your back."

His gaze met my glare.

"If it's any consolation," he said, "I never share my donuts with him."

The corners of my lips began to turn up against my will. "Okay, funny man. The least you can do is tell me how he got onto Anbu's drive."

"Hospital IT." He looked at his watch. "Oh, crap. I've got to get to work, young lady." He stood up and pushed in his chair.

I stood up and did the same. "Okay, old man."

He shook his head, unable to hide his smile. He put his hand in the small of my back as we exited the cafeteria. I reminded him to tame his hair.

Chapter 11

HALLOWEEN HORROR

Halloween. One of my favorite days. The university daycare children were outside my window in their costumes, ready to come in and load up on more candy. One little elephant tripped over a tree root, and his plastic pumpkin rolled on the ground. Candy scattered everywhere. The other children swooped in and grabbed the loot, while the poor elephant wailed. Just goes to show, no matter how old you are, someone's always waiting for you to slip up.

After every last candy was snatched, the children lined up and followed the teacher into the building; the elephant was last. Not two minutes later, there was an urgent tap at the door. A good excuse to set down my red marking pen. I grabbed the bowl of caramels and chocolate bars. Hopefully, the elephant made it to the front of the line.

I opened the door. "Fennel! I wasn't expecting you."

She brushed past me. "I just got my anatomy mark." She threw her exam onto my desk. "Thanks, a lot," she said. When she turned and saw the look on my face, she apologized. "It just doesn't seem like a fair grade."

Fairness. Now there was something to contemplate. Was it fair that I'd be there until midnight, preparing a lecture for her class, the one in which she apparently hadn't been paying attention.

"There's no mystery to marking an anatomy exam," I said as I passed her and sat back down at my desk. "You either answered correctly, or you didn't."

"Yeah, but there's so much to do in this program, and I spent so much time studying about the rib cage that I deserve —"

"The mark reflects performance. Need an example?" I flipped to the second page of her exam. "See here? There's more than one part to a muscle. If you don't specify that, you lose marks."

She rolled her eyes and fell back into the chair. "I could tell you those parts. I just didn't think it was important on the test."

"Okay, show me all the questions you're worried about."

She flipped through the pages and pointed out at least five of them.

"Just as an exercise," I said, "let's see how your grade will change if you get credit for the questions you think I've marked you unfairly on." I typed the numbers into the grade spreadsheet. Her mark went from forty seven to forty nine percent. This meager improvement wasn't unusual. Many students had tried it before, and the result usually sent them scurrying out of my office. She stayed firmly planted, though, and fought to keep her bottom lip from trembling.

"My father is going to kill me," she said in a high-pitched voice.

"It's just one exam."

"You don't know my father."

She was right about that, but I could imagine.

"I didn't even want to do this stupid master's degree." She wiped her tears with a tissue from her pocket. "Or the last one."

"What did you want to do?"

Her face turned bright red. "It's silly."

"It's not silly if it's what you want to do."

Her eyes darted to the candy on the corner of my desk. "Can I have one?"

I pushed the bowl towards her. She picked out all the Mars Bars, ripped the wrapper off one, took a bite, and slipped the rest in her purse. "Sorry," she said. "I'm pretty sure I'm having low blood sugar today."

"So?"

She dropped her shoulders and began to explain. Apparently, what she really wanted to do more than anything, more than an MD or eventually a PhD, was to become a veterinary acupuncturist. She had told her father and shown him a picture of a dachshund with thin wire needles sticking out of his head and neck. Her father ripped the picture in half and proclaimed that his money wasn't going to be spent on any 'hocus pocus'.

"Oh." I couldn't think of anything else to say.

"I know. It's dumb."

"It's not dumb. It's just pretty far off from where you are now."

"Doesn't matter."

Her mascara was smudged. I hated to think it, but it made her look like a raccoon. A raccoon who asked me again about her mark.

I had to be firm. I couldn't change it. She still had two more exams to write, I explained, including a practical one in the cadaver lab, which she may find easier. If she applied herself, she could bring up her grade easily.

"God! You just really don't understand." She stormed out, nearly knocking over the little grey elephant and his friend, a lime-green frog, who had just arrived at my door. They watched her for a moment and then turned to me and held out their trick or treat pumpkins.

A deep throated laugh rattled out from behind them. They flinched.

Schlemmer appeared in the doorway. "I see you're working your usual magic with the students." A grin stretched across his face. The frog froze, with the golden Styrofoam eyes on top of his head looking in different directions – one at the candy bowl and the other at Schlemmer, who now had his hand on the frog's shoulder. The elephant just looked sad. I got up and took the bowl to the children. Both took a handful of caramels and ran. Schlemmer stood and stared.

"Can I help you?" I asked.

"Looks like you're the one needing help."

"Don't you have anything better to do?" I pushed on the door to close it, but he flipped it back with the toe of his shoe.

"She's a bit of a loose cannon," he said, smirking at me.

"Either tell me something useful or leave."

"Useful. Hmmm." He scratched his chin and feigned deep thought.

"Yeah," I said, "like what you were doing on Anbu's computer."

"What do you want to know?"

"Next time you want something from *my* lab, ask."

"Relaax." He stretched the word out like a string of caramel. "I followed protocol. Didn't touch anything but what we needed."

"I don't care. You had no right to do that."

"Take it up with Luke."

"I already did."

Schlemmer cracked a smile. "I'm sure you did."

"Are you done?"

"Yes. As a matter of fact, I am." He looked down the hall. "Looks like you are too." He raised his hand, waved at whoever was approaching, and winked at me before leaving.

There was a distinct clack of heels coming closer. I knew exactly who'd caught his attention. Elizabeth appeared in my doorway. "We need to talk."

My favorite day. Officially vaporized.

She strutted in, slapped the palms of her hands on my desk and leaned across. "We've got one very upset student."

"She already talked to you?" I asked.

"Yes. Last night. Remember who her dad is?" Her

fingernail, painted gunmetal blue, tapped my desk. "Make it better. I don't need this to turn into, what shall I call it?" Her eyes rolled to the ceiling. "A problem."

Her departure was as abrupt as her arrival, and like the north wind, left a cold air mass in its wake.

Fennel stood at my office door the next day, looking as despondent as Diesel after being scolded for chewing a shoe. She didn't come in until invited.

"I'm sorry," she said. "I shouldn't have gotten mad at you about the exam. I was just so worried. I had a good talk with Luke, though. He knew exactly what to say."

A slight flush washed over her face.

"Unlike my father," she continued, "who just unloaded on me, like he always does when I do something wrong." The heat from her face was gone. "I'm so sick of trying to please him. Seems like that's all I've been doing since my mom died."

Her mother was dead?

Fennel looked at me, expectantly, like she wanted me to ask her about it. "It was a car crash. I was six."

"Oh, Fennel, I'm sorry to hear that."

She began to shiver while she told me about the drunk who ran a red light and broadsided them, only two blocks from home. "I can still smell it, you know. The blood. The metal."

My stomach lurched. All I could see was Anbu's car covered with a yellow tarp.

"I've never really had anyone, you know," she cleared

her throat, "to talk to about things."

It felt like a chasm was opening up before me.

Her knee bounced, double speed. "I'm not sure how to say this."

I waited.

"You don't have kids, do you?" she asked.

I shook my head to say no.

"Well," she said, "what I want to say is that, if I had a choice, I'd choose you as a mother. I mean, you're successful, brilliant, and beautiful for your age."

I tried to intercept, but she kept going and when there really wasn't more to say about my positive attributes or how she'd love it if I'd take her shopping, she left my office and, this time, closed the door gingerly.

Chapter 12

CONSENT TORMENT

Genie was sitting behind her desk, inspecting her manicured nails.

"Hi Genie. Is Dr. Schlemmer in?"

"No. Didn't you hear?"

"Hear what?"

"He's at city hall today. Getting a special Mayor's award."

"For what?"

"A music program he started in the inner city."

"Schlemmer?"

"Yes."

"He plays a musical instrument?"

"Yes."

The image of a caped figure with arms raised above the keys of a pipe organ formed in my mind. "Let me know when he gets back."

Genie looked over my shoulder and flicked her chin

toward the clinic door. "He's back."

In walked Schlemmer. He was near glowing, until Genie said, "Dr. Smith wants to talk to you."

"Can't," he said. "Got a patient." He breezed past me down the hall. I followed.

He unlocked his office door, flicked on the lights and threw his suit coat over the chair. "What?"

"Congratulations."

He grabbed his white lab coat from a hook behind the door.

"What instrument do you play?" I asked.

"I don't."

"Well, you must've at some point."

"Do you need something?"

"Piano?"

"No."

"Drums?"

"No." He put his hands on his desk and leaned towards me. "Strings. Satisfied?"

"Cello?"

"No."

"Guitar?"

He cupped his ear with his hand. "I think I hear your rats calling."

"Banjo."

"No."

"Harp?"

Schlemmer glared.

"A harp?" I tried as hard as humanly possible not to laugh.

"What do you want?" he said, while he buttoned

his white coat.

"You wouldn't have accidentally taken a video from Anbu's computer?"

"No, Mackenzie. I didn't."

"Well, there seems to be a file missing."

"Wasn't me."

"You were the only one on there."

"Would you like to see the files I took?"

"Yes."

"Jesus." He flipped on his computer, grabbed a USB stick from his drawer and plugged it in. On it, was a file folder named *Anbu*. "Go to town." He waved his hand toward the computer and walked out.

Seriously? Did he actually mean it? Or was he calling my bluff? Screw it. I clicked through each document, all the while remembering that Schlemmer was bright enough to have gotten rid of anything incriminating. It was all benign. Who was to say this would be the case for the rest of his computer, though? I glanced over my shoulder to the door before opening the search window and typing in *HDL82much.mov*. Nothing.

"Find anything?" Schlemmer's voice came from behind.

I jumped and waited a second for my heart to stop racing. "Nothing notable."

He shook his head, when I walked past him out the door.

Steven wasn't happy when I told him I was going in

to work on a Saturday morning. He attempted to keep me in bed. Might've been successful if it weren't for what I'd found besides the consents in Anbu's manila envelope. I needed to get into the sleep clinic, when no one else was around.

I secured my hair with a bobby pin, put on a little lipstick, and came out into the bedroom. Steven had buried himself under the covers. I drew them back. When I kissed him on the forehead, he smiled and pulled the covers over his head again. Diesel hopped off the bed and followed me to the basement. He watched while I dug around the tool box for a screwdriver and was like a shadow while I collected other essential items. He sat by the door while I tied my shoes. I reached over and scratched his ears. "Wish me luck, heavy D."

While I waited at a red light, with my bag of tools beside me, a dusting of snow in front of my car swirled on the pavement. It spun at the same speed as my thoughts, the ones about the yellow post-it note. I hadn't said a word about it to anyone. It was stuck between the three consents. I didn't notice it that day with Conner, but saw it when I sat in my office, alone with the envelope. Scribbled on the post-it in Anbu's hand writing was the message '*Get down on your knees and pray*'. Now, being enigmatic was not out of the ordinary for Anbu. In fact, at least once a week, he'd throw a puzzle or riddle at me, just to see if I could figure it out. This was different. It stirred a sick feeling in my stomach.

All was dark in the clinic, except for the security light that glowed above the reception desk. There was no aroma of coffee brewing, nor Genie's vanilla perfume. I flipped on the light in the file room and made my way to the *Guarafit* cabinet. In my planning the week before, I'd noticed that the key with the mandarin orange tag was no longer hanging with the others. Each day I checked, it wasn't there.

I took the screwdriver out of my bag. It gleamed. No nicks, scuffs or scratches. It reminded me of my general uselessness at domestic tasks, never mind crime. I inserted the tip of it into the top of the lock, and pulled the bobby pin from my hair. I held the screwdriver steady and wiggled the bobby pin up and down and side to side in no particular order. The lock didn't budge. Bloody *YouTube*. Made it look so easy. I began to jam the screw driver around in multiple directions at the same time as the bobby pin. It felt as uncoordinated as the night Dan McNeal lost his virginity with me: hands and legs and lips, jerking here and there and everywhere. With a click, the lock let go. I turned the screwdriver and opened the drawer.

Inside were the hundred or so neatly filed *Guarafit* research folders. My fingers scrambled along the top of the first six. Noticeably absent, still, was number 7. And 15. And 20. Luke told me it had all been solved, so where were they? I needed to see them. Anbu wouldn't have gone to the lengths he did, pasting the manila envelope in the most obscure place, if there was nothing about these three that made him anxious or curious.

Why didn't he ever mention it, though? Because it was Luke's project? Or perhaps he thought I had enough going on with the rat deaths. The only rat I could think of now was one whose last name started with an S. Genie deserved credit for the way she always looked after him, always being ready when he locked himself out of his office, which occurred at least twice a day. She got extra credit from me that Saturday morning. A key, marked with an S, was stuck to a magnet on the side of her unlocked desk drawer.

I slowly opened the door to Schlemmer's darkened office, half expecting to see him, lying in wait behind his desk. His high back leather chair sat pointed at the door, vacant. The light from the hall was enough to illuminate the cabinet beside his desk where I'd initially seen the orange file folder. I pulled the drawer open, expecting to find three fat research folders, but there was only one thin one with an orange label at the back of the drawer. Inside of it, the contract from the funding agency for the money to study *Guarafit* and a lone picture of an attractive woman with auburn hair. She looked to be about twenty. On the back was written *Kathryn 1985*. I slipped it back, shut the drawer and scanned his bookshelves. A miniature golden harp had been propped against some books in the corner of the top shelf. It stirred the same sense of amusement in me as the other day.

Deflated, I left his office empty handed, and pondered my options. I really had none, other than to break every ethical code of conduct I had agreed to, as well as the promise I'd made to Luke. I needed to get into the patients' medical files. This time, looking for more than just a signed consent form. A complete invasion of patient privacy. If it meant somehow understanding Anbu's riddle, it'd be worth it.

The master list was locked in the consultation room cabinet. I pulled it to once again break the study codes and find the last names associated with the three numbers. I decided to start with number 20. When I saw the name associated with it, the pen fell out of my hand. Participant F020 was Brenda Deswicki. Dead Brenda Deswicki.

The sound of the clinic door opening echoed from the reception area. My heart stopped and re-started with a thump against my rib cage. By the time I shut the computer, put the master list back and locked the drawer, footsteps were coming down the hall. I waited, hoping they'd go the other direction. But their military rhythm became continuously louder and, just when I expected to see Schlemmer, Luke appeared.

"Mackenzie! You nearly gave me a heart attack. I saw the light on and thought someone broke in."

My heart rate began to slow.

"From the look on your face," Luke said, "You nearly had one, too."

"A little. Sounded like Dracula coming down the hall."

Deep lines appeared in between Luke's eyebrows.

"Never mind," I said.

"What do you got there?" Luke was looking at the envelope in my hand.

"I found the missing consents."

"Really? Where?"

"Misfiled with some of Anbu's things. In the lab."

"That's a relief." Luke held out his hand.

"I was just going to re-file them."

"No worries. I'll get Genie to do it."

I passed the envelope to him. "One of the consents is Brenda Deswicki's."

"So?" Luke pulled them out and looked at them.

"So, she's dead. Don't you think it's a little odd that her research file was one of the ones Schlemmer had? Separate from all the others?"

"Not really. But if you're worried, we can take a look together."

I followed Luke, fully expecting him to head to the filing room, where he'd see that her file was missing. Then, maybe he'd finally start to wonder about Schlemmer. But, instead, he went into his office and directly to a shelf behind his desk. Three orange folders had been squeezed on top a stack of books. "Guess I should get Genie to file these, too," he said as he pulled at them. "Didn't think of it after I got them from Schlemmer. What number was she?"

"Twenty."

Luke sat down at his desk. I pulled a chair beside him.

Inside the file were several visit reports, all with nothing that would cause alarm. She was feeling good, happy about the weight loss, sleeping well, and had more energy than before. Her symptoms of sleep apnea, like falling asleep at the wheel, had subsided, and she was no longer using her CPAP machine to help her breathe at night. Her body temperature, blood pressure, and heart rate were all average. The latest laboratory tests all had values within normal for liver function, blood sugars and cholesterol levels. The woman was a picture of health.

"How does someone like her die of a heart attack?" I shook my head.

"Previous poor health. If you look at some of her early lab tests, they're not that great." He flipped to the back of the folder. "Like here. Look at her blood sugar levels." He closed the file. "There are also things we can't measure, like genes."

Luke leaned back in his chair, swivelled to face me, and smiled. "I'm glad you've got good genes. Don't know what I'd do without you around here."

"Really. What is it exactly that I've done for you lately?"

"Well, let's see. You solved the mystery of the missing consents, and you just generally keep me sane."

"Glad I can be of help, my friend." I stood, moved the chair back around to the other side of the desk, and wished him a good weekend.

On my way out of the hospital, I flipped open my brief case to be sure I had handed Luke the correct envelope, and not the one with the yellow Post-it note and the copies I'd made of the consents.

Chapter 13

DOG SITTING JITTERS

I spun through the rotating hospital door into the warmth of the lobby. There, people in winter coats, hospital gowns and scrubs browsed Christmas craft tables. Cinnamon candles, walnut shell ornaments, and green knit socks. It was only November. With so much to do before the holiday, I couldn't even begin to think about presents. Most pressing, the presentation for the conference in Banff. Data analysis was taking hours, ones that I didn't have. I enlisted Fennel's help and, even though I was still met with her blank stares in class, we were having success in the lab. More importantly, since the day in my office, there was no mention of my fulfilling the role of surrogate mother.

In the lab, Brittany turned from her computer and waved; she was working on the layout of my presentation. There was no purple. Fennel was absorbed in work on a spreadsheet. The last bits of data for the conference.

The phone in my cubby rang.

"It's been ringing incessantly since we got here," Brittany said.

I ignored it, knowing how much work we needed to get through, but it started again not half a minute later. I answered it, and got the unwelcomed news that our dog sitter's father had died. She was leaving for Ontario that night. What would we do with Diesel?

"Don't look at me." Brittany scratched her arms as though she had fleas. "Dogs give me hives."

"I could do it!" Fennel looked at me with bright eyes.

"Um, well, maybe I'll just see if any kennels have room."

"I'm serious," she said.

"I don't know."

"I love dogs! And Diesel is so cute."

The hairs on the back of my neck prickled. "How do you know?"

"I saw him when I was over for dinner at–"

"Right."

"Please," Fennel folded her hands together in a prayer position. "I'll take really good care of him."

"The problem is that he doesn't do well outside our house."

"I can stay there."

That was the real problem. The thought of a student in my house gave *me* hives.

"I'm sure your place is nicer than mine." Fennel blew a puff of air through her nose. "And I promise. It'll be just me and Diesel."

The next morning, Diesel sat and watched me pack my suitcase. I couldn't help but worry. Mind you, disaster scenarios ran rampant every time I had to leave him. What if he bolted out the front door, never to be seen again? Or what if he stopped eating because he was so lonely? To think – Diesel wasn't even my idea. Steven had yearned for a dog from the age of five after seeing the movie *Benji*. Aware of my resistance, he convinced me to see *Marley and Me*. It was only three weeks after my mom died. I was a wreck at the end of the movie, when Marley left this world, and sobbed all the way home. Steven apologized for suggesting the movie and claimed to be a bad husband. It wasn't his fault; it was just horrible to see Marley die. Steven agreed, emphasizing what a great dog Marley was and how he was such a big part of that family. And that's all it took. Pairing the word 'dog' with 'family'. I caved. I no longer had a mother and I wasn't one myself.

I threw my swim suit into my suitcase. There I was, leaving the closest thing that I'd ever have to a child with someone who, for all practical purposes, I didn't really know, never mind a student, who wouldn't mean to but would somehow find herself rooting around in my bedroom drawers. The biggest problem? My discomfort with the shrinking distance between Fennel and me. I needed the relationship to remain professional; it was part of my personal code of conduct with students. Steven didn't seem concerned. He said that, just because she'd been a little "needy", didn't mean she couldn't look after a dog. Still, as Diesel poked his nose around my suitcase, my stomach churned. It got worse when the doorbell rang.

I opened the front door. Fennel stepped in without hesitation. A white ski jacket curved along her chest like a fresh layer of snow. With luggage at her feet, she pulled off her blue angora toque. Auburn curls, which had been tucked underneath, flopped to her shoulders.

"Wow," I said, "that new hair color looks–"

"Just like yours?" She smiled and tilted her head to the side. "Hope you don't mind. When your hair dresser called the lab to confirm your appointment last week, I asked if she could fit me in too. Had it done last night after I left the lab. I told her not to make the color too close to yours, but you know how they never listen."

Steven dropped our bags at the door and extended his hand to Fennel. Smiling, she said how nice it was to meet him, how he reminded her of an old friend. She didn't let go of his hand until Diesel started rooting around in one of her bags and tipped it over. A book slid out, cover side up. *Fifty Shades of Grey.* Fennel didn't seem the least bit fazed. In fact, she seemed to be taking her time, bending over, grasping the book in her fingers, and sliding it back into her bag.

She straightened herself and removed her coat. The jacket obviously needed more insulation: her nipples were like two darts trying to poke through her spandex ski top. Steven's eyes just about bugged out.

"Here – let me take your suitcase upstairs for you," he said.

"I can handle it." Fennel flexed her arm muscle. "I've been working out."

Steven asked if Fennel knew how to use the cappuccino maker. When she said no, he put his hand on her shoulder and led her to the kitchen. "Every hardworking student needs caffeine," he said.

She giggled and, while they walked together, told him how much she loves coffee. The two of them chattered about the machine, and she said how great it was of him to show her how to use it. When the steam jet hissed, she let out a whoop and made a comment about all the pressure that must've been building.

"Hey you two – the taxi should be here soon." I stuffed one last pair of shoes in my bag. "Better show Fennel the security system. And the guest room."

A series of beeps echoed from the back door while Steven armed and disarmed the security pad.

"Okay – I totally get it!" she said.

"You're a quick study. Come with me. I'll show you your bedroom." Their voices trailed off as they headed upstairs. Fennel's new improved look crossed my mind; hopefully, she'd warmed up.

A yellow taxi slid to a stop in front of the house. I called to Steven, who finally got down to the door five minutes later. If we didn't hurry, we'd miss our plane to Calgary.

Inside the car, the artificial pine smell was thick and powdery. There weren't any unadulterated oxygen molecules left. In the pine haze, I realized that we didn't cover the list of 'what ifs' – *What if Diesel gets sick? What if he won't eat?* Dammit. The car was already rolling.

Maybe she was reading it at that very moment, seeing as how she was nowhere in sight. Diesel, on the other hand, was watching from the bay window with perked ears. He stretched his neck as we pulled away.

"He'll be just fine," Steven squeezed my hand.

"Did you see the way he looked when we were leaving?"

"Yeah – he was saying sayonara dudes. I'm on holiday with the hot chick."

"Nice." I pulled my hand away.

"What?"

What? I couldn't stand the grin on his face. That's what.

Across the river, the Hotel MacDonald glowed orange against a background of grey high-rises. Fog plumes shot from the tops of them into the dark morning sky. A thick crust of snow had buried the river bank and hoarfrost coated the skeletal trees. It was as cold in the taxi as it was out there.

Steven put his hand on my knee and whispered, "I'm just kiddin', Red."

"Did you get a hold of her?" Steven's head was the only thing sticking out of the hot tub at the Banff Springs. Steam swirled in the frigid air around him, and a full moon hung in the sky just above distant snow-capped mountains. The ice-glazed sidewalk made my walk to the edge of the pool treacherous, but didn't prevent me from putting a little extra swing in my hips.

Nor did the glacial air stop me from lingering on the top step, just to be certain that Steven noticed my new bikini. When I finally plunged in, the water stung my goose flesh.

"She said he's doing great."

Steven stretched out his arms to me. "Come here." The combination of his flushed cheeks and frozen hair was such a nice contradiction. And, we were all alone.

He hoisted me onto his lap and brushed a wisp of hair from my forehead.

"He's eating," I said. "And apparently even behaving on walks with her."

"Mhmm." He ran his fingers along my back.

"Hasn't chewed anything and only got into the garbage once."

"See," he said as his hands came to rest on my hips. "I told you she'd have everything under control." His fingertips slid down my outer thighs. "Just like you."

"Mmmm."

He put his nose against mine. "Not only cute, but smart."

I wriggled from his grasp.

"What?" he said.

I pushed away from him.

"You! You're cute and smart. Not her. Aw, come on, Mack. Come back."

I floated to the other side of the hot pool. His voice was still pleading from somewhere behind the rising steam. Sometimes, he could be such an ass.

Chapter 14

COMING HOME

Home. There was always this moment, a feeling of warmth, that settled over me with the familiar smell of home. That night, after the icy road trip from Banff to Calgary and then the delayed flight from Calgary to Edmonton, it was even more comforting. We hadn't been gone for long, but I missed my bed and I missed Diesel.

A note had been placed on the kitchen counter.

Dear Steven and Mack,

Diesel was an angel. Nothing exciting to report. He ate before I left this morning. Thanks for all the food and everything. I enjoyed my time in your home. I'll throw your key in the mailbox.

Fennel

X

I wasn't sure what to make of the smiley face under her name.

"What's wrong with it?" Steven asked.

"It's weird, don't you think?"

"It's just an emoticon — a smiling stick angel." Steven took the stairs two at a time to let our angel out of his crate. The two of them started romping. It sounded like twenty circus animals had been freed from their cages. I dragged myself upstairs. My suitcase bounced on each step behind me. The bed in the guest room was made, with the spread tucked in as if I'd done it. Good girl. The towels in the guest bathroom were placed in neat piles in the stand, and the sink and shower looked as if they hadn't even been used. But the comforter on our bed was disheveled and the pillows jumbled.

Diesel darted into the room and jumped on the bed. "Oh you bad dog!" I ruffled his ears. "Been on the bed? Get off." He obeyed, bumping the dresser on his way out. Not a minute later, he barrelled back in and jumped on the bed again.

"Off!"

Diesel didn't move.

Steven came into the room.

"Since when does he think he's allowed on there?" I said.

"Looks like he got spoiled by the dog-sitter." Steven walked over to the bed. "Off."

Diesel jumped off and ran into his crate in the corner of the room.

I slipped into my nightgown and climbed onto the bed. Diesel tried to jump up again, but averted when

Steven snapped his finger at him.

"I knew this dog-sitting thing with her was a bad idea," I said.

"We'll get him back into shape. Don't worry." Steven got into bed.

He was right. Worrying about retraining Diesel was a waste of energy. I needed sleep. I plumped my pillow and pulled up the bedding. But when our feather duvet, with its soft bamboo cover, settled in around me, something felt amiss. Was there a foreign scent?

"What are you doing?" Steven asked.

"Nothing."

"You just smelled your pillow!"

"No I didn't."

Steven sighed and, in less than a minute, his breathing was rhythmic and heavy. I smelled my pillow again and decided that my imagination was working overtime. A streak of orange from the street light shot through the space where the blinds met the window frame. My eyelids, heavy, began to drop. The orange spear that the light cast onto the wall split into two and then was gone.

Through a partially-opened door, a slippery voice whispered '*This is not yours!*' Where was Diesel? Dirty dishes and rotting food cluttered the kitchen. Parrots and parakeets were trapped in the guest room, bald, and squawking, pecking at each other's oozing sores. One naked parrot mocked, *Hello ugly, Hello ugly.* Another taunted, *Where's Steven? Pretty boy, Pretty boy.* The master bedroom. A woman with auburn hair was straddling him, on our bed, giggling. He grabbed her hips, pulled her down, and moaned. She looked back at me, but needn't. I already knew. A polluted grin crept onto her face and black sludge dripped from her lashes. She lunged at me with a piece of broken glass from a picture frame and plunged it into my eye.

The orange spear from the street light blasted into focus. My heart thumped in my chest. Steven was still sleeping peacefully beside me in the dim amber glow of the room, his eyelashes resting on his cheeks.

What would Ninsun have to say to Gilgamesh about that one?

What would *my* mom say?

She'd probably tell me it was just a dream.

I had thirty minutes to spare before Fennel was due to arrive at my office. I'd asked her to meet me there, so I could give her a small present for watching Diesel. My latte was strong, the news was dull and, before long, I was at the end of the paper, on the page with the obituaries. Not sure what prompted me to linger there. Morbid curiosity, I guess. That's when a picture sprung off the page. My eyes fell to the name underneath. Angela Ashbury. The patient who wanted to fit into the pink size six dress by Christmas. Under her name, the words '*Gone too soon*'. A list of family members – brothers, sisters, nieces, nephews, aunts, and uncles who would never forget her big heart and dancing green eyes – were under that. And one line lower, a message from her husband, of his undying love for her. Then nothing. No indication of the cause, nowhere to send donations.

I closed the paper. I needed to find Luke, but in walked Fennel, unexpectedly early. She wanted to know all about the conference. Her eyes fell down to the small gift-wrapped package sitting on my desk. She smiled when I pushed it towards her. Without wasting a second, she proceeded to rip off the pink paper. "Oh it's beautiful! Thank you. Please be sure to thank Steven." She clipped the amethyst necklace around her neck and ran her fingers along the silver links. "Diesel was such a little angel."

I stood and started to pack things into my briefcase. She continued to sit.

"He visited me in that soft cozy bed every night."

It felt as though a spider ran up one arm and down the other. "Didn't you sleep in the guest room?"

"Of course I did!" She uncrossed her legs and crossed them the other way.

"Did you really find that bed comfortable? It's hard as a rock."

"Oh sure, I'm not picky. Besides, everything in your house is so beautiful. It'd be hard to find something wrong with *any* of it. Not like my place."

This from the girl whose father could afford to buy three houses like mine. Her being obtuse bothered me, but where was I supposed to go with it? Come out and ask if she slept in my bed? Maybe she ate my porridge, too.

I looked at my watch. I needed to get to Luke before the department meeting. "How did everything go with the alarm? Did the code we set work for you?"

"Yup. No problems."

I started to ask her about Diesel being on our bed, but Luke appeared at my door.

Fennel turned partially in her chair and slung her arm over the back rest. "Hello, Luke. Love your tie."

He grinned and then looked at me. "Thought we could walk to the meeting together."

We all left my office, and when I expected Fennel to go the other way, she simply clung to us. To Luke, actually. Shoulder to shoulder, they talked about a movie they had both just seen. It wasn't until we reached the meeting room door that she detached. Luke headed in before I could pull him aside.

The meeting room was divided as usual, MDs on one side of the table, PhDs on the other. Luke and I ignored this unwritten rule and sat together. Schlemmer followed us in. He looked down his nose at me and planted himself on the other side of Luke. The room was full of chatter.

"Need to talk to you," I said quietly to Luke.

"What's up?"

"Another patient."

"Another patient…"

"Dead."

"Who?"

"Angela Ashbury." I lowered my voice as much as possible. "I'm getting really worried."

Schlemmer leaned around Luke. "People die all the time, Mackenzie. Especially when they're carrying around a hundred extra pounds."

His hearing should've been as bad as his vision.

"Thank you for your informed medical opinion," I said, "but I don't remember asking you."

Schlemmer snorted.

Luke leaned over to me and whispered, "Never mind him. I'll look into it."

Elizabeth, MD and PhD, sat down at the helm of the table and started moving through the agenda like a shipmaster. "Okay. Next. Student issue. Who asked for this to be on the agenda?"

The head of neurology cleared his throat. "I have a concern about Fennel Gutterson."

"Fennel Gutterson. You're her advisor, aren't you, Mackenzie?" Elizabeth asked, as if she had never talked to me about Fennel before.

"You know I am."

Elizabeth lifted a paper off the table and peered at it through reading glasses perched on the end of her nose. She waved her hand towards the neurology professor. "Continue."

"She was supposed to hand in an assignment three weeks ago. I asked her for it repeatedly. Nothing. She also failed my midterm, and from what I hear, I'm not the only one."

"Who else?" Elizabeth took off her reading glasses and avoided looking at me.

One other professor put up his hand.

"What's the problem here? Our students are cream of the crop. They just don't start failing!" A red blotch in the shape of a tarantula appeared on Elizabeth's neck. She dropped her hand and hit her pen, which flew across the table and onto Schlemmer's notepad. Too bad it didn't bounce up and stab him.

"Mackenzie, you're her advisor. What's going on?" Elizabeth asked.

"Not sure. She came into the program a straight-A student just like everyone else. She works hard in my lab and completes all tasks. Having said that, she did fail one of my anatomy midterms – as you know – and had trouble with the second."

"If she fails any of these courses," Schlemmer piped up, "she's dead weight and should be expelled." Schlemmer rested back in his chair with his hands cradling the back of his head.

"I see." Elizabeth put her glasses back on. "We cannot afford to have her flunk out…now can we? Get to the bottom of this, Mackenzie."

Before I could open my mouth to speak, she was already steering the ship in a different direction.

Chapter 15

CHEATER CHEATER

I swiped my identification card. The door to the anatomy lab swung open and a rush of warm air blew past me. The thermostat was at twenty five Celsius. The cadavers wouldn't complain, but the students certainly would. They were coming in for a lab exam. The storeroom at the back was sweltering and the smell of formaldehyde inside overpowering. The buckets with heads were on the shelf labelled 'necks', and the ones with rib cages were stuffed behind the limbs. I began to load what I needed on two carts. Sweat trickled down my back. The containers barely fit, and when the pail of half heads nearly tipped onto the floor, I cursed whoever turned up the thermostat.

At the first lab table, I pulled out 'Henry' – half his head, anyhow. Formaldehyde rolled over his brush cut and into the pail. He hadn't changed in four years. He looked at me with a partially-opened eye and stunned mouth. His head wobbled when I set it on the tray.

"Don't mind me, Henry." I slid my gloved fingers along the nerve tracts in his brain. There it was. What was once dubbed the 'third eye'. The pineal gland. Over the years we had come to understand that what it really does is control circadian rhythms. I stuck it with a pin and smiled. The purple flag on the end stood at attention. This would be a hard one. Not far below that, I poked a pin into the breathing centre. That one should be easier.

Next came the disembodied rib cages. I had no pet names for these even though, at some point, they breathed, danced, and made love. Now they were just headless, limbless torsos submerged in oversized Rubbermaid containers. Their leathery brown skin was coated underneath with hardened fat, some more than others. Sad to think how that simple yellow substance could cause so much strife. I pulled it all back and began marking bones, muscles and cartilage. Twenty numbered pins later, the torsos were ready.

Two minutes to go and I still had to mark the necks. While I stuck pins into the throat and trachea, voices began to collect in the hall. The door rattled. They were eager to get in and get this part over with. Finally, at five minutes past the hour, a knock. I ran between tables and spread out the dissection trays.

I opened the door. "Ready to face mortality?"

A few of them laughed.

"Please line up at the far side by the whiteboard."

They filed in, dressed in their lab coats and clutching their clipboards.

"Grab a pair of gloves on your way in."

Fennel walked in behind one of the men, Josh. He grabbed two pairs of gloves and passed one to her. Josh was one of the younger students in the class and had a reputation for partying more than studying. He pulled on the middle finger of one glove and flicked it at Fennel. She laughed and swatted back at him with hers. Someone made a comment about how hot it was in the room. I ignored it.

"Okay, everyone," I said. "Get yourselves into groups of five at each table."

Fennel and Josh, shoulder to shoulder, giggled about something on their way to a table.

I handed out a sheet with numbers and blanks beside each of them. "You'll have four minutes at each station. You are to identify each flag."

"How do we know which pin is which?" Fennel asked.

"They're numbered," I said. "When the timer sounds, you'll move clockwise to the next station. There's no going back. Just do your best at each place. And don't touch the pins. Ready?"

The timer sounded and off they went. The silence was eerie, as if only Henry and I were in the room, but when time was up, the quiet was broken by groans and shuffling feet. After the second bell, the group that Fennel was in moved to the table at the far end of the room. She was unusually close to Josh. Shoulder to shoulder again. He appeared intent on the task. In fact, he almost looked like he wanted to shoo her off like a fly. I slowly made my way to them. Fennel's eyes flicked from her paper, to the cadaver, to Josh's clip board, and back to her paper. I moved closer, slowly. Sure enough. Paper, cadaver, Josh's clip board. Then she'd scribble something down. I watched until the timer went again. She did the same thing at the next table. This time, I counted. Ten times.

The bell sounded and, as the groups rotated, I approached her. When I put my hand on her clipboard, her eyes opened wide. I took it from her.

"What are you doing?" Fennel asked.

The students stopped rotating and turned to look.

I handed Josh a new sheet. "Please continue on this page and give me what you have. Everyone else, just stay where you are for a moment. No talking."

"What's going on?" Fennel stood with her hands on her hips.

I took her by the arm.

"I wasn't finished!" she said.

I pulled her close to me. "You were a little too close to your classmate."

"I'm just really hot." She tried to pull away. "I was gonna faint. That's why I was close to him."

"You can cool off out here." I led her through the doorway and closed the door behind us. "You're free to go."

"You can't do this to me." Her face was flushed.

"Don't worry. I'll be in touch." I went back into the lab and closed the door. Even though it still was hot in there, the students were standing between the dissection tables, frozen in their spots. They all looked guilty.

"Move to your next station."

Three more table rotations and the exam was finished. No one said a word to me as they handed in their test sheets. Josh came up last.

"I hope this won't affect my mark."

"You'll hear back from me."

"I seriously had no idea. I didn't even realize she was close."

"We'll talk later." I side-stepped to get around him and walked towards the storage closet. Moments later, the lab door clicked shut. I put the two pages I had confiscated side by side. Josh and Fennel. Sure enough. Fennel's answers were an exact match. Even the ones that were wrong.

Chapter 16

BITTER PILLS AND TARTS

Luke's voice called from behind. It sounded thin in the cold morning air. I turned and nearly slipped on ice.

"Careful," Luke smiled.

I wasn't in the mood. The past couple days hadn't been the best.

"Ooh, that's not my usual happy Mack," he said. "Let me guess. Fennel?"

"How'd you know?"

"Had a conversation." Luke opened the door to the building and waved me in. "Guess she thought I might have some advice."

"And did you?"

"I told her I didn't want to get involved."

"Well, now that you are, any advice on dealing with Elizabeth?"

"Nope. Good luck with *that*." He patted me on the shoulder and began to walk away. I called for him to stop.

"I've been waiting for you to get back to me about Angela Ashbury," I said. "You ignoring me?"

What I couldn't say was that I had once again breeched patient confidentiality. Or should I say I tried to? My afterhours visit to the medical record room behind Genie's desk left me empty handed. Angela's file had been missing. I searched the rest of the clinic but couldn't find it. Problem was, I couldn't talk to Luke about it. This time, I was certain he'd have my head for snooping through his patients' records.

He smacked his head with his hand. "I completely forgot to let you know. I'm sorry. I know how concerned you were about it. It's just that I've been so busy."

"So? What was it?"

"It took a while to find out. Maybe I just didn't want to think about it. Or maybe I was afraid to tell you."

"What? Was it her heart?"

Luke looked down. "No. Car accident."

"Oh."

"Hit a little close to home, you know?" His eyes began to mist.

I knew. It had been just over five months since Anbu's death, and it still felt like yesterday. "Man," I said. "Anbu, Fennel's mom, Angela. Should anybody be driving anymore?"

"Makes you wonder, doesn't it?" He patted me on the shoulder again. "Truth is, you know this little meeting you have coming up? Your life will be in more danger there than in your car driving home tonight." He smirked.

I thanked him for his support and walked towards Elizabeth's office.

Elizabeth pushed a plate of butter tarts across her desk. She baked them. Who knows why she thought I wanted one; half of them were collapsed, and the edges of all were burned. When I told her no, she pushed the plate a little closer, so I took the one that was lightest brown.

"I understand you've accused Fennel of cheating," Elizabeth said.

The tart tasted like baking soda, leaving me with the dilemma of whether to spit or swallow. "I've discussed it with her," I said, and swallowed.

"The only proof you have is that her answers were similar to one of her classmate's?"

"They were exact."

"Perhaps they're just two really bright students."

"The mistakes were exact."

"Who's to say that Josh didn't cheat off Fennel?"

"Me."

"No proof." Elizabeth's stare bored into me. "Your accusation is weak."

"She was right up against him."

"Apparently the room was very hot. Several students have confirmed that. Fennel felt faint and was leaning on him for support."

"Are you kidding me?"

"Not to mention that you started the exam late. You

know how that can stress out students. Especially ones like Fennel who seem to have some exam anxiety."

"I started only five minutes late."

"Quite frankly, this *accusation* poses a serious problem. Fennel's very upset."

"Hmmm."

"She's a fragile girl, with what happened to her mother and all." Elizabeth let out a sigh, flush with feigned concern. "Not only that, but her father promised two more very generous donations. Without these, say goodbye to two department members."

Tempting, if one of them would be Schlemmer.

"Of course," she said, "those without tenure are at greatest risk."

"Is that a threat?"

"How do I put this?" She spun a pen on her desk. "Guess I just have to be blunt." She stopped the pen. "Your tenure application has a few glaring weaknesses. It could go either way."

My cheeks got hot. "Then why did you encourage me to put it forward?"

"Now, now, Mackenzie. All I'm saying is that the dean is on the evaluation committee and, well, let's just say that he's gotten to know Fennel's father." Elizabeth took off her glasses, leaned across her desk and got so close that her coffee breath choked me. "Why make your life more difficult by sending this report to him?" She lifted a copy of the report I'd drafted and let it drop.

"Because the academic integrity code says that I'm required to."

"Not if you didn't actually see what you thought

you saw."

"So, you want me to unsee what I saw? I'm stunned."

"Yes, sometimes you are stunned, aren't you? Just do the right thing."

On the way out of her office, I wanted to punch the wall, even though I had no idea how to throw a proper punch. *Stunned.* What made her think it was okay to say something like that? It almost topped an incident that had happened a year before in Sweden. Mind you, trying to convince an international colleague to tell me to fuck off, when I stopped at their table to say goodnight and then doing it herself when he wouldn't, is hard to beat. What made her think it was okay to say *that*? Besides fifty shots of Akvavit? Who knows. No one believed that story. They probably wouldn't believe this one either.

I walked into the Dean's office, shoulders back, solar plexus forward, and dropped my report on his desk.

Chapter 17

LUSCIOUS LUCY

Halfway down the hall, Fennel was weaving back and forth while looking at her mobile phone. Nearly ran into a hospital laundry cart. She flicked her auburn hair to the side, looked up and saw me. She froze, spun on her foot, and began to walk the other way.

"Fennel."

It was as though I had just told her, if she didn't stop, I'd shoot.

"We need to talk." I said.

She turned to face me. "I need to eat lunch."

"Fine. Nothing that we can't discuss over food."

We walked towards the cafeteria in silence. Small particles of dirt crunched beneath her spiked heels. I hoped she wore boots to work and changed in the lab; we were in the depths of a cold snap. When she turned to go through the cafeteria doorway, I noticed, for the first time, a tattoo of a black panther with bright yellow eyes on her ankle. The lemon irises bored into me, warned me to keep my distance.

More silence while we got settled at a table beside the courtyard windows. Fennel had no lunch and refused to let me buy her anything. Her jaw was clenched so tight that, even if she had let me get lunch, she wouldn't have been able to open her mouth to eat it.

I told her that she passed the final anatomy exam, although barely. She looked relieved, but not for long. The problem was that, for the cadaver exam, I couldn't give her anything but a zero. It pulled her final grade below a passing mark.

"I did not cheat." Fennel's voice sounded thin and tight.

"We've already been over this."

She stared out the window. "Fine, then. Just tell me what I can do to make this go away."

There really was nothing she could do, I explained, and until the dean made a decision regarding her behavior in the cadaver exam, it wasn't clear if she could even take the course again. If he agreed that she cheated, then she would not be able to repeat the course. Without the course, she wouldn't be able to complete the master's program. I outlined this in detail to her.

With her elbows on the table, she put her hands to her forehead, as if she was blocking the sun. Her fingers were shaking. "You obviously don't get it!" She dropped her hands. "My dad is going to kill me, and he's gonna stop supporting the program."

The wooden stir stick that I'd been bending back and forth snapped in two. Fennel's eyes got wide.

"Your dad is a problem for you, not me."

"I thought, out of anyone, you'd understand." She paused for a moment and then lowered her voice. "Just remember, we've all done things that would be embarrassing, if they got out."

My mind flashed back to the deck in the summer.

Fennel threw back her chair and stormed off. On the way out, she bumped into Luke. Spun him halfway around and just kept going.

Luke took her place at the table and promptly gave me half his donut. "Problem?"

I nodded. "Trying to be nice, but I feel like killing her."

"She's probably not the right one to kill."

"Mmmm."

"She still working in your lab?"

"Like I have a choice."

"Did that come from the top top, or just the top?"

"Just Elizabeth. Apparently, I don't have a case to fire her. Elizabeth started talking wrongful dismissal and a bunch of crap like that. Jesus. It makes me wonder how much dough Fennel's dad has forked over."

"Talking about dough," Luke said, "I have good news about our fund-raising gala for Ninsun. Guess who's coming to town to help out?"

"Brad Pitt?"

"Close. But not quite. It's your good buddy Raucket."

I coughed in the middle of my swallow. "And this is good news *how*?"

I hadn't given serious thought to Raucket since he retired to a small island on the east coast, but now his image crashed out from the recesses of my brain. Every little bit of him, every contradiction. His wild hair, his perfectly-groomed beard, his god-awful polyester clothing, his fine Italian leather shoes, his refined use of the English language, his delivery of words that were like well-aimed daggers. When I made it through my PhD, no thanks to him as a supervisor, I packed him up into a neat little box and tried not to think of him again.

"I know, I know," Luke said. "You guys didn't have the best of endings. Or middles or beginnings. I can see you're not pleased, and I certainly understand why. But it'll be great for publicity. The guy still carries a lot of weight."

The stir stick was now broken into several pieces. A small pile of destruction. A crow landed in one of the trees in the courtyard. It opened its beak wide and began to squawk, thrusting its head forward with each call. I felt like doing the same. Protesting Raucket's visit.

"Mackenzie, look at me."

I did, but was filled with anger that made my eyes water.

"Lots of people who were around then, have left," he said. "And those who haven't, mostly have forgotten. You need to as well."

I laughed to get rid of the constriction in my throat. "Okay, I'll just forget it, Luke."

"You just wait until he sees the empire you've built here. He'll crap his pants. There's one more thing," Luke said, "and here she comes." He nodded his head towards the sliding glass cafeteria doors.

Lucy Briggs – a PhD classmate from years ago – with

her cinnamon brown hair and long legs was walking towards us. Even though she wasn't Raucket's student, he had a special affection for her and hired her as a research assistant. He even went so far as to question why Luke would think of hiring *someone like me*, and that, if it were up to him, he would hire Lucy because she had more experience. Rumor had it that the only place she had more experience was in Raucket's bed.

"What the hell is she doing here?" I asked.

Luke cleared his throat and stood up. "Lucy! I'm glad you found us." She extended her hand. He clasped it with both of his.

"Your receptionist told me I'd find you down here," she said, locking her eyes on him.

She finally looked at me. "Oh, Mackenzie. So good to see you."

I bet.

"What brings you to town?" I asked.

"My little brother is getting married. You'd think he could've planned it better. Two trips home from Ontario in only six months."

"Two trips?" I asked.

"I'm coming back for the gala. Wouldn't miss it."

"We were just talking about that," Luke said.

"Love to stay and chat," I said, "but I've got a class to teach."

Lucy laughed. "I remember those days. Release time from teaching is glorious."

"How did you manage that?" Luke asked.

"Salary award. They're hard to come by."

Of course they are.

Luke looked at his watch and then to Lucy. "We should go. Patients will be here soon. The documents are in my office."

As we exited the cafeteria, he put his hand on her shoulder blade to guide her in the right direction, I'm sure, and left it there. I walked behind the two of them in the cloud of her floral perfume. Her pencil skirt was skin tight, and there wasn't an ounce of fat where it shouldn't be. As we neared my lab door, Lucy wrinkled her nose and said, "Geez, you'd think they could've put you in a better part of the hospital." Without another word to me, and before I could come up with any kind of witty retort, the two of them continued on their way to the sleep clinic.

Later that week, Fennel was in the animal room with two females, unfamiliar to me, but friends of hers. They were in the university drama program. Fennel explained that they wanted to see the rats. Had I neglected to discuss my visitor policy with her? I couldn't imagine I had, but I also couldn't remember doing it.

"I'm going to have to ask you to leave," I said. "This is a secure lab."

One of the women, Rebecca, prickly as a Brillo pad, made no effort to move. She scrutinized all the rats and focused in on Huey, Dewey and Luey. "I think it's so cruel that these little guys have to spend their days donating their bodies to science."

"They're treated better here than they would be in a

gutter in New York City," I said. "They aren't wanting for much."

"Except their freedom," Rebecca said, as she walked out of the rat room.

The other drama student paused at the doorway. "Is it true that you're trying to make them fat?"

I didn't answer, just moved myself into their space and began to usher them out.

"Don't you think it's cruel to intentionally give them a disease that's going to make them sick?" Rebecca asked.

"No. I think it's cruel when we fail to do everything we possibly can to understand a disease that causes people to lose their lives behind the wheel, because they haven't gotten a good sleep."

"When they get too fat to move, what will you do then?"

"Get them a gym membership."

Rebecca's face hardened. She turned and left without even saying goodbye to Fennel. The other woman slipped out behind her.

The lab door slammed shut.

I turned to Fennel. "Did I not talk to you about the visitor policy?"

"Not that I remember."

I pulled out the policy and procedures manual and pointed to the page on lab access. "Read this."

"Well, it didn't seem to be a problem for Dr. Briggs earlier this week."

"You let Lucy in here?"

"Luke did." Fennel tapped her foot and smiled. "She

sure is great, by the way. She's so smart and has so many ideas."

"I'm sure she does." I handed over the lab manual.

Fennel snapped it from my hand, stuffed it in her bag and exited.

That Lucy. She always had a lot of ideas. Most of them bad.

My stomach growled. It was seven in the evening, and if I didn't hurry, there'd be nothing left to eat in the cafeteria. I had an evening of writing ahead of me. And if Fennel would ever get the data analysis completed, I could actually write up the results, and spin a conclusion. The rat paper would be a slam dunk. The editor of the Journal of Respiratory and Sleep Medicine told me as much. Elizabeth could, then, stuff her comments about my research productivity.

In the cafeteria, only one piece of lasagna remained in the metal heating bin, its edges curled and nearly an inch away from the side of the pan. Disgusted, I turned and accidentally drove the corner of my empty tray into the back of a patient who was picking at wilted leaves in the salad bar. I apologized. The woman spun around. Her eyes widened when she saw me. "Dr. Smith!"

Her face was familiar.

"Jacklyn Gardner," she said.

Still nothing.

"I was in the weight loss thingy. I met you when you were training Anbu. Terrible to hear about him."

"Oh, Jacklyn. Sorry. Didn't recognize you. Must be the outfit."

She laughed and tugged at her hospital gown. "Yeah. Ticker problems."

"Your heart?"

"Mhmm. Would just start racing like a jack rabbit. Felt like I was dying. Couldn't breathe."

"Did you tell Dr. Schlemmer?"

"Yes. He said it was just an anxiety attack. But, yesterday, I started blacking out. I'm here for some tests. They're keeping me in for a few days. Do you think I should tell Dr. Schlemmer?"

"I'll let him know."

She held up a limp lettuce leaf, tarnished around the edges. "Hah! I don't think even rabbits would eat this."

"Suppose not." I tried to laugh. "Hope they figure out what's wrong."

"Me too. Can't stand eating this green crap." She flung the leaf back into the salad bar. "Nice to see you," she called out as I walked away.

My empty tray clanged when it hit the metal conveyor.

Upstairs in the Ninsun clinic, light from under Luke's office door glinted off the floor tiles. When I knocked, the door opened, courtesy of Schlemmer.

"Hey Mack," Luke looked at his watch. "What brings you to my door this late? On a Friday, no less."

"I need to talk to you."

"About what?"

Schlemmer stood there and smirked.

"About the *Guarafit* trial."

"What's up?"

I glared at Schlemmer, hoping he'd leave, even though Jacklyn was his patient. He didn't budge.

"I ran into a study patient in the cafeteria. She's in hospital under observation for what sounds like heart arrhythmia. Between her and Brenda –"

"Who is it?" Luke said.

"Jacklyn Gardner."

"It's just anxiety," Schlemmer said.

"Didn't sound like it," I said.

"Since when did you become a physician?" Schlemmer said. "Besides, what happens on the trial isn't really any of your business."

"It sure as hell is. I enrolled some of them. Remember?"

"Now now, Mack," Schlemmer cracked a wide smile, "the risk of atrial fibrillation in obese patients is about fifty percent higher than normal. We learned that on the first day of medical school."

"Maybe," I said, "you just don't want to hear this because you're worried about your precious funding."

"Okay, you two," Luke said. "That's enough." He informed me, in the pleasant and reassuring way he always did, that there was nothing happening that wouldn't be happening anyhow. If there was, the Phase III trials that were going in full force, both here and at other institutions, would never have gotten off the ground. And so far, there were no unexpected events.

"Maybe it's too soon," I said. "Maybe you should follow up with your subject group from Phase II."

The two of them stared as if I just suggested that

the moon was made of cheese, and we could prove it if we'd just send up another shuttle.

"To find what?" Luke said, his voice now angry. "That half of them have what they'd have anyhow? Hang out in emergency tomorrow and there'll be another one. You're over-reacting."

Heat radiated off my face. Coming from Luke, the message had twice the gravity. I took a deep breath and looked at Schlemmer. "Don't you think you should at least call her or the ER and check in?"

Schlemmer's face reddened. "Don't tell me what I should or shouldn't do."

"Listen," Luke rolled back his chair and stood. He looked at Schlemmer. "I know you're flying out early tomorrow. I'll call first thing in the morning just to make everyone happy, okay?"

"Fine." Schlemmer stomped away to his office.

Luke stared at me for a moment and then shook his head. "You need to relax or you're gonna end up in the ER beside Jacklyn."

Chapter 18

FENNEL'S FREEDOM

Unbelievable. I sat there stunned. Elizabeth's words still echoed in my brain. What I was, and wasn't going to do. There was no proof, Elizabeth said. The administrators in graduate studies apparently agreed, and the dean was annoyed at even having to deal with the issue. I was to pretend, when it came to Fennel, that the cadaver exam never happened. Take the percentage that was allotted to it, add it to her final exam, and recalculate. This gave her an overall passing grade for the course. But barely. Her transcripts would be changed to reflect the decision. The only repercussion to her? An 'honesty in academia' course, which was optional for all graduate students anyhow.

I stomped into the sleep clinic, past Genie, who was looking at Facebook, and down the hall to Luke's office. When I got there, his door was partially closed. And there she was. Fennel. Inside. Thanking him, and saying she didn't know what she'd have done without him. While I stood there listening, I became acutely aware of a presence behind me. It was Schlemmer. Smirking.

"If it's any consolation," he said, "I was on your side this time."

Seriously? What angle was this? We were done teaching, so he didn't need me to cover a lecture. I begrudgingly agreed to put his name on the last paper I submitted, even though he did nothing to contribute. So, it wasn't that. We were done running Phase II of the *Guarafit* trial. Wouldn't need my help there. Maybe it was the patient, Jacklyn Gardner, the one with heart issues, which he so easily dismissed. He could think again.

I'd already tried to pull her medical file one night, when I was alone at the clinic. Wasn't certain what I was looking for, just hoped it would be obvious. I abandoned my quest, though, when I thought I heard someone behind me. His sudden camaraderie wasn't going to stop me from going back and digging into her file. I just needed to find the right time.

Schlemmer didn't wait for me to respond. He just walked away with his right hand up in a goodbye salute.

I pushed open Luke's door. Fennel turned. No one said anything. The triangle of silence was broken when Fennel said she had to run to class. She thanked us both for all our help on her way out. Her heels clicked down the hallway.

"Maybe *you* helped her," I said. "She's deluded if she thinks I did."

"Some advice?" He didn't wait for my answer, just

told me to let it be, for my sanity. And tenure.

"How exactly did you help her?" I asked.

"I simply listened. Nothing more, nothing less."

I asked him if he had any advice about how I was supposed to work with her in my lab. He just smiled his Luke smile and told me he was certain I'd find a way. I wasn't so sure.

Chapter 19

DATA DEBACLE

The rat manuscript. I avoided writing it for some time. There had been other things to think about over the past couple months, like figuring out exactly what to do with Fennel. The deadline for submitting the manuscript was looming, however. I had one weekend at home to make headway. So what did I do? I stared at my screen. Typed a sentence. Deleted it. Made a cappuccino. Wrote another sentence. Deleted it. Scratched Diesel's ears. Thought about a sentence. Forgot it. Folded my underwear. Changed the title. By Sunday night, I had accomplished a mere introductory sentence.

In the lab on Monday morning, I still didn't feel like writing about what might as well be called the "ooga booga" study. It'd taken two years, two long years, to get to that Monday morning. Up to then, everything that could've gone wrong with the study, did – from the animal MRI equipment failing, to the rats not being cooperative. Couldn't blame them. If I had my head put in a restraining device and my body encased in a small tube, I also may have been obstinate. As usual, Anbu was the one who figured out how to deal with the rats. A mild sedative, lots of treats once they were in the tube, and mock MRI trials, including recordings of the noise, until the rats acted as if the whole thing was just another day at work.

Unlike any other paper, though, there was something about writing this manuscript that was creating a dull pressure under my skull. The journal editor had promised me, if I met his deadline, he would fast track the paper without a full peer review. Maybe that was it. That kind of thing was risky and not always appreciated by the research community. But it was his free will.

My fingers hovered over the keyboard. I waited for creativity to kick in. Just as I was about to type the second sentence, Fennel burst into my cubby, hands firmly planted on her hips.

"All the data I've been working on are gone!"

"Okay. Whoa. What?"

"The rat data. For your paper. You know, the stuff I've been analyzing forever."

The earth slipped from beneath my feet. This bloody study was possessed. "Are the original data, the respiratory traces and the MRI scans, still on the computer?"

"No, they're gone too."

Perspiration broke on my upper lip. Brittany came up behind Fennel.

"She thinks I did it," Brittany said, popping her head to the side of Fennel's shoulder. "I can't even get onto her drive, and I certainly wouldn't erase data!"

I looked to Fennel. "What about the external drive? You back up, right?"

I didn't wait for her to answer. The two of them parted to let me pass and followed me to the cupboard where the external drive was housed. The lights on it were blinking, a sure sign that it still had a heartbeat.

"It's not there either," Fennel said.

"What?" I dropped my head. "Didn't you back up?"

"Of course I backed up."

My heart drummed in my ears and miniature black dots began to prick in my vision. If this study didn't give me a stroke, Fennel certainly would. I understood how the data could disappear from one drive. But two? Yet, after a thorough check of the network, including Fennel's drive, reality hit. The data weren't anywhere. I got up from her computer. She was right behind and barely moved out of my way, when I told her I needed to think.

What if my second copy of the original data was deleted? The one I secretly made and stored on an alternative drive? Anbu had suggested it to help me sleep at night.

I went into my cubby, alone, and typed in the password. A message popped up. The drive was not accessible. This could not be happening. I took a deep breath. Calmed down. Typed again, one key stroke at a time. The drive opened, and the original unanalyzed data were there. My heart rate slowed to normal. But still. What was I going to tell the editor now? I'd already been waiting on Fennel for weeks.

"Fennel. Come here please."

She walked into my cubby. A lemon yellow scarf hung around her neck. She flicked one end over her shoulder. The silk fluttered through the air like a feather.

"I'm not sure what to say about this," I said, trying to whisper.

"Well, there really isn't much to say except that someone in here is sabotaging me," she said, loud enough for Brittany to hear.

I wanted to take that yellow scarf and twist it. Unfortunately, she was the only one trained to link and process the data. To train anyone else now, even Brittany, would take too long.

"Start over from the beginning," I said.

"How?"

"An IT friend told me how to recover the original data."

Surprise flitted across her face.

"I'll do the reliability check," I said. "Whatever you've done by Friday."

"A reliability check? *Before* everything's done?"

Anxiety swelled in my stomach. She was right. I should do a random re-analysis on the whole data set, but I just didn't have time. My schedule was stacked after the end of the week.

Fennel left the lab without saying anything more. I felt a palpable sense of relief. But not Brittany. She was on the brink of tears at the edge of my cubby, swearing to God that she had nothing to do with it.

"I know," I said.

"Yeah, but she made it seem like it was me. I'd never

do something like that."

"Why don't you take a little break?"

When the door closed and there was no one but me and the rats, I picked up the phone and called the one person who I knew could help. Twenty minutes later there was a knock at the door.

"Conner." I immediately felt a sense of relief, just saying his name. "Good to see you."

He blushed.

"Come in."

He went straight to Fennel's computer. Focused as a pin of light, he pulled up system windows I didn't know existed, popped in a memory stick, and proceeded to click away.

"You got a horse." He nodded his head at the computer while the names of hundreds of files flew by. "A Trojan."

"A what?"

"You know, malware."

"Is it a virus?"

"Not really. Just a program. Downloaded, to hack in."

"And then what?"

"Crazy shit, I mean, stuff. Keystroke logging. Watching someone's screen. Crashing a computer."

"Is that what happened?"

"Maybe. Anyhow, this'll get rid of it." He pushed up his glasses on his nose and worked some sort of computer magic. "You're gonna want to beef up your security."

"We're behind a firewall here. Shouldn't that be secure?"

"Should be." He watched the program as it continued to scroll. "Inside job, maybe."

"Hey Red," Steven's voice came through the phone. Throaty. Sexy. "Guess what? I made reservations. Just you and me. Tonight. Our favorite place."

"Oh man, Steven. I can't. There was a complete blow up in the lab today."

Dead silence.

"Do you even know what day it is?" he asked.

Searching, searching. *Oh God.* "Of course I do."

"Well don't you think we should celebrate?"

"Yes. But if I don't work through tonight and the rest of the week, I'll never get this paper out on time. It was invited. I've got a hard deadline."

"And they can't cut you a few days' grace?"

"No. They can't."

He was surely going to say he understood, wasn't he?

Nope. There was only the buzz of the telephone.

"If the situation was reversed, Steven, and you had a deadline to meet, I'd understand."

"Well, that's exactly the point, *Mackenzie*. The situation is never reversed. I'm always the one waiting. I wait for you to get home from work every day. I wait for you to eat with me, to listen to me. I wait for you to come to bed and, maybe, just maybe, have sex, or at least tell me you love me."

"I'm sorry. But, what's the big deal if we celebrate a few days from now?"

"Wow. I should sign up for the monastery. I'd get more action with a nun and a little communion wine."

"That's really nice."

He hung up.

Heaviness set in my chest, an ache to be ignored, pushed down, compartmentalized. My hand was still on the phone, when I realized that Fennel had been standing at my cubby.

"Um, I feel really sick," she said. "Think I'm gonna puke."

She looked fine to me.

"I know you need stuff done." Her voice squeaked. "I'll make it up to you. Promise."

I stared for a moment in dismay. This day couldn't get any worse. "Fine. Get better."

It was three in the morning by the time I got home. The back porch light was off, and there was no moon to illuminate the path to the entrance. My vision was blurry from having stared at the computer screen for so long. In the shadows, the door lock was invisible. I overcame that challenge but tripped on the ledge of the door frame when I walked in. I wanted to throw my bag across the floor. You'd think Steven at least could've left one light on back there.

Inside, the spotlights over the eating bar were the only source of brightness. A box, wrapped in silver paper with a red bow, sat directly under one of the beams. A card was leaning against it. The envelope was blank.

I ripped it open. On the front of the card were the scripted words, *'Love You'*, encircled by pink foil hearts. Inside it said *'Today and Always. Happy Anniversary'*. It was signed 'Steven'. He usually signed cards with something like 'You are the love of my life' or 'I'm the luckiest man on earth'. There was nothing like that. No x's. No o's.

Inside the box was an ostrich egg, glossy and red like a candied apple. It was nestled in navy velvet. The egg was from Cape Town, from a little store on the water front. It was one of the most beautiful Steven and I had seen on our trip there, but it was expensive and we agreed that it was too fragile to carry home. It'd be just like Steven to figure out how to do it without me knowing. God, I was an ass.

The bedroom was dark. Steven's breathing was heavy and rhythmic, and when I slipped under the covers and touched his shoulder, he remained motionless.

"Steven," I whispered.

"I'm tired."

The bottom of my stomach fell out.

"Would you mind explaining this?" I stood in the bathroom doorway the next morning with a lemon yellow scarf in my hand. Steven stopped shaving for a moment to look back at me in the mirror. The circles under his eyes were as dark as mine.

"Looks like a scarf," he said.

"No shit. Looks like Fennel's scarf. What's it

doing here?"

It was on the floor by the front entrance. I found it when I went to get a pair of shoes for work.

"She stopped by last night," he said.

"Fennel. Stopped by?"

"Yes."

"What the hell for? She was supposed to be sick."

"She needed someone to talk to."

"And so she chose you?"

"Mhmm." Steven stretched his neck and felt for spots he might have missed.

"You don't even know her? You met her for, what, five minutes?"

"Guess she thought I could provide some insight."

"On what?"

"Your moods."

"What is that supposed to mean?"

"She felt really bad about what happened in the lab. Knew you were steamed and didn't know how to approach you. She said you were pretty cold when she left."

"You've got to be kidding me. And you fell for this?"

"For what?"

"For this thing she does. This sucking up."

"Cut her a break." Steven breezed past me. "She's just a little lost."

"She found her way here pretty easily."

"Bloody hell, Mack. I don't really care about her."

"Well that's good to know."

"Maybe you could try to be a little less selfish, though."

"Me?"

"Yes, you."

"Now what is *that* supposed to mean?"

"With me. With her. She looks up to you, don't you see that?"

"I think I've seen all I need to see."

I stuffed her scarf to the bottom of my bag and, on the way to work, contemplated throwing it out my window into the path of an oncoming semi.

"I've seen that look before." Luke sat down in the chair on the other side of my desk. "What's up?"

"Nothing."

"Mack, I know you better than that. It's about that patient, isn't it."

In all the fuss, I'd forgotten about Jacklyn Gardner in her blue hospital gown.

"That's why I'm here," he said. "I called her, but forgot to tell you. Her tests were all negative. She had esophageal reflux, masquerading as heart trouble." He leaned forward. "But, you got me worried. So, I looked into her file. I really shouldn't have. She was one of Schlemmer's. Anyhow, she was fine during the trial. All tests normal there, too."

"Yeah, but when was the last time he saw her?"

"I don't recall exactly."

"How far out is she?"

"Didn't you hear me? She had heart burn."

I sat silently, and fought the urge to retaliate.

He reached his arm back and pushed on the door. It clicked shut. "Okay. Spill." He sat and waited. "I'm not leaving until you do." He definitely looked comfortable, leaning back in the chair with his ankles crossed.

"It's Fennel."

"What'd she do now?"

"Besides losing a shitload of data? Hit on my husband."

"Huh? When?"

I told Luke about the anniversary fight and the yellow scarf in my front entrance. "She heard me on the phone. Knew we were fighting. Suddenly had to puke."

He smiled and shook his head.

"Think I'm being paranoid?"

"Not at all." He stood and walked over to the window. Touched one of the blooms on the orchid he gave me. "I wasn't going to get into this with you." He turned and leaned against the shelf in front of the window. "She hit on me, too."

"Fennel?"

"The one and only."

"When?"

"A couple of times. Once when she was dog sitting for you. Called me over, because there was a bee in the house. She was in hysterics. Said she was allergic."

"What? It was winter? How come I never heard about this?"

"It was so ridiculous, I didn't think it was important. Second time was when she came to talk to me about the cadaver lab cheating issue. Both times it was nothing, really. Just verbal innuendo. Still. You might want to keep an eye on her. Not that you and Steven have anything to worry about."

I tried to remember the last time Steven kissed me. I mean really kissed me. Jesus. When was the last time we had sex?

"Do you?" Luke asked.

"Of course not."

Andrea Bocelli's voice glided out my office speakers and floated into the air. It filled the room with a kind of magic. I couldn't understand the words, but they sounded like love. Like the anticipation of seeing a lover, of touching skin, of hearing a warm and familiar voice. He sounded as though he was reminiscing about the first time he felt the warmth of her body and the softness of her lips under an Italian night sky, filled with falling stars. Steven crossed my mind, and the spell was broken. Since the Fennel episode a week ago, we had barely communicated.

My office phone rang. I hoped it would be him. It was Brittany. She said she needed to chat. Could use a coffee. And while trying to be casual, there was an urgency in her voice. We agreed to meet at the Wren's Den, an old corner store converted to a coffee shop.

The hinges of the wooden door creaked. A bell jingled overhead. The smell of browned butter, sugar and cinnamon, and freshly ground coffee reminded me of my grandma's house. Brittany was perched on a couch by the window, reading a book. Lace curtains rippled from the open window beside her. For a moment, I imagined Fennel's yellow scarf floating to the floor in the entrance of my home.

"Hey you." I said. "What'll it be? The usual?"

"How could I say no?"

The Den's cinnamon buns were always fresh-baked, warm, and sticky, with just the right combination of cinnamon and pecans. The sweet buttery smell wafted up from the bun on my walk back to Brittany. She glanced up from her book and closed it wistfully. "Just reading about Frederico."

"Since when are you into trashy romance novels?"

"Since I needed some sort of escape from real life."

"That why you want to chat? Boys?"

"No." She rolled her eyes and pulled off a quarter turn of the bun. A string of caramelized sugar stretched from the edge. She caught it with her finger. While she wrapped it around the dough, she said, "Know all this weird stuff around Fennel – with data going missing?"

"How could I forget?"

"Well, the other day I was going downstairs to the lab. I heard a conversation in the stairwell." Brittany put the cinnamon bun into her mouth, closed her eyes and sighed. "Delicious."

"And?"

She finished swallowing. "It was Fennel and Luke. She said something about a cadaver, but I didn't quite catch it."

"Okay…"

"How do I say this?"

"Just say it."

"I know you like Luke and everything, and I don't want to say anything bad about him, but I think there's something weird going on between the two of them."

"Like what?"

"There was a whole bunch of, um, well, giggling in the stairwell."

"Hmmm."

"You know. Sexy like."

"Gawd. Okay, listen Brit. I've already talked to Luke about it. Don't read too much into it. Best not to give it another thought."

The curtains blew out from the window. In blew a bad feeling. It'd be hard not to give Fennel another thought.

All was quiet while I worked in my lab cubby. The rats were fed and happy, and my morning coffee was hot and comforting.

The alarm system on the lab door beeped. I wasn't expecting anyone for at least another hour. Fennel's footsteps crossed the floor. Bold and assertive, until they came to a sudden stop. She must've seen it. Hanging over her computer monitor like a Jolly Roger. She took a few more steps, quieter this time, then her bag hit the floor.

She appeared at my cubby. Scarfless. "Um, thanks."

"For what?"

"My scarf?" She raised one eyebrow and didn't take her eyes off me. When the silence got to be too much, she continued. "I was just really worried about you."

"Let's get something clear. I am your supervisor. You are my student. My personal life is none of your business."

"I was only trying to help."

"The only place I need your help is here. Do it again and your time in this lab will be cut short."

"Don't think my dad would like that."

"I don't really care what your dad likes."

"All I meant was that he will have my head, if I screw this up."

"Then I guess you better not screw it up."

Chapter 20

SLEEPING STIFF

The hallway to my lab was eerier than usual. The lighting from the emergency panel barely reached my door. What caused the power outage this time? Bad wire? Surge from the MRI machine? Ghost from the morgue? He'd have no trouble getting into the lab, because without power and with only ancient generators in the hospital, the security pad was dead. So were the lights inside the lab. I had opened the door with a key. It was unusually silent inside, which meant that, in the rat room, all environmental controls – the ventilation, temperature and light regulation – were compromised.

A pen light, barely brighter than a firefly, was enough to illuminate my way to the back of the lab. The rat room was as warm as Grandma's house, but smelled sufficiently less pleasing. Without ventilation, the ammonia vapors had grown thick. I flashed the dim yellow beam of the pen light across the cages. Paper bedding rustled while the rats scrambled for cover. Not a single crackle, though, from my favorite rat cage, and inside, arranged in a bizarre lineup, were what looked like three tree stumps. Huey, Dewey and Luey, all quite plump, were on their hind feet, clinging to the metal bars with their front paws. Their chins were propped against the cage and their obese bodies motionless. Terror struck. Did they somehow not receive any ventilation during the night? Had rigor mortis set in? I moved the light closer. Dewey's fleshy belly bulged rhythmically against the crosshatches of the cage. The same for Huey and Luey. Their pink noses jutted into the air, conduits for gentle breaths slipping in and out of their lungs. They were sleeping.

The skin on my neck tingled – rats don't sleep standing up. Rats curl up, and cluster in their pack for warmth, comfort, and companionship, and they usually don't sleep when it's dark. Before I could capture the image with a camera, all three began to stir and retreated to the cage floor, yawning and stretching.

"Hey!" A voice came from behind.

I flinched. The pen light clinked against the wall before it hit the floor.

I turned to see Brittany's outline. "Don't sneak up on me like that!"

"What's going on?" She smirked. "A séance?"

"Almost."

Brittany and I sat out in the dark lab with only the pen light on the table. She soaked in every word about the rats and what it might mean about sleep apnea in humans. The only obvious explanation for their behavior was that when they laid down to sleep, their airways collapsed. They couldn't get enough oxygen, so they stood up and let gravity pull the fat towards their feet. The most amazing thing was that the three of them adapted. Humans don't. They'll gasp for air throughout the night without a clue. Then, walk around the next day in a stupor, wondering why they're so tired.

The power came back on. Brittany squinted as her eyes adjusted. "What's next?" she asked.

"Not sure. Not a word, though, Brit."

"Of course not."

I didn't know what was next. I was still recovering from the *ooga booga* study. It had finally been published, but only after what seemed like an excruciatingly long time waiting for Fennel to reanalyze the data. Throughout those days, her yellow scarf hung from a coat hook in the lab. Something to wrap around her neck and pull, if her behavior got out of line. It didn't. Other people's behavior, however, was suspect. Especially Schlemmer's. When it came to order of authorship on the manuscript, he somehow thought he should be first. If not first, certainly second and before Luke. He claimed that it was he who conceptualized the whole study, even though he did nothing after that to contribute. I mean, weren't the five papers from the *Guarafit* trial that he had published, in one year alone, enough for him? In the end, I couldn't believe my eyes when I clicked on the link to the published version of my paper. Schlemmer's name was there alright, second to mine, but Luke's didn't appear on it. Anywhere. Turned out that Fennel had forgotten to attach his signature page with the rest of ours to the email she sent to the editor. In usual Luke style, while I'm certain he was upset, he didn't hold it against me or make my life difficult. He simply said that I owed him big the next time around. The relationship between him and Fennel seemed to cool after that, however. Which was probably for the best.

In the end, the whole drama around that paper had worn me down. But that morning, what I witnessed with the rats, was the first thing that had given me a buzz of excitement in weeks.

"We need to talk." The irises of Elizabeth's eyes, usually dark brown, looked black.

"If this is about Luke not being on the paper, we've already worked that out."

"It's not." She motioned me into her office, went around to the other side of her desk and sat down. "Let's just say Luke must have a horseshoe you know where."

"What's that supposed to mean?"

"The paper you just published."

"Yeah?"

"The one that you were so proud about being fast-tracked." She had opened her arms wide when she said the word *proud*. She still had them spread.

"Is this about Schlemmer?"

She folded her hands in front of her. "Tell me what rats you used."

"All of them." Except for Huey, Luey and Dewey.

I was saving them for the replication paper, but she didn't need to know that. "Why?"

"Who analyzed the data?"

"Fennel."

"Something happen to it?" She tried to ask this innocently, but her voice was pregnant with expectation.

"Why?"

"Just answer my question."

The last thing I wanted was to get into that. Damn, Fennel. Sometimes, I wish she would just disappear. Elizabeth didn't flinch, didn't even blink, while I spilled the gory details of the missing data incident.

"And, so, you re-analyzed the original data?" she asked.

"What's up with the twenty questions?"

"What's up?" She laughed and shook her head. "Let me tell you what's up. I got a call from Bob. The editor."

"And?"

"There's a problem with the manuscript."

"Typo or something?"

"No. A bit more serious than that."

Here it comes…Schlemmer. I knew he'd find a way to get me.

"A formal complaint has been lodged against you," she said.

"A complaint? About what? That Schlemmer wasn't first author?"

Elizabeth raised her eyebrows. She shook her head.

"What? That it was fast-tracked?"

Elizabeth sat, stone faced.

"Oh man," I said. "I knew I shouldn't have agreed

to that."

"Just stop, Mackenzie." Elizabeth glared. "A whistle-blower called. Told Bob your data were fabricated."

"What! That's crazy. Who?"

"Whoever it was said you made up the data to show the effect you reported."

"That's nuts. The results came from *real* rats and *real* data."

"That Fennel analyzed?"

"Yes, and the reliability analysis on that checked out."

"Glad to hear you're confident, because you're going to be audited."

"Are you kidding?"

"The VP Research talked me through the process."

"You've already talked to the VP?" The room started to spin.

"I'm to notify you in writing that a complaint has been lodged."

She pulled a sealed envelope from her drawer. I couldn't bring myself to look at it. The world around her was fuzzy.

"There'll be an inquiry," she said. "If anything comes of it, there'll be a full investigation. The VP suggested that Bob choose the expert. It'll have to happen fairly quickly."

"Not Raucket. I couldn't handle him rifling through my lab."

"Such petty worries, Mackenzie. You should be more worried about preserving your reputation. And the university's, of course."

The room went into a full spin. I think I heard her

calling after me while I ran down the hall.

The metal door of the bathroom stall clanged against the brick wall. Vomit splashed into the toilet bowl and splattered back at me. I leaned back onto my heels, wiped my face, and fought another urge to heave.

"Listen," Luke said, "people aren't happy that you beat them to the punch. It's novel research. Someone's jealous." He reached across the table and patted my hand. "From the sounds of it, everything is under control and this is just a blip on the radar screen."

A blip. This was more like a blight – an enormous one.

"By the way," he moved his hand back to his coffee cup, "Let's keep this quiet. With the gala and all."

Of course. Anything Luke did had to be no less than a smashing success. Never mind a black-tie affair, filled with MDs and prominent medical researchers from around the world that was sponsored by *Zirica*, the start-up pharma company that was running the *Guarafit* trials. This blemish on my lab and Ninsun wouldn't quite equate with that mystique.

Chapter 21

THE RAUCKET HAS LANDED

Outside my office door was a face I should recognize. It took a couple of seconds to register. Skinnier and saggier than before, but framed with the same disheveled, curly hair.

"Mackenzie Smith," Raucket said, as if nothing had ever transpired between us. He moved forward with open arms, forcing me a step back. His sunken eyes, those same lifeless marbles, inspected me.

I backed up another step.

"I see they put you in old Dorothy's office." He rubbed his hands on his thighs and looked around the room. "Hear you got a lab at Ninsun, too, and that you may even have some non-human forms in there." His eyebrow hairs, even longer than before, stretched halfway up his forehead.

"I've crossed over to the dark side," I said.

He looked to my bookshelf and laughed. "Boy, I'd

like to see that."

I started to pack my briefcase.

"Heading out?" he said.

"Going to the clinic."

"Me too. For my lecture tomorrow, you know, and my speech at the gala on Friday." He tugged on the lapels of his light summer jacket. "Guess I still got it goin' on."

God help me.

He wasn't leaving and I was late. Reluctantly, I invited him to accompany me to the hospital. The walk there was stale. We had nothing to say to each other. Like a fruit fly, he followed me. All the way to the lab. I felt compelled to use my body to block the security keypad while I punched in my code.

"Wow. Some system you got there," Raucket said with a grin.

"It does what I need it to do."

He stuck his fingernail into the gash on the door from the pocketknife. "You should get that fixed."

The alarm sounded its all-clear. I was glad to see it was working again.

Brittany turned from her work station. I introduced her. Fennel was in the animal room, watching the rats as instructed and waiting with a camera. She was drumming her fingers on the door window, preventing any hope of catching them sleeping, never mind in an upright position. I opened the door.

Huey waddled to the front of the cage.

"Wow," Raucket said. "Fat little buggers, aren't they? What the hell are you feeding them?"

I stood quietly.

"Well," he said, fixated on the three rats, "everyone is entitled to their secrets now, aren't they? If I'm allowed to ask, what are you studying?"

"The relationship between weight and sleep apnea."

"That's been done," he said.

"Not like this." I walked out of the rat room. Fennel trailed behind. My comment wasn't enough to wipe the smug look off his face. I considered telling him about the rats sleeping upright, but thought I'd let him read about it one day instead. What a prick.

Fennel pulled a document from a folder by her workstation. "We just published this."

It was the bloody *ooga booga* study. Raucket looked at the title and raised one eyebrow. He flipped to the third page, studied a figure, and tossed the paper on the table. "Huh."

Brittany looked at me with wide eyes. Fennel dropped her head and smirked.

There was a knock at the door. Everyone looked relieved.

Luke appeared much happier than the other day, when we discussed the whistleblower news. Then, again, his name wasn't on it, so I imagine his stress levels were significantly less than mine.

"Herb! So good to see you!" Luke thrust out his hand. Raucket grabbed it and pulled him in for a half-hug, and a pat pat pat on the back.

"Likewise," Raucket said. "I was just having a look at my protégé's lab here."

Ugh.

Luke smiled. "You don't have to go far to find people trying to emulate her work."

"Well, she learned from the best, didn't she?" Raucket grabbed the lapels on his jacket again. He was going to tear them off if he wasn't careful.

Luke forced a laugh. "So tell me, Herb, what do you need to get ready for your lecture?"

"Access to a computer would be nice."

"I'm sure Mackenzie wouldn't mind lending you a space here," Luke said as if I weren't standing right there. "We're so cramped up in the clinic."

"Great," Raucket said. "I'll come back after dinner. Gonna meet an old buddy for a steak at The Keg."

"I can't be here this evening," I said.

Luke barely let me finish. "I'm sure we can lend Professor Raucket a code for the evening. That way he can access it at his own convenience."

Was he kidding? I hoped my disbelief was obvious. He knew how much I disliked this man. "The only problem is that the security system—"

"Ah…the good old security system," Raucket sighed. "Are those crazy *CAFÉ* people still around? Waving their stupid little banners and fighting for the lives of all rats?"

"No disrespect, Professor Raucket," Fennel said, "but I can see their point. My friends showed me some websites. Of course, this doesn't apply to Huey, Dewey and Luey." She rolled her eyes. "They're treated better than the average kid in the inner city."

"Who the hell are Huey, Dewey and Luey?" Raucket asked.

The space under my desk was too small to crawl under.

"They're the stupid fat rats who won't sleep," Fennel said.

"You named your rats?" A joker smile materialized on Raucket's face. "Ha! Ha! Oh man – you named your rats!" He slapped his leg. "You've gone soft, Mackenzie. Rule number one – don't get close. By the way, they're rats, not ducks. Not sure if you realize that."

"Do you know what, *Herb*? I'm fully aware of that."

A look of disbelief crossed his face. When I was a student, he always insisted we call him Dr. Raucket.

"Time to go." Luke took Raucket's elbow and guided him towards the door.

"I'm done here," Raucket said.

"Mack, see that Dr. Raucket gets a code to your lab." Luke popped his head back in before the door closed. "We need to talk. Noon."

Brittany was the first to speak after the door closed. "I don't mean to sound rude, but Dr. Raucket was a real jerk."

"I thought he was charming," Fennel said.

The clock on the wall read eleven. I had precisely an hour to stew about Luke wanting to give Raucket access to my lab.

It was noon. Exactly. Luke was sitting in front of his computer, staring at something on the screen.

"I don't want Raucket in my lab."

Luke jumped and clicked shut his screen.

"I thought we agreed," I said, "after the little pocket knife incident, that access would be tightened. Giving Raucket a code, even a visitor one, violates it. No one else will be there."

"Seriously, Mack. What harm can come of it?"

I closed his office door. "With everything that's been going on? Lots!"

"Like what?"

"Digging around for more ammunition."

"Think about it. He's retired. He has no reason to bother with petty grievances. Whoever is making up these lies about you is in your sphere right now. A competitor. Speaking of which, who's doing the audit?"

"Andrew Pickett. Flying in from the UK on Monday."

"Thank God the gala will be over," Luke said. "Can't imagine him showing up in the middle of it."

"I'm not done with the Raucket issue."

"Just let him use your lab tonight."

"I'm not comfortable with it."

"Why? It's not like we're letting some unknown into your lab. We know this man."

"Exactly."

"Come on. You need to put your differences aside. They're personal. This is business. And he's not a criminal."

Luke got up from his desk and politely informed me that he had to go. And, just like that, he opened his door and left.

When I finally closed the document on my computer screen and blinked, it felt like a layer of my corneas peeled off. It was almost seven o'clock in the evening, and Steven was expecting me home for dinner. First, I needed to put away a stack of files, safe from prying eyes. Raucket hadn't shown up. Who knew if he even would. Next, I needed to check the rats.

"Goodbye boys." Huey, Dewey and Luey toddled to the front of the cage, when they heard the treat bag crinkle. Despite my dread of seeing Raucket again, and the fact I was going to be late for dinner, the rats needed a little extra love. They'd been deprived since Anbu was gone.

I reached in and picked up Huey. His plump body was warm against my cheek. I told him he was my favorite fat rat and put him down. He skittered to the back of the cage with his treat. Dewey was next. His four pink paws dangled above my head from his sloth-like body. With my index and middle finger touching his two front paws, I told him that he was my favorite lazy rat and set him back into the dent in the shavings where he'd been laying. Finally, Luey. Tummy up, his body stretched from the tips of my fingers down onto my wrist. I scratched his belly, told him that he was my favorite docile rat, and put him back in the cage beside the others.

All three of them lined up, side by side, six eyes gazing out as if to say thank you for the love and come back soon.

A loud crash of thunder rumbled the ground beneath my feet. Outside on the deck, the kitchen light radiated through the window, and in the middle of it was Steven, washing something at the sink. The back entrance was dark, but the smell of curry made me suddenly aware of the hunger I'd been ignoring all day.

A plate, wrapped in foil, was sitting on top of the stove, and a glass of white wine was on the counter beside. My 'hello' got no response. Steven started the dishwasher and turned to leave the kitchen. Without looking at me, he said, "There's a plate for you on the stove."

"Sorry for being late." My apology fell flat. Steven disappeared downstairs to the TV room.

While I ate cold butter chicken and drank warm wine, thoughts swirled about rats that slept standing up and rats that had come back from a previous life.

Chapter 22

THE TRIO

On the way to work, the radio announcer was making a big deal out of the summer storm the night before. It created a power outage in the university area, brought the light rail transit to a halt, and stranded a full train of passengers for over an hour on the bridge that crosses the river. With that having gone on in the area, I knew I'd find the power out in my lab. It didn't matter, though. I had a key as a backup. And I'd already been coming in without turning on the lights, just to observe the rats sleeping upright. The tricky part was getting into the animal room without making noise or startling them with the pen light.

That morning, the outline of their upright chubby bodies was obvious again. A rush of excitement fluttered in my stomach. What a nerd. Honestly! There had to be better things in life to get excited about than fat rats. I crept closer, slow, silent, and careful not to flash the light directly on them. Something was different. They weren't leaning against the cage. Instead, somehow, they'd propped themselves up in the middle. I got closer. Brightened the light.

The beam clearly illuminated Huey's feet. What I saw couldn't be right. It just couldn't. His toes were dangling above the paper bedding. I flashed the light up to his head. A thin cord, with one end made into a noose, was pulled tight around his neck. The other end was tied around the cage's wire mesh. His pink eyes were completely lifeless and his lower belly was stained with urine. He wasn't the only one. Dewey and Luey also were dead. Tied in a row beside him, hanging.

The rats in the other cages were hiding, in whatever way they could, with only a tail sticking out here and there from under bedding or behind a ledge.

I crumpled to my haunches and inhaled deeply, but it still felt like I couldn't get enough oxygen. There was a lingering presence of evil in the room. It made the hairs on the back of my neck prickle. I sensed a presence behind me, waiting with a rope, slack between two bony hands, ready to sling around my neck. I stood and spun around to find only an empty space filled with an invisible horror. I fled.

In the darkened corridor, the cement wall was cool against my back. I slid down until my butt hit the floor. Even with my eyes squeezed shut, the image of their dangling bodies wouldn't go away. I had to get myself together and fix this before anyone else arrived. I took a deep breath. And another. And still another. With a whir, the start of the air conditioner made the vents in the ceiling buck. Power had returned and the corridor was now brightly lit.

I stood up and inspected the door. There was nothing – no scratches, no broken locks, no signs of forced entry. The nick was still there, but no new note attached. *CAFÉ* would've left their calling card. More importantly, they would've needed access. Fennel's annoying friend, Rebecca, could've gained access through her. Would Fennel have let her in to spite me? No. Even though she hated me, anyone who wanted to be a vet acupuncturist would not let harm come to an animal. Furthermore, why would Rebecca hang them? Was she so insane to think that, by sacrificing those three, who were already suffering *according to her*, the rest of my lab would be closed down and the others saved? No. She wouldn't have killed them. She'd have stolen them and shown the media how *I* was killing them with obesity. I ran my finger back and forth over the nick. This was an inside job. Could Raucket be so mean-spirited? Could he not stand that I'd succeeded in spite of him? Or Schlemmer. Lazy Schlemmer. Was this his revenge for not putting him as first author on the last publication? No. I'm sure he was happy about that little fact now.

Whoever it was, their next move would be to expose this.

Alone, in the silence of the lab, the horror of what was behind the animal room door loomed. I couldn't bear to see it again but had no choice. Inside the cupboard labelled *animal care* were the supplies I'd need for cleanup. When I reached in to pull out the disposal bags, the policy and procedure manual for animal care and ethics tipped over. I stuffed it back in and slammed the door.

In the animal room, the ventilation had started to erase the fumes that had built up overnight. The door of their rat cage creaked. I cut the wire that was knotted around Huey's neck. His lifeless body was rigid, but his fur was soft against my hand and, even though he was just an experimental animal, a lump grew in my throat. I was his custodian. I was to care for him in the most humane way possible. He trusted me, and I failed.

I put him into a red plastic disposal bag and slid Dewey beside. His black-spotted belly pressed up against Huey. Luey's body was still flaccid when I cut him down. Inside the bag, he settled into the space between the other two. Motionless, all three lay together, back in their huddle. Luey must've been the last to watch the others die. Probably from the corner, trembling, with frightened eyes, watching while Huey hung there and Dewey clawed for his life. I hoped that the last thing Luey did was to bite whoever killed him and his two friends. I zipped shut the bag and opened another. With gloved hands, I filled it with paper bedding from the cage bottom that was splattered with blood and excrement. I wanted the world to disappear.

Out in the hall, I ran into Schlemmer. He glanced at the shoe box in my hands. "Mighty early to have been shopping," he laughed.

"Sure is." I kept walking with my left hand under the box and the other pressing down on the lid.

The biomedical waste containers were in a locked

room beside the morgue. One of the containers had an orange flame on the side and was labeled 'Burn-up Bin'. The contents would be taken to the incinerator in a day or two. I removed the bag with the paper bedding from the shoebox. It rustled when it landed on other dirty things in the bin. I picked up the bag with Huey, Dewey and Luey. It was not as easy to let go. Before I did, I thanked them for all they'd done and wished them well in their next journey, whatever that may be for a rat. When the bag slipped from my fingers into the waste container, my chest felt as though it would cave in. I realized, too late, why you should never name your lab rats.

Back in the lab, an eerie silence had descended on the animal room. As tears flooded out of me, memories of Anbu flooded in. The pain in my chest was terrifying. It was pure grief. There I stood, almost a year after his death, sobbing like he had died the day before. The keypad on the lab door beeped. In strutted Raucket, whistling. Before I could close the animal room door, there he was. At least the cage door was closed. He stopped when he saw me.

"Ooh. Did one of those fatties bite you?" He honked like a goose.

"Did you come here last night?" I walked towards him, made him back out of the room, and closed the door.

"Nah. Was in no shape to work on a presentation. My old buddy Rod and I got into the te-kill-ya at the Keg."

I wished the tequila *would* have killed him. He sat

down at a computer without another word, straightened his suit coat, and typed in a password. It was the visitor logon, which I hadn't given to him.

Later that day, only a few seats remained in the lecture hall – one beside Schlemmer and a few others scattered in the back of the room. Wasn't hard to decide where to go. The air buzzed with excited voices while a technician tapped his finger against the podium mic. The room was arranged with about three hundred seats that formed a semi-circle around the stage. A massive screen hung above the podium, half of which projected the presentation and the other half Raucket's enormous head.

He launched into his lecture with a joke about a marital dispute over a husband's snoring. At least he found a new joke. At about slide twenty-five, I realized I hadn't heard a word he said. My life was unraveling, as if someone found a loose string on the bottom of my sweater and was running away with it. I'd been accused of fraud. My lab had been penetrated by the enemy. My rats were dead and I'd decided not to say a word.

Finally, Raucket got to his last slide. On it was a picture of him, back in the day, holding one of his experimental rats by the scruff of its neck. He looked up to the audience, in my direction, with a shit-eating grin on his face and said, "Amazing how these guys just hang in there." The audience laughed. A shiver traveled down my spine.

I lay in bed, alone, and stared at the ceiling. It was late. Steven wasn't home, and I had no idea where he was. He wasn't answering his phone. I closed my eyes. The image of the three of them, hanging from a wire, blazed in front of me. Squeezing my eyelids didn't help; they were still there. I'd need a gavel to get this image out of my mind. Diesel got up from his open crate, walked over to my side of the bed and rested his head on the mattress. He nuzzled his nose into my pillow and waited. I scratched his ears and drifted away.

Chapter 23

THE REVEAL

In the morning, it felt as if a brick had dropped on my head. The other side of the bed hadn't been touched. I wanted to call in sick. A hot shower and make up didn't help. The mirror told the truth. I selected the reddest lipstick I could find.

"Hey," Steven's voice came from behind.

Jesus! I hated when he sneaked up on me.

"Where were you?" I asked.

"Slept downstairs. Didn't want to wake you."

"Where were you before that?"

"Out with the boys."

"You don't answer your phone?"

"I forgot it in the car."

"Right."

"You don't believe me?"

"I believe you."

"Doesn't seem like it." From behind, he stared at

me in the mirror. "I've been trying to give you some space. I know the pressure you're under."

"What do you mean?"

"With the gala, having Raucket around. Can't believe Luke did this to you."

"It's business."

"It's not business! It's ignorant after what Raucket did to you." Steven waited and when I didn't respond, he huffed. "Oh right. I forgot. Luke rescued you."

I walked away. What was I supposed to say?

At one point in my life, when the world conspired to create the perfect storm, Luke did rescue me. It was years ago. My mom was told that she was terminally ill. My PhD candidacy exam – a long, and usually painful, intellectual grilling – was quickly approaching. And I found myself pregnant from a one-night stand with Steven. He stepped in, said he'd support the child and me, and that it didn't mean the end of my PhD or my future career. I came to know, trust, and fall in love with him. He remained true to his word, even when the first ultrasound revealed I was pregnant with twins.

Nausea plagued me all day long for the first four months. When Raucket found out I was pregnant, he was incensed. He started working me hard in his lab and spewed off-hand remarks about women with children, how they didn't amount to anything in academia. Good old Lucy Briggs, who was his student at the same time, couldn't wait to tell me that Raucket said I better not think about getting pregnant again, if I wanted to stay in his lab. When I confronted him about it, he told me to get over myself. If I couldn't handle it, I should leave.

Then, when I was five months pregnant, I made a mistake. A big one. I reversed the sign on a series of numbers. Lucy caught the error. Raucket called a meeting of my PhD committee, as well as a 'mediator' who happened to be the dean of the faculty. I felt like a rubber duck in a carnival game with a bull's-eye on my wing. The dean instructed each one of them, when it was their turn to fire. Most fired blanks, but when it was Raucket's turn, the big guns came out. I was irresponsible, insubordinate, disengaged and distracted. As he continued to reveal all my inadequacies, a tightness started in my abdomen and continued to press until I was doubled over with blood dripping down my legs and onto my sandals. The inquisition came to a grinding halt. Voices cried out to call an ambulance.

The emergency room staff had barely wheeled the stretcher through the delivery room doors, when I had a contraction so strong that, before the nurses or doctor could do anything, fluid gushed out of me and, with it, two silent babies. They weighed less than a pound each. Neither had a heartbeat. After it was all over and the stretcher had been wiped clean, a porter wheeled me away. The fluorescent lights on the ceiling flashed by in slow motion. He transferred me back to the sterile white emergency room where it all began. I curled into a fetal position and listened to the sound of my tears hitting the paper that covered the stretcher beneath.

Somewhere amidst the unbelievable heartache, a warm hand touched my back. It was Luke. A man I hardly knew at the time. He found out somehow. I didn't ask. Didn't care. He was horrified to hear I was there alone and that Steven was away on business and couldn't be reached. Luke stayed with me that night, held my hand until I fell asleep, and took me home in the morning, where he stayed with me for the next two days until Steven returned. Two weeks later, when I was back at work in Raucket's lab with a wicked fever and abdominal cramps, I called Luke. He marched me down to the ER and slipped me through the queue. The ER physician delivered the news that I'd need an emergency gynecological procedure and walked out of the room as if he'd just told me I had a cold. Luke went after him. He dragged him back into the room and made him explain in detail the D&C, which, unbeknown to me then, would result in complications. I'd never have children again.

Luke was young, and beautiful, and kind. He instinctively knew how to comfort me, how to make me laugh, how to make me forget. And, in the background, he supported me when I took Raucket to task for harassment.

So how, with Steven still standing outside the bathroom that morning, could I refute his comment about Luke rescuing me? I didn't even know where to begin.

"The gala is tomorrow night," I said to Steven as I passed him on my way out of the bathroom. "Don't forget to pick up your tux."

Chapter 24

THE NEWS

Traffic around the university was stop and go. Temporary spaces between cars were being hijacked by impatient drivers. My cell phone rang. I tried to dig it out of my bag, just to see who was calling. A Mario Andretti wannabe cut me off. I stomped on the brakes. The contents of my purse scattered to the floor. My cell phone flew the farthest. It was stuck on the upper edge of the rubber mat, buzzing like a fly.

I ran through an amber light on the way, parked the car in my usual parking space, and reached for the phone. Luke called ten times in fifteen minutes. He got like this before a big event. Who knew what it would be this time. Probably stressing about the color of napkins that were to be used at the gala.

When I dialled him, the phone only rang once. There was no hello. No formalities.

"Fuck, Mack! What the hell is going on?"

My mind raced. "What are you talking about?"

"Have you seen the front page of the *Sun* today?"

"No. Why?"

"Let's see. How does this sound? *Sweet dreams aren't made of this: Ninsun Sleep Clinic gala to proceed in the wake of nightmarish rat hangings.*"

"What?"

"*What?* That's all you have to say?"

"Luke, I have no idea what's going on." That was the truth. Just not the one he was looking for. Luke continued to spew profanities, while I started to piece things together. It must've been Raucket. Had he spent the last fifteen years plotting his revenge? I took such pleasure in his embarrassment, when he had to defend his stance on pregnant women in academia. Never mind that it was to the Dean of Students, who had surrounded Raucket with the very same panel that a few months earlier were traumatized by the sight of blood running down my legs. While Raucket got only a hand slap, it must have silently killed him to be civil to me in his lab after that. The panel was watching.

I tuned back in to Luke. He was saying something about a reporter who had been calling repeatedly.

"*CAFÉ* idiots," he said. "It was them. I know it. Those fuckers must've found out we were in line for more funding." Luke threatened to cancel the gala. He'd invited several government ministers, including the one for health. "Do you think he's gonna fund a clinic that hangs rats?"

There was a pregnant pause. To my surprise, when Luke started talking again, his voice had a ring of optimism in it. He said he had a plan. "I'm gonna send this reporter down to your lab. She can see for herself that everything is okay. Let her take pictures. Post them. Whatever it takes to show that your rats are fine."

I didn't waste any time reminding him about laboratory policy, but he wasn't buying it.

"The benefits outweigh the risks," he said. "Where are you?"

"Um, just leaving home." A wave of nausea rolled through my stomach. I don't think I'd ever lied to Luke before.

"Thirty minutes?" he asked.

"Forty-five."

I nearly tripped over my feet in the parking lot. I had to get to the lab before anyone else. After yesterday morning, I'd given Fennel the rest of the week off. Told her to help Luke get ready for the gala. Thank God.

The lab was dark and the animal room was the way I left it. I arranged new bedding in their empty cage, and chose three of the heaviest rats, one from each of the other cages, to replace them. As I closed the cage door, a knock sounded out in the lab. I took one last look at the new rat grouping and left to open the lab door. Standing outside was a woman in a navy suit with perfectly coiffed blonde hair. It was the kind of hair that would crunch under your fingers.

"Dr. Smith?"

"Yes."

"Diedre Noshan, from the *Edmonton Journal*." She overextended her hand. "Dr. Hesuvius sent me."

"Miss Nosham —" I reluctantly shook her hand.

"Noshan." She tilted her head and smiled; her hair didn't move. "It's Noshan."

"Miss *Noshan* —"

"Was there a break in?" She leaned in and inspected the door frame. "Doesn't look like it."

"No."

"Is it true that the rats were hung by wire from their cages?"

It was time to give entrance to Sherlock. I swear I could feel her breath on my neck as we walked to the animal room.

I turned and blocked the doorway. She stopped on her toes and dropped back onto her heels.

"This must be really hard for you," she said.

"Miss Noshan, you should know, better than anyone, that you can't believe everything you read."

I flipped on the lights to their brightest setting. The rats scurried. "You can see for yourself that all is well. All is quiet. And all cages are full of healthy rats." I went on to explain how I had no idea where the story came from, which was the truth. Again, just not the one she was looking for.

She put her face right up to the death cage. "Can you tell me, then, what kind of testing you're doing with the rats?"

"No."

"Well, I'm gonna need some sort of story. A source told me you research sleep apnea. Do you do drug testing?"

"No."

"Can you explain what you're doing if it's not

drugs then?"

"No."

"So then it is drugs?"

"No! They were on a simple weight gain program."

"Were?"

A sick feeling slid down my breast bone and settled in my gut. "You know what I mean."

She scribbled onto her note pad. "That's interesting. *CAFÉ* always has concerns about cruelty to animals. Are your rats force fed?"

She'd obviously done her homework and, from her next comments, was intent on resurrecting Anbu's last days. I needed to rebuff her attempts to stir up the past. Current details about their diet and how they were fed seemed to work.

"Aren't you putting their health in jeopardy – the same as a human's – by severe weight gain?"

"Miss Nosham…"

"Noshan."

"Yes, *Noshan*, I've nothing further to say. Take a picture, if you like."

The camera flashed. At best, she got a tail sticking out from the bedding.

I answered my phone after one ring.

"She there yet?" Luke's voice was pressed.

"Just left."

"And? Everything good?"

"Yes." The sick feeling in my stomach kicked me,

just to remind me that it was still there.

"Hopefully that takes care of it. I don't need any reporters or *CAFÉ* showing up tomorrow night. Better call campus security." Luke hung up without saying goodbye.

Back in the animal room, I started to move the rats back to their original cages, but stopped. The chance of Luke inviting someone else in was high. An empty cage would be hard to explain. I'd confide everything to him, but only after the weekend. I pulled shut the lab door, checking twice that it was locked, and turned to leave.

Outside, down the corridor, was Diedre Noshan talking to Fennel. As I approached, Fennel looked over her shoulder and caught sight of me. Their conversation ceased. Diedre scribbled in her notebook, shut it, and tucked it under her arm. "Thank you for talking to me, Fennel. I appreciate your insights."

"For you, any time, Diedre. If you need any pictures of me, well not now of course, because I haven't had time to put on makeup, but I'd be happy to –"

"Fennel," I said, "if you don't mind, I'd like to have a word with Miss Noshan. Privately."

Fennel didn't say a word, just smiled and left.

"Miss Noshan, I'm not sure what game you're playing here. Just remember, students may not have all the correct information. Misinformation could affect people badly."

"Are you referring to yourself?" she asked with a smug smile.

"No – I'm referring to the patients' lives that are

affected by the research we do."

"I'm just trying to get to the truth. You seem reluctant to participate."

"That's because *I* still don't know how that article appeared. How can you expect a student to know?"

"I report only facts."

"And how will you be sure of those?"

"I plan to interview others until the story comes together."

"Well, I hope you get your story straight." I wanted to say more, but walked away.

"Thank you, Dr. Smith," her sickly sweet voice called out after me. "Look forward to hearing from you in the future."

Chapter 25

THE GALA

The night of the gala arrived and not a word from Diedre had been printed in the *Journal*. Still, I was sick inside. This was not how I imagined the evening, when I dropped a small fortune on a new black dress. Never mind the black bustier, garters and stockings. They cost about as much as the dress. It was obviously not how Steven imagined it either. He'd arranged weeks before for a limousine. A bottle of Dom Perignon was chilled and waiting.

We were stuck in a lineup of town cars in front of the Faculty Club along Saskatchewan Drive. The sting of our fight from the previous morning still prickled. We'd become good at pretending, though. In fact, Steven was acting like nothing happened. He was making heroic attempts to distract me from thinking about the newspaper article in the *Sun* by cracking jokes and being sure that my champagne glass was always topped up. On any other day, I'd have knocked on the privacy window and told the driver to pull out of line and do a loop around the city. But thanks to all the stress, the word libido had fallen from my lexicon, and certain body parts were at risk for becoming vestigial. Not even the expensive undergarments could give me my *sexy* back.

A group of men and women in tuxes and gowns exited from a car in front, and as they promenaded up the walk, one man squeezed his wife's ass. Apparently she had her *sexy* exactly where it needed to be. Mind you, she probably hadn't been dealing with scoundrels and dead rats. Our driver inched the car forward.

Bam! A hand smacked the back passenger window of our limousine. The driver slammed on the brakes. Champagne splashed out of my glass and onto my dress.

"Sorry," a man's voice called from outside. "Wrong car."

Steven ran his hand along the back of my hair and, while I wiped droplets of champagne off my lap, asked if I was okay. Was I okay. Did it look like I was okay? I smiled and steeled my nerves.

We stepped outside the car. There were no cameras, microphones, or Diedres in sight. Only two campus security guards patrolling the perimeter around the front door and an empty unmarked police cruiser across the street.

A lilting melody – piano, brass, and strings – floated out from the Faculty Club. Blue miniature lights had been hung inside the windows on the second floor. It looked like a starlit sky. Outside, the stars weren't yet visible in the evening sky, but a faded crescent moon hung just above the tree tops in the river valley. The summer air was warm against my shoulders, and when Steven put his hand on my back, gently between my shoulder blades, the sick pit in my stomach eased.

Inside, the ten-piece band played an undulating version of *Moon River*. A group of women in jewel-colored gowns flowed across the floor. They stopped to accept champagne from a young, attractive, server in a black and white uniform – a penguin who suddenly found himself amongst a muster of peacocks. And just like that, Angela Ashbury was in my head, six feet under, with damp, cold dirt leveled on top of her. Sad that such a bright, sparkling woman never reached her target, her pink size six.

From behind them came Luke, the man whose past couple of days were brought to him by the letter 'f'. It wasn't clear if it'd gotten any better. No frown lines, but no smile either. Finally, when he was two steps away, the levee broke. "Mackenzie!" He laid his hand on my arm and whispered in my ear, "Don't worry. Everything's been taken care of. And…you look beautiful."

My chest felt light and warm.

Luke stepped back, looked to Steven and nodded. Steven nodded back. I was scrambling to find something to say, when the young waiter interrupted with a tray of champagne. Steven said that he'd prefer not to have any and that he'd be back after he got a drink from the bar.

Side by side, Luke and I assessed the crowd – government ministers, renowned scientists, their girlfriends and wives, boyfriends and husbands. There were also people from *Zirica*, including the CEO who was approaching. Luke extended his hand. The CEO grasped it and, while he shook, complemented Luke on the success of the reception. Luke retorted by saying how he appreciated their sponsorship. The CEO quietly said it was a small investment in return for the connections in the room. They'd be good for business and the soaring stock price, he said out of the corner of his mouth.

"Have you met Mackenzie?" Luke said.

"Don't believe so. Pleasure." The CEO took my hand.

"She's a star," Luke said. "Don't know what I'd do without her."

Really? The CEO should've heard him yesterday morning. Speaking of being without people, I realized that it had been at least fifteen minutes since Steven left. He wasn't anywhere in sight. I wished I could say the same about Schlemmer, who was on his way over. Definitely my cue to exit, but not before inspecting Schlemmer's hands for scratches or bite marks. There were none.

The band picked up the tempo with a rendition of *Cherry Pink and Apple Blossom White*. Steven loved the song. Even more so after a drink or two. I wouldn't be surprised to find him in a corner somewhere, pretending to play the trombone, even though it should've been a trumpet. Where was he?

Over in the far corner, one head taller than most everyone else and wearing three-inch heels, was Lucy Briggs. Her gown, black and sequined, hugged her curves. Satin evening gloves stretched up her arms, past her elbows. Fennel was right beside her, in a red backless dress that revealed flesh down to the dip in her back. Her auburn hair was swept up. A few loose curls brushed against her shoulders. She shook her head in humorous disbelief at something Lucy said. I tried to imagine what they had to talk about. They barely knew each other.

Like a bee going for honey, Raucket buzzed across the room and put his hairy claw on Fennel's shoulder. He leaned in and whispered in her ear. She responded by laughing. I walked over and interrupted, not really to say hi, but to check his hands carefully, even more so than Schlemmer's, for any signs of struggle. There weren't any. I couldn't watch another minute of him pressing up next to Fennel and telling limp jokes. I left to find Steven.

Finally. There he was, standing at the fireplace, by himself. The deep frown lines and lack of smile were clear. I apologized and asked him to join me at the table. Dinner was about to be served. We walked side by side in silence.

As if losing him before dinner wasn't bad enough, though, it happened again after dinner, somewhere between speeches and schmoozing. Brittany hadn't seen him; she was too busy watching the young waiter. Schlemmer was at the side of the bar by himself, looking wobbly with a drink in his hand. Doubtful he knew what planet he was on, never mind where I might find Steven.

Laughter rang from the terrace, where guests were milling in the fresh air with after-dinner drinks. Lucy stepped in front of me just as I was about to cross the threshold. She started to tell me something about her research in Ontario. A flash of red out on the terrace caught my eye. Fennel was talking to a man, whose elbow was the only thing visible from my where I stood. She leaned in to say something, so close that her breath must've been moist on his cheek, and her breast warm on his arm. Lucy stepped into my line of vision and continued on about her research. Two men, snifters of brandy in hand, approached to exit onto the patio. Lucy moved to the side to let them pass, clearing my line of site. Fennel was twisting a loop of hair while listening to whatever her male guest was saying. He shifted, just enough so the side of his face was visible. That's when Lucy's voice became an incomprehensible murmur, and all I could see was Fennel's breast against his arm. The object of Fennel's affection, Steven, smiled as she spoke. He looked down at the ground and shook his head, took a sip of his drink, and looked up at her, at her chest, the same one that was inviting him to bury his face in it.

The distance between them increased, when they saw me approach. I interlocked my arm with Steven's and, when I did, told Fennel that Schlemmer was looking for her over by the bar.

She blew a small laugh through her nose. "Steven, it was so nice talking to you. I hope we can do it again."

"What was that all about?" I asked.

"What was *what* all about?"

An icy feeling that hadn't been around since I was young and self-doubting and dating the wrong kind of men settled in. I dropped my arm from his.

"Mack, it was *nothing*."

"It didn't seem like nothing."

"Oh come on, don't be crazy." He reached out to touch my shoulder, forcing me to back up against the railing.

"What exactly did you want me to do?" he asked.

"I don't know, how about not flirt with my students?"

"I was *not* flirting with her! I was simply passing time, while you were off doing whatever it was you were doing."

"I was working. And I certainly wasn't flirting."

Steven mumbled something that sounded like it contained the name Luke.

"Let's go." I stomped off.

"Whatever you want."

On the way out, Fennel twiddled her fingers goodbye. Happy to see Steven four feet behind, I'm sure. The initial sickness of the night was back in its entirety.

Sunday morning came quickly. I was barely awake, having my first sip of coffee, when I saw it. Diedre Noshan's article that was printed in the *Journal*. Not only did she expose in detail what Fennel told her about the obesity experiments in the era of Anbu, but she also described a scene at the Faculty Club with *CAFÉ* protestors, who lay waiting in the bushes for the party to start. I had no idea of that, until I read it myself. Apparently, campus security spotted the protestors lurking and called the police, who dragged them out from the bushes, kicking and screaming. When the protestors started batting at the police with their signs, they were restrained, cuffed, and loaded into a van. One woman got a black eye in the process and, of course, her picture showed up in full color beside the article. Worse, however, was the other picture that took up twice the space as the protestor. A 5x7 of three pairs of rat feet, dangling, with toenails grazing paper bedding. It was the first thing anyone would see. I pushed my coffee away and tried to breathe.

From down the hall, in my study, tucked away in my brief case, my cell phone started to ring. I knew exactly who it was, and there was no way I was going to answer.

Chapter 26

PICKETT FENCED IN

On Monday morning, Andrew Pickett, the auditor from the UK, was sitting at the meeting table in my lab, twirling a pen between his fingers as if it were a baton. He wore his thick gray hair like a badge of authority, even though he had only five years on me. We'd met before at conferences, briefly, in polite unmemorable exchanges, where his British accent made even the most banal words sound clever. That morning, after some courteous conversation, his face took on a seriousness that seemed there to stay.

"All laboratory activity must be suspended at once." He held each *s-sound* in the word *suspended* just a little too long, like Kaa the snake from the *Jungle Book*. "You will need to vacate the premises while I am here and refrain from taking notes, folders, or anything of the sort. Of course, these requests apply to you and all your students."

"Fine."

"I will need all your data and will interview each of you about said data. Separately." He did the *s-thing* again on the word *separately*.

"You have full access to anything and anyone."

"Very confident." He looked out the corner of his eye at me.

"Of course."

"Very well, then."

"There will be one disturbance today," I said. "I'm having the security codes and locks changed."

"Oh yes," he nodded and smiled. "I heard you had some *problems* recently."

"I've instructed the locksmith to leave you a key," I said.

He looked perturbed that I was still around and simply sat like a king who was waiting for a servant to leave. Oddly, he was the least of my worries. I was about to face Luke, who must've called every half hour, until I answered the phone at 6 pm on Sunday evening. We didn't talk about it, just made a time to meet.

Luke looked up briefly from a file and waved me in. He told me to shut the door. The moment it closed, he leaned back in his chair and sighed. "You want to explain?"

"Not really."

He didn't smile.

I told him what had happened.

"And you didn't think it would get out? Especially

with that first article? Obviously someone knew, Mack!"

"My first concern was not to destroy the gala for you."

"Who cares about the gala! This is worse. At least if I knew I could've tried to do some damage control. You realize what's going to happen, don't you?"

I couldn't look at him.

"Animal welfare is going to be all over it," he said.

"I know."

"You're going to get shut down. Between this and the complaint against your paper." He stood up and looked out his window. "Geez, Mackenzie."

"Do you think I'm enjoying this, Luke?" My voice shook. "None of it makes sense!" My eyes filled with tears.

He walked over to me and before I knew it, he was embracing me and telling me how it was going to be okay. How we'd come too far together and how he was just as worried as I was. He leaned back and took my face in both his hands. His eyes locked on mine. He moved his face towards me. I pulled away and slapped him.

On the way out, I heard Genie calling after me. I didn't stop until I got to the lab door and then remembered Pickett was there. I leaned against the corridor wall. My hand still stung. What had I done? Did I really think he was going to kiss me? I looked up to the heavens, as if that would help me. I stared for a minute before it dawned on me. My eyes focused in. In the corner above the door was a video camera that potentially had seen things that none of us could imagine.

The guard in the security booth had a puzzled look on his peach-fuzzed face. "You must have some super secret stuff going on in that lab." He glanced away at one of the video monitors and adjusted the camera linked to it. "There are always people here asking for videos."

"What do you mean by that?"

"Well, just the other day, there was a woman here asking for one. I couldn't help her though. The cameras had been wiped out by the storm. No video."

"What did she look like?"

"Had hair the same color as yours."

"Did she give a name?"

"She did, but I don't remember."

"Was it Fennel?"

"No. I'd remember a weird name like that. Isn't that a spice or something?"

"You said that there were lots of people. Who else?" I asked.

"Well, a while ago, when the guy who got killed in that car accident was still around, I was helping him with a video from that door."

"Anbu?" It came out louder than expected.

His eyes went wide. "I swear, I didn't know what he was up to. Just read about it after in the newspaper."

"Don't worry," I smiled and softened my voice. I couldn't risk him clamming up. "It's not a problem. So, did you give him anything?"

"Yeah. It took a while to figure out how to convert it for him, but we got it."

"You still have it?"

"Nope. Too long ago. Can't keep backups that long.

Maybe he gave it to the other person who was asking for it?"

"Who was that?" I asked.

"One of the docs from upstairs, I think."

I pulled out my phone and showed him a picture of Schlemmer. He said it wasn't him. Then, against every fibre in my being, showed him one of Luke. It wasn't him either. He said the guy was younger. Maybe a resident. Problem was, there were no residents or fellows with us during that time.

"Whoever it was, did you give him a copy too?" I asked.

"Couldn't."

"Why?"

"Something got fried when I copied it for Anbu. The doc was really good about it, though. Didn't seem mad or anything."

I walked away, feeling the gravity of the missing video from Anbu's computer. I had let that slide. But with a lot of free time suddenly on my hands, while Pickett rifled through my lab, I'd get back to it.

I studied the timeline that stretched out on the scroll of paper in front of me. It had taken me the better part of a week to sketch it. I didn't want to miss a detail about places, people or time. It was fairly linear except for a few stray branches where I'd inserted several question marks. One stray was the envelope that Anbu had taped to the underside of the drawer. Along with his message about praying. I would come back to that. While I studied the sequence, one thing became clear. Anbu wasn't responsible for the original rat deaths. I had to admit that without any proof, I sometimes wondered if he might have accidentally fed the tube the wrong way. I was wrong then, and I was wrong now. And Raucket hanging the rats? That was way beyond him. It stunk of *CAFÉ*. They'd orchestrated a string of events from the time of Anbu and rolled them out cleverly.

At the end of one stray branch, I'd sketched a car with its wheels up in the air. It was time to make a visit to someone I hadn't seen in a long time.

His eyes were as piercing and as blue as the first time we met. He leaned across his desk. The months in between our last meeting slipped away when I began to tell him about recent events.

"So, what you're telling me," Armstrong said, "is that you've got a group of animal activists who like to dress up as doctors, kill your rats, and sabotage your work in order to shut down your lab."

I nodded.

"I'm sorry, Dr. Smith, but this really is a university matter. The police don't usually get involved in these kinds of murders," he grinned.

"Look, I'm not an idiot. I understand that."

"Then what is it that you think I can help you with?"

"Anbu."

"Anbu?"

I explained how I couldn't get the odd series of events on the morning of his death out of my head. How his car supposedly went off the road, how he sounded so frantic, how they never found his cell phone.

"What are you saying?" His eyes looked back and forth between mine.

I hesitated. I didn't want to start a chain of events. On the other hand, if what I suspected was true, Anbu deserved justice and I needed to protect myself. "Have you ever looked online at cases of animal researchers and the threats levelled against them?"

"Can't say I have," he said.

"Do it sometime. You'll find everything from threats about slitting throats to bombing labs. In my mind, if they can do that, what makes it so hard to believe that they wouldn't run a car off the road? Especially if that person had evidence against them."

"You mean a video of them entering your lab."

"Yes! They drowned animals with food in the name of their cause."

"You have no proof of that," he said.

"That's why I'm here. I need your help."

"I'm not sure there's much I can do."

I sat back and sighed, not sure why I expected a different response.

"I suppose," he said, "I could interview a couple of them, just to see. You understand that this might be like stirring a bee's nest. It may put you at risk."

It didn't matter. I was at risk, however you looked at the situation.

Andrew Pickett summoned me. Get to the lab, he said, as soon as possible. When I arrived, he was sitting at the lab table, which was now covered with papers, files, and notebooks.

"Let's get to the point, shall we?" Andrew said. "I've found inconsistencies that warrant a full investigation." He pulled an envelope from the mess of documents in front of him. "This outlines the process and what your rights and obligations are over the course of the investigation."

It became apparent in that instant. I was with the enemy, with no shield, no sword.

"What I need from you now, Mackenzie, are more data."

"What I gave wasn't enough?"

"I need more. I need the data from your last five published studies, as a start."

"Why?"

"For verification, shall we say." He smiled.

A deep loathing began to fester. I trusted him about as much as a black mamba.

I went to my filing cabinet and pulled the paper records from the studies that he wanted. I had electronic data for all those studies but felt a certain sense of satisfaction making him sift through reams of paper. I set down the folders on his messy table with just a little extra force and a *Girl Guide* smile on the side. "Good luck," I said and left.

Certain mores must be followed between professors and students, such as don't relieve yourselves in the same bathroom. It was awkward. The bathroom on the main floor was always filled with students, but there was one upstairs on the second floor that was tucked away in a corner and was almost always empty. I went there after my meeting with Pickett.

I'd almost made my way around the bathroom's privacy wall. Not sure what made me stop. Maybe the fact that I hadn't seen her since the gala last week. What exactly would I, should I, say to her? She was staring intently at her reflection, completely unaware of me and humming a familiar song. I couldn't place it. When she stopped, the air was blank, just waiting for a sound. She brushed her fingers across her collar bone and caressed something under the neckline of her top. When she moved her fingers just a little, a pearl necklace, disturbingly like my mom's, was hanging around her neck. She fondled the pearls, one by one, knot by knot. I stepped back and, when I did, she broke the gaze with her reflection.

I bolted. Did she see me? Our eyes didn't meet. But then again, maybe they did. Maybe just for a split second.

Chapter 27

PEARLS OF WISDOM

I kept my mom's pearls nestled in their case at the bottom of a drawer in the guest room, hidden elaborately in a folded sheet, so that should we be robbed, they were nowhere near my other jewelry. But after rifling through the sheet, there was nothing. No box. Not even after the sheet was completely unfolded. There was still nothing, when the drawer was completely emptied of all other sheets and pillow cases. Nothing in the other drawers. Nothing under the mattress. Nothing under the pillows. Diesel sat in the doorway with his ears pinned back. He didn't even move with the sound of Steven coming through the front door and up the stairs.

"Whoa!" Steven slid to a stop as he was passing the guest room door. "What is going on?"

"My mom's pearls! They are...Fuck! Fennel took them!"

Bark, bark, bark. Diesel jumped on Steven.

"Jesus." Steven pushed him off. "Calm down."

I didn't know if he was talking to me or Diesel. Diesel came back and pushed his rump against Steven's leg. Steven just stood and stared.

"I saw her wearing them today," I said.

"You must be mistaken."

"Of course you'd think I'm mistaken! Why're you standing up for her?"

Steven sighed. "Diesel needs a walk. Help you look when I get back?" He tried to touch my hair.

"Just go."

The moon beamed through the window. It created a silvery sheen on our bed linens, which were tucked around my body like a cocoon. "Steven, we need to change the security code."

"Why?" He shut the blinds.

"This whole thing with Fennel."

"She only had a contractor code. It expired the day we got home."

"Well how did she get in then?"

Steven didn't say a word. He slid into bed beside me.

I turned on my side after contemplating it for a bit. "I guess she could've taken the necklace when she was here. Or…"

Steven's chest was rising and falling, rhythmically, peacefully. Glad to see he was taking this seriously. Diesel snorted inside his crate, scratched around in a circle, and laid down. But I couldn't sleep. This was the last thing I needed amidst everything else. Yet somehow, it eclipsed all that. I certainly wouldn't be able to rest until those pearls were back in my hands.

Fennel knocked on the frame of my open office door. She was wearing a sundress with a scoop neckline, which exposed her bare neck.

"Shut the door," I said, as she walked in. "I need to talk to you about a personal matter."

"Sounds serious."

"It is. I'm missing a string of pearls."

"Oh, and you think I took them?"

"No. I wondered if you saw them, when you were staying at our place."

"No, I didn't see them. And even if I did, I wouldn't have taken them."

"I didn't say you would have. I just wondered if you laid eyes on them, that's all."

"No." She stared at me with eyes as frosty as ice. "Can I go?"

I motioned to the door. "Be my guest."

After a few days, I decided it was time to deal with the chaos in the guest room. I folded the sheets and pillow cases that were scattered about and opened the drawer to put them back where they belonged. I couldn't believe my eyes.

"Steven!"

Footsteps slammed up the stairs.

There, all by itself, in the top drawer, was the jewelry box. I grabbed it as if pulling it from a fire. The brass hinges creaked when I lifted the lid. Inside, resting peacefully on the velvet, were my mom's pearls.

Steven burst into the room and stopped dead, when he saw what was in my hands. "Where were they?"

"In the drawer."

"Hmmmpph." He shrugged.

A surge of anger exploded from the center of my chest. "That's it? That's all you have to say? I went through this drawer a million times, Steven. I wouldn't have missed them."

He stared as if I had a third eye in the middle of my head. Then, in a calm and reassuring voice, tried to convince me that I was just stressed out and tired.

"Too tired to see them? No way. I could've been up for forty-eight hours straight, with hot pokers stuck in my side, and I still would not have missed that box. You need to change the code on our alarm. Now."

The pearls were beautiful, polished, and smooth, but when I lifted them to my nose, they smelled like musk. After a gentle, prolonged wash with soap and water, the scent was extinct. The knots between the smooth ivory drops were still moist against my fingers when I fixed the silver clasp at the back of my neck. Somehow, having this around my neck steeled me for what I was about to do next.

The knock came precisely at nine o'clock. When Fennel walked in, her eyes widened momentarily, as if she saw a phantom hovering around my neck.

We sat across the desk from each other, silent, having taken up our rightful sparring corners. I swept my fingertips along my mom's pearls. How exactly did I want to throw the first blow? Jab? Hook? Undercut?

"You're fired," I said.

"You can't do that."

"Watch me."

"Elizabeth won't let you."

"Dr. Montgomery has no say in this. And neither does your father, by the way. I hired you. I can fire you."

"You know, I really tried to like you. I mean, I do like you. Even after you accused me of cheating. But you've really got problems."

"You're the last one to be saying things like that. You need to grow up. Stop living off your father."

"You want me to grow up? Hah! Maybe you should tell your husband to grow up."

"Fennel. Seriously. I'm not going to start talking to *you* about my husband."

"Maybe you should talk to *him*, then. Ask him why he gave me those pearls and then returned, like a stupid school kid, begging for them back."

"Get out of my office."

I tried not to think of what she said, but it kept reeling in my mind. She was surely playing with me. I started writing a text to Steven but stopped. This needed to be a face-to-face conversation. And, unfortunately, it would have to wait a few days. Steven was away on business. It gave me time to think of how to broach the subject so that he wouldn't accuse me of not trusting him.

Chapter 28

COMING UNDONE

The envelope that Pickett gave me was still sitting on my desk, sealed. I'd developed a sixth sense over the years about which envelopes would be pleasing to open and which ones wouldn't. This one was sure to cause grief. I squeezed my pinkie under the seal and ripped.

Dear Dr. Smith,

Further to the allegations launched against you regarding falsification of published data, we have been advised by Professor Andrew Pickett that the results of his inquiry warrant a full investigation.

At this point, several processes are required. First, we are bound to inform the complainant of the investigation. Second, an ad-hoc committee will monitor the investigative process and hear the findings of the investigation. Third, an agreement has been reached to second Professor Pickett for a period of not less than 30 days to complete the investigation. Professor Pickett will produce a formal document outlining his findings. This will be circulated to you and the committee. In that document, Professor Pickett will conclude that:

Serious research fraud or academic misconduct has been committed, or

No fraud has been committed, but serious scientific errors have been made, or

No fraud has been committed and no scientific errors have been made.

In the case of a) or b), we are required to inform the agency that sponsored your research about the investigation and its resultant outcome. As well, we are required to inform the journal/s that have published any findings related to the investigation.

Interim administrative actions related to teaching, committee work and expenditures out of your research accounts will be decided upon between you and your department chair, Elizabeth Montgomery. Throughout this process, all findings will be held in strict confidence to minimize any damage to your reputation that could occur as a result of inaccurate allegations.

Sincerely,

Dr. Zachary Tellrom

Vice President, Research

"I need to see you in my office. Immediately." Elizabeth said.

"I was just about to go into a meeting with —"

"Cancel it!" The line went dead.

A flutter stirred in my chest, like a moth in a jar, beating its wings against my rib cage. It felt like the walls of my office were collapsing and all oxygen had been sucked from the room. I was sure I was dying, gasping for my last breath. Calm down, my logical brain told me. No! Get out. Run. Get out, or you will die, my emotional brain said. I fled outside and doubled over. My hands clasped my knees like vice grips. I drew long hard breaths into my lungs. The chickadees in the elm tree above sang a rhythmic song, while the ground beneath swirled. Eventually, the spinning turned to a gentle sway, and I was able to stand up straight. The long walk round the building to Elizabeth's office was unbearable, though. I must've stopped ten times in an attempt to calm myself and rationalize what had just happened to me. By the time I knocked on her door, the panic attack, or whatever it was, was over.

Elizabeth was sitting behind her desk. Her lips were pressed and white. I barely sat down before she started.

"Do you mind explaining how things went to hell while I was away? How dare you fire Fennel?" Although her words were hot, the air that carried them was filled with ice crystals.

"Seriously?" I felt my face crumple up in disbelief. "She's been nothing but –"

"You had no right to go over my head."

"I had every right to," my voice shook. "As it was, I put up with her for way too long. She's completely untrustworthy."

"*She's* untrustworthy?"

We sat, neither of us flinching, neither talking. Just glowering at each other. Finally, Elizabeth said, "I've reviewed the letter from the VP research and talked with Luke about your rat situation. The animal welfare people filled in the details. They're certain you're trying to cover up more rat deaths in your lab by making it look like sabotage. Then, there's the police coming around wanting to ask me about *CAFÉ* and Anbu."

While she continued to talk about how inappropriate it was of me to get the police involved, my insides burned. I felt like I was growing claws.

Elizabeth shook her head. "Honestly, I'm not sure what to say."

"Really? You? Lost for words?"

"Getting snippy is not in your best interest right now," she hissed.

I clenched my jaw so I wouldn't say another word and glared at her.

"Here's what's going to happen," she said. "You're going to stay away from the university and your lab.

For some time. Hopefully, it'll give you perspective. You're going to stay out of Andrew's way. The rats that managed to survive will be transported to another lab."

A flutter beat in my chest again. I pushed through it. "I have commitments that I can't break. My students. A keynote in London."

"A keynote? You sure they still want you?" She leaned forward as if to tell a secret. "You know how these things get around." She leaned back into her chair. "Do what you want with it. But, you will *not* take any new students. Your current students will be assigned to interim supervisors. I'm going to find coverage for your teaching in the fall. And, no more expenditures from your research accounts."

Time stopped and the world around was hollow. "Don't you think that's taking it a little too far? Pickett is *not* going to find anything. I can assure you. And while I didn't handle the rat situation the way I should have, I absolutely did not harm those animals."

"Let's be honest, Mackenzie. If Pickett wouldn't have found anything in the inquiry, there'd be no reason for a full investigation. And exactly how do you propose to prove otherwise about your rats. They're dead. You burned them without allowing due process to take place."

"Are you saying you don't believe me?"

"This is not a case of believing or not."

"I think it is."

"Mackenzie, your nerves are raw."

I wished that she would stop repeating my name.

"Just take the next month or so to recover," she said.

Recover. She sat there so self-assured and smug. Not worrying a flip about the future of her career. In fact, she saw all this as my just reward for Fennel's firing.

"How will you explain my absence?" I asked.

"It'll be a temporary medical leave."

"Oh please. How will you answer questions about my supposed illness, when I don't have one?"

"Do you have a better idea? Oh, and next time, do use a little discretion when you decide to engage in exhibitionism. Even if it is in your own backyard."

I felt heat rush up my cheeks and radiate off the top of my head.

"You're lucky I talked her down," she said and stared.

I stared back.

She smirked. "You're awfully quiet now. Guess there's not much for you to say."

I stood up and turned to leave, but stopped. When I turned back, she was still sneering.

I stepped toward her desk. "The only thing I have to say is *watch out*. People aren't always what they seem."

The smirk drained from her face like dirty bathwater. She told me to get out.

The clock on the stove read noon. I swore I heard the wine fridge begging me to open it, to grasp the slim neck of a bottle. Any neck, any bottle. And so I did. The purple foil ripped easily and the cork squeaked as the opener rotated into it. Then, pop. The best sound I'd heard all day. Glass and bottle in hand, I slid into the hammock. Diesel sat on the deck, facing the house; he occasionally looked back to assess the situation.

One glass down. Warmth tingled in my legs. Leaves fluttered in the trees above. Two glasses down. The clouds began to conceal the sun. Three glasses. Rain soaked through my T-shirt. Four glasses. Diesel was still sitting patiently, wet. He stood and shook his body every so often, sending a spray of droplets in all directions. The last glass. My tears blended with the rain on my face.

A tune looped in my mind, in time with the back and forth of the hammock and the thump of my foot pushing off the fence. *Mocking Bird.* That was it! The song Fennel was humming in the bathroom. What a piece of work she was.

I tipped the bottle. The last few drops of wine rolled onto my tongue. Then, as loud as I could, I sang, "Pappa's gonna buy you a doggie named Rover." Diesel stood up, shook like a maniac and ran to the back door.

"Hah! My sssinging hurting your earsss, little doggie! Funny sssilly dog. L'il Rover. Oh – funny little dog!"

The garage door started to go up.

"Uh oh. Big cheessse is ffffinally home. In his fffancy business sssuit." I tried to focus. Wondered why he was holding his coat above his head. He looked worried, poor guy.

"Hey handsssome! Or should I sssay boomerang man. Give a gifffft. Take a gifffft."

"Mack! What the hell are you doing out here?"

"Washing off thisss nightmare. Fffuckin' nightmare, I tell ya."

"You're shivering."

"As ifff you care."

He pulled me out of the hammock and put his coat around me, like a good husband.

"How did I get sssuch a good husband? Too bad I haven't been laid, in like, two monthsss. Oh yeah. I fffforgot. You're ffffucking Fffennel."

I started pounding on his chest with my fists and stumbled backwards.

He grabbed both my arms and stood me straight. "Stop it, Mack. You're talking crazy. Let's get you inside."

We made it in without me falling.

"Read it." I chucked the envelope from Andrew at him, but missed. Diesel the mad dog got it.

"Hah! Maybe he can read it to you." I slid to the floor. "Ha! Ha! Thiss is really funny. So funny! Lissten, I'm laughing like a hyena. Right fffrom Affffrica. Land of big pusssy."

"Diesel!" Steven yelled, "drop the *god-damned* letter!"

"Jus' let 'em eat it, for Chrise sake. Ooooo-eeeee. I said Chrise, not Christ's. Don't wanna go to confession. Diesel's gonna have to go to confession for being sssuch a bad dog."

Steven chased Diesel around the table.

"Look at them run! Ooo-eee. Diesel's winning 'cause he's sssmarter."

Steven stomped to the closet, got some dog treats, and threw them at Diesel.

"Hah! Now who's the ssssmart one? Diesel jus' dropped that god-damned letter."

Steven read it. Didn't look good. He had those nasty frown lines.

"Come here, sweetheart," he said.

"Don' sssweetheart me, Fffennel lover."

"Stop it. We'll talk about her tomorrow. Let's get you to bed."

"Gonna hafta ssscrape me off the floor 'cause I ain't movin'."

I let him pick me up. Why fight a good thing? My arms and legs were limp noodles. Before I knew it I was on the bed and he was taking off my shirt. The guy moved fast.

"Aw, you jus' gonna tuck me in? No nooky nooky? Tha'sss okay. 'Cause there are two Dieselsss over there, watching usss."

The blinds in the bedroom skidded up the window casing and clicked into place at the top. The bright yellow light of the sun jabbed my eyes. My head was splitting. Steven offered to stay home with me. I mumbled from underneath the covers that I didn't want him to.

We need to talk, I heard him say. I pulled the covers down beneath my eyes but kept my nose and mouth covered.

"I want to tell you about Fennel," he said.

I pulled the covers over my head again.

"I need you to listen."

The bed rocked when he sat down beside me. He pulled the covers down to my chin. I didn't dare move my head, because when I did, the world spun.

"This is eating me up inside," he said.

That was it. There could be only one thing that would come next.

"I gave her those pearls."

"What!" I bolted straight up. I felt like heaving but still managed to say "Fuck you" before I laid back down.

"Just listen. Remember the scarf night?"

I stared at the ceiling. Wasn't going to say a word.

"That night was weird," he said.

"I bet. Did you have to peel her off you?"

Steven looked down at his hands.

My stomach squeezed.

He looked me directly in the eyes. "She just wanted to talk. It was all cryptic though. I got the feeling that either she was in trouble or that you were."

"Did she mention Rebecca?"

"No. Who's that?"

"Her little friend from *CAFÉ*."

"She didn't mention her or them at all. She just said she didn't know what to do. I assumed she meant about you and about you being pissed off at her about losing data."

I shut my eyes and took some deep breaths.

"Then, at the gala," he said, "she was even odder. Asking a bunch of questions about your rats and what really happened. Also asked if I was worried about you. Then she got into a whack of questions about Luke. How well I knew him, what kind of guy he was, if I liked him. So, I turned it around and asked her if she liked him. She said no, that she liked me. And that she'd be happy to tell me a few things that I'd probably find interesting, if we could have some time alone. That's about when you came and found us on the terrace."

"So you *were* flirting."

"No. She was."

"And somewhere in all of this you decided to give her my mom's pearls?"

"She came over here."

"Oh God."

"A few nights after the gala. You were late at a meeting."

I put my hands over my face. "Please tell me nothing happened."

Steven was silent.

"Steven! Tell me."

He turned away and looked at the bedroom door. "She tried to kiss me, but I pulled away."

It felt like a pair of bony cold hands had wrapped around my heart and were attempting to rip it from my chest. "Why did you even let her in?"

"She said she needed to talk to me about you. That you were in trouble."

"Well that wouldn't take a genius to figure out."

"She said she had to tell me something about Luke, but that she needed to know beyond a doubt that I could be trusted. She suggested there was one way I could convince her."

"Please tell me you didn't –"

"No! Of course not. I told her I'd give her something instead to show her how much I liked her. She knew about the pearls. It made me sick to hand them over."

"I bet."

"Mack, obviously someone is out to get you. This is serious."

"The only thing that is serious is that she was over here alone with you."

"Geez, Mack. I wasn't going to let it go anywhere. I was trying to help. She definitely knows something."

"No!" I sat up. I didn't care if my head spun. "She conned you. And you conned me. Making me think that somehow she got into our house. Guess she wasn't lying when she told me you came back begging for the pearls."

Steven's eyes opened wide.

"That's right," I said. "She told me right after I fired her."

"Mack —"

"She's just full of shit and was trying to get in your pants. I didn't think you'd be that gullible."

Steven stomped out of the room. The door slammed shut after him. I didn't care.

Chapter 29

PREPARIUM ULTIMATUM

Preparation was the cornerstone of my professional life. I prepared for meetings, classes, grants, conferences. Come in unprepared for one of those, and consequences were delivered swiftly. The investigation with Andrew Pickett was no exception. So sitting at my computer, I typed in 'academic misconduct'. A list of links popped up in my web browser. The first one looked like it might hold potential. I clicked on it and scrolled down until something caught my eye. *Research fraud…rarely the result of a conspiracy to commit it…usually pinned solely on the person in question.* I shut my computer and stood up but then imagined Pickett sitting at my lab table, smirking. I sat right back down.

There were several categories of fraud that fell under academic misconduct. Three, to be exact. The first? When a researcher creates non-existing publications or false titles. Not my issue, but it made sense. After all, academics were judged by their number of publications and honors. Category number two included plagiarism – copying someone else's words or ideas. I hadn't ever done this, but I always worried about it with students. It came down to trusting them. Even with Fennel in the mix, this wasn't my problem. Next – invented experiments and nonexistent or exaggerated research results, data fabrication. Exactly what I'd been accused of by the whistleblower.

That category was scattered with phrases like *worst kind of fraud, public harm, erroneous conclusions*. Andrew Pickett's voice was as clear as if he were standing beside me – 'inconsistencies in the data'. A knot grew in my stomach. Reading on didn't help. This kind of thing could land you in jail. Like Scott S. Reuben, an anesthesiologist whose prolific work changed how patients, all over the globe, were treated for pain during and after surgery. Problem was, the data were fake in over twenty articles. He went to jail for six months and had to pay back hundreds of thousands of dollars to pharmaceutical companies and the government. He's no longer a doctor, because convicted felons can't hold a medical license.

There were a million questions about him. '*How could this have gone on for so long without him being caught?*', '*Didn't any of his colleagues know?*', '*Why didn't the peer-review process of publication catch this?*', '*How many patients have been hurt by what he did?*', '*How many thousands of dollars have been wasted on needless interventions that were based on his research?*' I could sum it up in one word that we can all be victim to, if we're not careful. Ego.

Fuelled by fame and recognition and undying gratitude of patients. Never mind the pressure to publish or have your colleagues see you perish or lose your research funding.

I clicked on another link. It took me to *Retraction Watch*, a web site with the epitaphs of many a scientist – *Here lies 'insert name of dishonest scientist', always remembered by those he misled*. The Who's Who of scientific misconduct was at my fingertips. Top of the list that day was Anil Potti, a Duke researcher whose papers, nineteen of them at that point, were being retracted or corrected under allegations that he falsified chemotherapy research. They speculated it was part of a plan to develop cancer tests that would lead to big money for him and all those involved. With another click I was watching a *60 Minutes'* segment. All those cancer patients, trusting and hopeful, just like my mom. She trusted anything her doctor told her, and if there was any hope that a new experimental treatment would've spared her, she'd have signed up immediately. It made me stop to think how this unwavering belief – that science is the one true thing – permeated the core of humanity, despite the fact that science is carried out by people who are fallible. Most people believe that if something is published in a medical journal, then it must be true. Not many people think of scientists as being motivated by greed and fame and fear and professional rivalry.

But just how much of a problem was this? At the bottom of the *Retraction Watch* web site, I found a link to a study. In it, the researchers reported that almost two percent of scientists admitted to having fabricated or falsified data. This intrigued me. How many scientists were there in the world? Maybe one million? I moved the decimal place in my head. If just one million scientists existed in the world, it would mean that twenty thousand of them had committed research fraud. *Twenty thousand.* I read on. In another publication, where researchers investigated how many scientists thought their colleagues falsified data, a whopping fourteen percent replied affirmative. In the scenario of one million scientists, that translated to one hundred and forty thousand instances of data fabrication.

The information was depressing and wasn't going to help me. I needed to find something different, something about scientists who were 'unjustly accused of research fraud'. The limited number of hits that came up were convoluted and mostly irrelevant. Except for one. In the mid-eighties, a biology professor named Thereza Imanishi-Kari, was accused by her post-doctoral fellow of fabricating data for a landmark article on the immune systems of mice. Apparently the post-doc, Margot O'Toole, wasn't able to replicate the results. It took ten years of back-and-forth, a requested leave of absence, and scads of legal bills for Imanishi-Kari to be vindicated of almost twenty initial accounts of fraud. She said she never dreamed the whole situation would turn into such a nightmare. Ten years. Ten years! Where did I picture my life in ten years? Certainly not just recovering from this vile situation.

I closed my computer and pulled out the sketch of events that I'd constructed. I stared at the point on the timeline, when I was accused of data fabrication. Someone from *CAFÉ* could've been the whistleblower. But on what grounds? I kept hearing Pickett's voice over and over again about data inconsistencies. There was no way *CAFÉ* could've orchestrated that. And then, a bomb went off in my head that sent shock waves out to my toes. I'd forgotten a point on the timeline. The reliability check. After the data loss in my lab, I'd only re-analyzed the first ten percent of Fennel's data. She was incensed about my accusation of her cheating and could've easily been swayed to retaliate. The more I pondered this, the more it seemed highly suspicious that her friend, Rebecca, the woman who was so upset about Huey, Dewey, and Luey, showed up in the lab just before the data screw up. How did I not see this?

CAFÉ found Fennel.

I hadn't seen him since I slapped his face. We agreed it would be best to meet off-campus, in a small coffee shop near the center of the city. A red Ferrari pulled up on the street and parallel parked in front of the shop. Luke stepped out. The money that *Zirica* was paying him and Schlemmer for working on Phase III of the *Guarafit* trial must've been paying off. He walked in the door and smiled when he saw me. We made our way to the counter to order and exchanged pleasantries while we waited for our coffees.

At a quiet table in the corner, we both started talking at the same time and stopped. He held out his hand for me to continue.

"I feel really, I mean —"

"Don't say another word," he said. "I know how it must've seemed. It wasn't. But I could see how it was misinterpreted."

"Can we forget it then?"

"Of course. Now, what's up?"

"I didn't know who else to talk to." I explained the situation with Fennel and *CAFÉ*, and asked if he thought I should talk to Pickett, which he didn't. He said it would make things worse at this point and that I should just wait until the inquiry to make my case there. If it even came to that, he added. He didn't come out and say it, but I sensed he thought I was being paranoid about the connection with *CAFÉ* and Fennel.

We walked out together. The Ferrari was gleaming. I told him how beautiful it was. I knew it was a life-long dream but hadn't realized he got one. He seemed uncomfortable talking about it and must've said at least five times how it was only a base model. I didn't realize that there was such a thing when it came to Ferraris. Leave it to Luke to play the whole thing down. That's just the kind of guy he was. We parted with a hug; the world felt right again in that moment.

I pulled into my garage, imagining what it must be like to pull in driving a Ferrari. My phone chimed. It was an anonymous text message.

Stop digging or you're next.

Chapter 30

BIGGLEDY WIGGLEDY

I smoothed the paper on the table. It was crinkled and coffee stained. I knew Conner wouldn't judge. I directed his attention to two random branches on the timeline that made no sense to me. The first was the phone call from Anbu the morning he died. I tried to explain to Conner what I thought I heard. *Save the rays*. Did this have some computer significance, I asked? A video? Maybe Blu-ray? Conner squinted as he thought about this and then said no, that Anbu would never have used a format like Blu-ray.

"Could he have said, *save the data*?" Conner asked.

"I suppose. But I don't think so. I'm pretty sure the last word was rays or something like that. What about this?" I pointed to the branch labelled 'envelope' and told Conner about the message on the post-it note.

Conner repeated 'get down on your knees and pray' several times. "Didn't Madonna write a song with those words in it?" he asked.

"Like a Virgin?"

Conner blushed and mumbled, no, *Like a Prayer*.

When I asked him what he thought the relationship might be to that song, he just shrugged. I was quickly coming to the conclusion that Conner wasn't going to be able to help me with these two unknowns, and I didn't know what to do with them. They didn't seem related to *CAFÉ*, but then again, maybe I was missing something. I'd look at the lyrics later, just in case.

Last but not least, I asked Conner to look at the text that arrived on my cell phone after my meeting with Luke. It had come from 888-888-8888. He snorted. Anonymous text. Good luck finding out who sent it, he said. Would even be hard for the police.

Diesel barked like a rabid dog at the front door. When I opened it, Armstrong smiled broadly until Diesel jumped on him and nearly knocked him backwards.

"Woah. Killer. You should sign him up for the academy."

I invited Armstrong in. Diesel calmed, but didn't leave my side the whole time Armstrong was there.

"The main people from *CAFÉ* have all been interviewed," he said. "There's nothing there."

I pulled out my phone and showed him the most recent text. He sighed and rubbed his forehead. Said he didn't know what to make of it. He'd make a note.

"A note? That's it?"

"What do you want me to do?" His icy blue eyes seemed to turn a shade of grey.

"I don't know. Maybe you could run a trace on it or something."

"You watch too much TV."

My cheeks burned. "Think whatever you like of me Corporal, but there is something absolutely wrong here. Are you going to just brush this all under the rug like Anbu's case?"

Now his cheeks were crimson. "Brush it under the rug? Is that what you think happened?"

"Yes. As a matter of fact, I do. Anbu took the fall for something he didn't do. I seem to be the only one, besides his poor wife and family back in India, who wants to set the record straight. Everyone else has been willing to let the truth die with him."

"That's between you and the university. The police have done their job. Case closed." Armstrong stood and walked to the front door. Diesel barked at him the whole way there and continued at the front window until Armstrong got in his car and pulled away.

I removed the manila envelope from the drawer in my home office and pulled out the three consents. I had no idea how they related to *CAFÉ*, if they even did, but there was something about them that Anbu needed me to know. If I followed his lead, maybe the connection would become clear. From my sleuthing, which now seemed long ago, I knew that number 20 was Brenda

Deswicki. Luke interrupted me before I could figure out 7 and 15. The only option that remained at that point was to go into forbidden territory.

Later that the evening, when I was certain no one would be around, I entered the hospital wearing a pair of scrubs I'd taken home as pajamas. I put my key into the Ninsun Clinic lock, not certain it would turn. It did. Guess they didn't think of everything.

I pulled the research file that had the master list in it and decoded the two subject numbers. When I saw whose name was associated with number 7 on the master key, the breath was sucked out of my chest. Jacklyn Gardner. I retrieved her medical file, not sure what I should even be looking for. After I'd seen her in the cafeteria, Luke told me all her tests were normal. He was right. As I poured over them, she seemed to be the picture of health, right up to February, which was her last visit on record. There were no reports from the ER, however, which was odd. Especially since Luke had said he was going to call them to check in. I wanted to see what kind of note he made about it in the daily log. I flipped to the front of the chart, looking for an entry in May or June. I couldn't quite remember when I'd run into her. There was nothing recorded. There should've been. Every contact with patients or other professionals was supposed to be recorded there. More concerning, however, was what seemed to be a truncated note in the daily log at the end of February and then nothing after it. There was the mandatory signature beside it, which looked like Schlemmer's, but it was in a pen color just a little different than the entry.

The blue light of the photocopier rolled back and forth over that page in Jacklyn's chart. As it came to rest, the reception door slammed shut. I froze. There was nowhere to hide. Footsteps crossed the floor. Before I could do anything with the chart, a security guard popped his head around the corner of the photocopier room.

"Oh, sorry doctor," he said. "I saw the light on and thought it was pretty late for someone to be in here."

"Just finishing some charting. Then I'm done. Thanks for checking in."

"You need a walk to the parkade?"

"That's so kind." A trickle of sweat rolled down my back. "I'll be fine."

"Don't work too hard." He smiled. "Goodnight."

I waited until I heard him go out the door and then pulled patient 15. Agnes Bantle. I didn't recognize the name, but wasn't going to stay and review the file. I copied the pages from it, stuffed them in my bag, put all the files back exactly how I'd found them, and left. I walked as quickly as I could. Not only had I disobeyed the university by going into the clinic, I had now committed a major infraction of the health information act. Fineable for a minimum of $10,000, and jail time.

The next morning, I took a deep breath and dialed from our home phone, which was unlisted. There were two rings before a woman's voice answered. I put on a big smile and pictured Genie in my head.

"Good morning," I said. "May I speak with Mrs. Gardner?"

"This is."

"Mrs. Gardner, this is Genie from the Ninsun sleep clinic."

"Who?"

"Genie. The receptionist from Ninsun."

"Oh?"

"I'm just doing a chart audit. We need to make sure all your information is correct."

"Such as?"

I tried to sound as bubbly as possible. "Just need to confirm your past appointments."

"Why?"

"To be sure we haven't missed any. Looks like your last appointment was in February. Is that correct?"

"No. It was May."

"You sure?"

"Yes. I stopped coming after that."

"How come?"

"You're sure asking a lot of questions."

"Oh, I'm sorry. We just want to be sure that you're getting the best care possible, and it sounds like maybe you weren't if you stopped coming."

"No, it wasn't that. I just wasn't feeling good. I went to the emergency and even ran into that lady doctor from your clinic. She said she'd tell Dr. Schlemmer. Didn't hear a thing, though."

"He didn't call?"

"No."

"Did a different doctor call? Maybe Dr. Hesuvius?"

"No."

"That's not right. We must've messed up in getting the message to him."

"I don't see why any of this matters."

"Are you still taking *Guarafit*?"

"Who did you say you were?"

"I'm the receptionist. I just need to make a note for Dr. Schlemmer."

"I didn't feel good from it so I stopped."

"My goodness! I'm glad I called. I'll chat with Dr. Schlemmer."

"Not necessary. I'm not coming back."

I wanted to ask so many other things but didn't want to give myself away. Genie barely knew how to spell *Guarafit*. I thanked Jacklyn for her time and said goodbye.

Luke had said he'd call Jacklyn for Schlemmer; apparently he didn't. Worse, though, Schlemmer obviously had altered her medical record. I couldn't fathom what Schlemmer would get out of lying about the patients' health, except another publication to support all the rest. In addition to that, I'm sure *Zirica* wouldn't want to hear about bad results. Were they pressuring him? After all, he was in their pocket, so to speak. But all that seemed shallow, even for Schlemmer. I needed to make notes about it all on my timeline. But where? I decided to park them in a corner of one page.

The bigger question was what did the consents have to do with my rats? I tried to think like Anbu. Three rats, three consents? All three rats were dead, but only patient 20, Brenda Deswicki, was dead. She was healthy during the trial, though. Luke had even reviewed her file with me and said that the damage was likely done early on in her life. Number 7, Jacklyn Gardner, withdrew because she wasn't feeling good. Was she a carbon copy of Brenda? Then there was 15, Agnes Bantle. She also was Schlemmer's patient.

I settled in with a coffee and scrutinized every copied page of Agnes' medical records. And they were all there – no missing dates, no missing pages. Turned out, she had spotless records. Steady weight loss. Normal test results throughout her participation in the trial and a discharge date with an ideal weight and resolution of all apneic symptoms. I collected all of the records I had copied from her file and went to my shredder. If anyone found these in my home, I'd be going to jail for nothing. The link that Anbu was trying to reveal was not death.

While I fed the sheets of paper into the shredder, I went through the facts in my head. Someone sabotaged my rats by feeding them improperly. Of that I was convinced. And it wasn't Anbu. First of all, he would've immediately recognized his mistake after the first rat went into respiratory distress. Secondly, even if he did it accidentally, he would've fessed up. That's just the kind of person he was. Like the time he enrolled a patient for Luke and made an error in recording the patient's weight, which resulted in an initial dose of *Guarafit* that was wrong. He told Luke as soon as he realized.

Schlemmer crossed my mind, again. There was no other conclusion except that he altered Jacklyn's records. Obviously he was hiding something, and I couldn't even confront him about it. Luke was my only hope to bring light to this whole situation. But if I told him what I did, that I went through Jacklyn's file, called her, and impersonated Genie, he wouldn't be able to support me. Not publicly, at least.

"You did what?" Luke's voice was tight on the other end of the line.

"I had no choice. There was a reason that Anbu set those three consents aside. You need to confront Schlemmer."

"Did you ever stop to think that maybe this has to do with Anbu and no one else?"

"What?"

"Maybe he had something to cover up. His life was not exactly stable, with all the stress of being a new father and trying to show his family back home that he could be a success."

"What are you suggesting?"

"He was tired. He confided that to me. He was making mistakes. Maybe there were too many and he thought he had to hide them."

There was a squeeze in my stomach. That was the last thing I wanted to believe, but it was plausible. I knew that his family's opinion of him was very important.

"Listen carefully, Mack," Luke inhaled deeply, "you need to let this go. Do you hear me? You already have too much at stake, with Pickett being in your lab and all the accusations against you. If anyone found out what you did, well, that'd be it. Lay low. Forget your rats. Forget the consents."

I agreed. Mostly just to get off the phone. There was more I had to do.

I typed in 'save the rays'. The webpage was full of information about saving sharks and manta rays. This would seem to point to *CAFÉ*, but what did manta rays have to do with rats? Nothing, as far as I could tell. Just another dead end. I typed in 'say a raise'. As expected, it revealed everything I needed to know, if I wanted to ask Elizabeth for more money. Unlikely she would entertain that idea. That wasn't it. Maybe I heard him completely wrong.

What I was more certain of was the yellow post-it note and the words Anbu wrote. 'Get down on your knees and pray'. I typed in *Like a Prayer* and watched the video. Burning crosses. Madonna in a bustier. Down on her knees. Kissing the feet of a black saint with roses and bringing him to life. Singing 'life is a mystery'. She got that part right.

Chapter 31

PICKETT PICKING AWAY

Pickett eyed me while I sat down at the conference table in the lab. His outfit, a light pair of brown pants and a purple shirt, made him look like an aristocratic grape. He ran both hands down the front of his shirt until satisfied that he was suitably unwrinkled.

"I have questions about some things," he said, holding on to the word *things* and dropping his voice so it rumbled. "Let's start with the reason I was brought here. As you know, I was asked to audit the data for your latest publication."

Why did he think he needed to remind me of that?

He opened a folder and began to shuffle through a stack of papers. "I've re-analyzed a godforsaken number of traces, and the majority of them don't correspond with any of the cells in the spreadsheet you gave me. They don't even come close, such that I could conclude the discrepancy was due to test-retest error. In fact, the numbers are so discrepant it suggests they *were* fabricated."

I craned my neck to see what he was referring to.

He closed the file and slid it under his hand. "The only accurate numbers are from the reliability check, which was done on selected data, I might add."

He sat and waited. So did I.

"Can you explain this?" His foot tapped under the table.

My mind raced up and down empty streets, looking for an answer, but there was nothing. Except for at the very end of one lane, where Fennel leaned out a door and waved.

"Fennel was responsible for data analysis," I said. "Our reliability checked out on the first portion of the data, so I let her do the rest."

"Why only the first portion? Why not random?"

"I was going away. We were in a time crunch. I needed Fennel to work on it while I was gone."

"Time crunch? Or poor planning?"

"No, Andrew, there was a plan. We had to deal with an unexpected event."

"Seems like there are a few of those around here. Care to explain?"

I took a deep breath and gave him the briefest account possible of the data loss.

"Interesting." He jotted a note into a book that was already half-full. His writing was small and obscure.

"Let's get back to the data in the manuscript, shall we? You say Fennel analyzed them?"

"Yes. The reliability check was excellent. I felt

confident of her work."

"And you never looked at the data again, after that, to see if she was still analyzing them reliably?"

"No. I like to put a certain degree of trust in my students' abilities."

"She's only a master's student, correct?"

"Yes."

"And there was some question about her cheating on an exam, correct?"

"There was no proof."

"If I have my facts straight, you were the one who accused her of it. Isn't that true?"

"Yes."

"So what would possess you to think she'd be different in your lab?"

"Are you implying that she did this?"

"Did what?"

There was a glint in his eye. I said nothing.

"Given everything," he continued, "don't you think your course of action was irresponsible? Aren't you the director of this lab? Her immediate supervisor?"

"Yes, as a matter of fact, I am." I leaned into his face. "Have you asked her how she thinks the data got so distorted?"

"Why, yes, I have. But that's of no concern to you right at this moment. Oh – and please – you're not to contact Fennel or any of the other people I've interviewed to do your own interviewing. Do you understand?" He opened his folder and flipped through the documents inside. "Moving on to issue number two, then. Your rats. The most recently dead ones," he smirked. "What happened?"

"I don't see what that has to do with the paper."

"Of course you don't. Please just answer my question."

Like a foreigner in a foreign land, sitting in the local police station with no rights or privileges, there was no option but to explain.

"Now, isn't it true," he leaned back and looked up at the ceiling, "that you were going to use those particular rats for a replication study?"

I nodded my head and cursed the day I ever told Fennel about it.

"Hard to replicate a study that has fabricated data. Even harder to replicate it with dead rats."

"Are you kidding me? What exactly are you suggesting?"

"I'll ask the questions now."

"Geez, Andrew, I feel like I'm on trial here."

"You are." He smiled.

Blood pulsed in the back of my skull, crashing like the ocean into my ear drums. "How did this go from auditing my data to questioning me about my rats?"

"It's funny in life how one thing leads to another, isn't it?"

"Hilarious."

"Well, then," Pickett snapped closed his notebook, "I'm not expecting to need to talk to you again until the meeting with the full committee."

"When will that be?"

"I thought maybe three weeks, but the situation has gotten rather complicated now."

Chapter 32

RETURN OF THE MAC

It had been four mind-numbing weeks of being clois-tered inside the walls of my house. A boring and suf-focating eternity. Steven and I hadn't been talking much, and Diesel and I had played so many games of fetch that even he didn't want to play anymore. Luke's invitation to meet for lunch was perfect. Campus was off limits, though. Luke suggested somewhere downtown. Fine with me; I just wanted some human contact, and a coffee would be nice. A cappuccino with more milk than espresso, gentle and sweet. He said I could have whatever I wanted, that he just wanted to see me.

We agreed on the Hotel MacDonald, where it would either be couples out for a romantic lunch or business-men trying to impress each other. Inside the lobby, my heels clicked across the marble floor. There was no one else around to hear except for the gargoyles perched on top of the stone arches. Their eyes followed me all the way to the Confederation Lounge. When I got to the entrance, a finger tapped my shoulder.

"Dr. Smith?" a male voice inquired.

I turned to see an overweight, middle-aged man. I scanned the area around him to see where he had been hiding. There were no pillars or big plants. He must've been stalking behind.

"Who wants to know?"

"You don't know me, but I've been following the story about you and your lab."

"I've said all I have to say to you guys."

He stopped, wide-eyed, for a moment. "Oh, no," he cracked a half smile, "I'm not media. My name is Brian Deswicki."

My heart skipped.

"Brenda Deswicki's husband," he said. "I used to come to every appointment with her at Ninsun."

In the awkward silence that followed, I told him how sorry I was to hear about her death. A film of tears stripped across his eyes.

"It's been tough." He looked over to the front door and cleared his throat. "But that's not why I stopped you." He stuffed his hands in his pockets and cleared his throat again. "Something has been bugging me, and when I saw you, it was like a sign from above. I wasn't even supposed to be here today."

I wanted to ask him how long he had been following me, but he didn't give me a chance.

"Brenda was healthy as a horse her whole life." He looked off to the distance, smiled a little, and nodded to himself in agreement. "Even though she was overweight,

I always swore she was going to outlive me."

He looked up to the gargoyles and blinked several times. I waited.

"With *Guarafit,* though," he said, locking his eyes on me, "it was different."

"How so?"

"At first, it was great. She was losing weight, and she felt good. But near the end of the trial, her heart would race and she'd feel like passing out."

"Did she tell Dr. Schlemmer?"

"She didn't want to say anything, because she didn't want to get kicked out of the trial. She was so desperate to lose weight, she made me promise I wouldn't say anything either."

The lobby was still, empty, silent. A hollow space was opening in my chest.

"But now I wonder if I did the right thing," he said.

I knew he was waiting for confirmation, but the words weren't coming.

"Can you tell me – did I?" he said.

"You did what you thought was right."

A woman crossed the lobby with a squeaky suitcase wheel. Brian watched her until she reached the check in, then looked back to me. "I guess what I'm really asking is whether any other patients got sick?"

The image of Jacklyn Gardner picking at lettuce leaves in her hospital gown popped into my head. "Not that I know of." As the words rolled off my tongue, the hollow space in my chest turned into a chasm.

The lines in Brian's face softened. He thanked me and walked slowly across the foyer and through the rotating doors to the empty world outside, the one without Brenda.

My chest still ached when Luke rounded the corner with his bright smile, jaunty stride, and crisp white shirt. My mind raced. Should I say anything to him? The picture that Brenda's husband painted was very different than the one Luke and I saw when we reviewed her medical chart.

Before I could make up my mind, his arms were round me, squeezing tight. He let go and started speaking with a Pickett-like English accent. "My dear, although the lounge is tasteful and well-appointed, today it just feels stuffy."

"I need to talk to you."

"So serious." Luke took my arm, his fingertips a feather touch on my elbow. "Come on, let's hit the patio, relax a little, then we can talk."

"No, stop. I need to say this here. There are too many people out there."

He dropped his hand from my arm.

"Brenda Deswicki's husband just found me. He told me she was having problems. Thought it might've been related to *Guarafit*. Something is going on, Luke. I don't know if Schlemmer is covering up something, and I don't know how *CAFÉ* fits in, but something is wrong."

"Oh my god, Mack." Luke flung his arms to his sides. "We've been over this time and again. You and I looked at her file. Together. Remember?"

I nodded.

"Listen," he dropped the tone of his voice and gently put both hands on my shoulders, "I'm telling you this because I'm your friend. You are stretching. You're trying to find a reason for why your world is turned upside down. If you're not careful, though, people are going to start to think you're losing it. You know, looking for all kinds of conspiracy theories. I don't want that to happen to you."

"I'm not losing it!" I flicked his hands off my arms.

A woman who was walking by lifted her eyebrows.

"Let's go sit outside," Luke said quietly. "Get some fresh air."

Sunlight washed over the patio. The perimeter was lined with rose hedges deftly hiding their thorns under petals of pink and white. The patio was packed with couples and suits, except for two empty tables, one at the far end and the other in a corner. Luke started to guide me towards the far end of the patio.

"Oh shit." He grabbed my arm and turned me abruptly back towards the door. He kept pulling me to go with him but not fast enough to keep me from looking over my shoulder.

"Stop!" I said.

"No, Mack. Just keep walking."

I dug in my heels, until I was certain of what I was seeing. There, gazing out towards the river valley, was a couple. The two of them, cozy at a setting for four, separated only by the corner of the table. Each with a glass of white wine, they appeared unaware of other patrons, servers, ambient noise. The woman said something, took a sip of wine, and looked off into the distance. The man touched her hand.

Luke dug his fingertips into my arm. "Let's go. Now."

"No!"

"Ssssshhhh," Luke leaned in. "You have to. You don't need any more public drama. Deal with it at home."

Yellow eyes glared at me from her ankle. I couldn't breathe. Couldn't think. Couldn't stop shaking. Steven had told me he was going to be in business meetings all day.

"Now!" Luke hissed and dragged me out to the lobby.

The Ferrari engine growled down the hill to my home. Luke insisted on driving me. Said I shouldn't walk and shouldn't be alone. He likely was worried that I'd go back to the patio and strangle her. I'd been silent for most of the car ride. It was Luke who was spitting venom, mostly about Fennel. When he finally quieted, I told him about Fennel wanting to confide in Steven.

"So let me get this straight," he said. "She's got some supposed deep dark secret. He wants her to feel comfortable, so he gives her your mom's pearls? Who does that!"

"Luke, you need to understand –"

"No, Mack. You need to hear this. I care too much about you." He took a sharp turn on the street before mine and pulled off to the side. He put the car into park and turned to me. "No husband who loves his wife would do that, nor would he do what you saw him doing today, under any circumstances."

"He's trying to help me."

Luke stared. "You don't really believe that, do you?

You're too smart a woman for that. Right?"

His eyes bored into me.

He took a deep breath. "You aren't going to like hearing this, but you and I both know what's going on. Don't try to tell me that he is only consoling her."

I stared straight ahead. My chest felt bound with wire. My eyes stung. "You don't know that."

"Fine." Luke pulled away from the curb, drove around the block and parked in front of my place. "Don't forget, I know what she is all about. Thank god I was never in closed quarters with her."

"You're such an ass!" I stepped out of the car and slammed the door. He called after me as I went up the walk. I fumbled with my key, not able to see the lock through my tears. His voice wouldn't let up. It kept getting closer and closer. I just needed to get inside. I pushed all my weight against the door and flew in. Luke stumbled in behind like a shadow. I stood there with tears streaming down my face. Luke closed the door and came around to stand in front of me. He tried to put his hands on my arms, but I backed up until I was against the wall. He came and stood in front of me and slowly stepped in until his body was pressed against mine. For the first time in months, with his chest against me, I felt safe. I wanted to just stay like that. He grabbed my face and this time kissed me. His lips were soft and full, and when his tongue tip touched mine, my heart felt like it was going to explode. I pushed him away and slapped him twice as hard as last time.

The door opened and slammed. I fell to my knees and collapsed. Pebbles of dirt that had been tracked into the house bit into my bare skin. Luke might've said something before he left, but I couldn't remember as I listened to the rumble of his car driving away.

I hated myself. I hated Steven.

Chapter 33

PAPA'S PICTURES

I squeezed shut my eyes and forced the kiss out of my mind. Every time I thought of it, my stomach lurched. The only thing that eased my conscience was the image of Steven's hand on Fennel's. It only helped for a bit, though, before the sick feeling of his infidelity carved a hole in my gut. When I saw him walk out of the garage that evening, my heart began to pound. I breathed deeply to slow it as he came in the back door.

"How was your afternoon?" I asked when he rounded the corner.

"Nothing exciting."

"Really? Nothing out of the ordinary?"

"Nope. Same old, same old."

"Just another busy day, huh?"

"Yup." He hung up his jacket.

"Meetings?"

"Yup."

"Lots of them?"

He chucked his shoes into the closet and slammed the door. "Yes, Mack, it was a very busy day with lots of meetings."

"Liar."

He set down his brief case. "What the hell are you talking about?"

"What the fuck were you doing with her?"

"With who?"

"Oh please! Don't treat me like an idiot. Fennel. That's who."

He walked away.

"Steven!"

He spun around. "She asked to meet me okay!"

"Oh, I see. And she forced you to touch her."

"Where are you getting this from?"

"Are you going to deny it?"

"Fuck, Mack. She's trying to help you. And so am I. So what if I touched her hand?"

"So what?"

"You don't want to know what she said?"

"No. But obviously you do."

"Jesus Christ. You can't even see when someone is trying to help you."

I took a deep breath. "Why don't you enlighten me?"

Steven paused. Looked back and forth between my eyes. "She knows something but is scared to say."

"Oh, poor Fennel."

"See! There you go."

I shot him a look. Silence extended between us like a highway on the prairies. He turned to leave.

"Who is she scared of?"

He stopped and turned back. "Her dad."

"Her dad. I'm so sick of hearing about her dad. Does she not have anything better to talk about?"

"Actually yes. Luke."

"Oh my god. You can never let it go, can you?" I leaned across the counter. "Just so you know, she slept with him too." The lie felt good. Like I had just thrown a machete at him.

"You know?"

"What do you mean, do I know?"

"Well do you or don't you?"

"Just get to the point, Steven."

"He's blackmailing her with photos?"

"Oh my god. Is that the story she fed you?"

"Whether you want to hear it or not, he's related to all this. And he's using Fennel. But she's been too scared to say a thing, even to me, because he threatened that, if she did, he'd send naked pictures to her dad."

"Holy, god, she is living in a dream world. And so are you, if you are sucker enough to buy that garbage."

"Aw, fuck you. I'm tired of trying to help."

"Fuck me? No. Fuck her. I'm sure you've been dying to."

Steven stomped into the basement. He returned up the stairs with a suitcase.

"Where are you going?"

"See, Mack. That's the problem. All that matters to you is your world. Your career. Your everything. You don't listen to a word I say. If you did, you'd remember that I'm going to Portland."

Dresser drawers banged upstairs. I grabbed my cell phone and went onto the deck outside. I dialed Luke's number. It rang at least ten times before he picked up. His hello was curt.

"Did you sleep with Fennel?"

"Jesus, Mack. You slap my face when I try to get close to you, and now you want to know if I slept with Fennel? You need help. I'm serious. And I think it's better if we don't see each other until you get some."

Emails from the university had been scarce, but that morning, there was one announcing a lecture in bariatrics, the study of obesity. I wanted to go to see if he'd address the link between obesity and sleep apnea. That, and it'd be a distraction from the past three days of constant worry about Steven. After our fight, we didn't utter another word, not even 'goodbye' when he walked out the door, bound for Portland. The lecture was going to be in Bernard Snell Hall, which was perfect. The entrance at the top of the auditorium, behind all the seats, would be ideal for sneaking in.

I decided to wear my favorite powder blue Armani suit. Might as well have put it to good use, before it got eaten by moths. When I emerged from the walk-in closet, Diesel sprang up and slapped his front paws on me.

"No Diesel!"

He recoiled and hunched in front of me, ears pinned back like a cape. Two perfectly-formed paw prints soiled each leg, right by my crotch.

"Dammit!"

He slinked away and squished himself into the back corner of his crate.

I changed outfits – a pair of ugly grey pants that barely fit and clashed with my suit jacket. I exited the closet feeling fat.

I slammed shut the crate door. Diesel flinched. His eyes were wide.

"Stupid dog. Stop looking at me like that."

Keys, check. Phone, check. House alarm, check.

The lecture had been a letdown. There was no novel information. Simply slides packed with bullet points and text about the rise of obesity. On top of that, Schlemmer was in the audience, in the front row with Luke. He and I hadn't spoken since my phone call about Fennel.

Luke kept popping into my mind, while I shopped for groceries after the lecture. Driving home, the sense of unease in my gut mounted to such a level that I stopped my car at a park, found an empty bench, and stared at the downtown skyline across the river. Like a computer that had been shut down, my mind went silent. I simply stared until the buildings blended into one. I came back to life when a man and his dog jogged past. My heart squeezed. I'd been awful to Diesel that morning. He was about the only living being who didn't think I was crazy. And he was loyal to me.

I walked back to my car, acutely aware that in my

race to some academic peak, I'd let friends fall off and hadn't cared. Those who'd been running with me, Anbu, Steven and Luke, were lost to me now as well.

The groceries for the evening – sirloin steak, baby potatoes and a bottle of cabernet sauvignon – were spread out inside the trunk of my car. One of the potatoes had rolled up to the top of the cargo hold. I slithered in. Couldn't care less if I destroyed the ugly grey pants. My neighbor across the street, Anne, was digging in her flower bed. She called my name, when I popped out of the trunk. I waved and started up the walk. She came running after me.

"We were sorry not to see you or Steven at the community meeting last night," she said.

"I totally forgot. I've been so busy and Steven is out of town."

"The new president gave a packet of information. I took one for you and gave it to your niece."

"Hunh?"

"She was here earlier this morning. Said she'd give it to you."

"My niece was here?"

"She was at your door. At first I thought it was you. I had the documents close by, so I ran them over. She said she was going to be leaving you something anyhow and didn't mind putting the package with it. She's a lovely girl."

The steps in front of the house were bare. "Where

did she leave it?"

"Somewhere in your house, I assume. She let herself in."

"She went into the house?"

"Yes."

"Did she say what her name was?"

"No, just that she was your niece."

I abandoned the groceries and Anne; Brittany didn't have a key.

Inside, the alarm warning didn't go off. The house was silent, the air still. The hairs on the back of my neck prickled.

The front entrance was void of a packet. So was the kitchen. There was only one person who it could've been, and this time Steven didn't let her in. She could've easily got a key cut when she dog sat. Or maybe Steven gave her one. Maybe in all of his wisdom, he gave her our alarm code, too. It'd be just like her to strike, to pilfer the one thing she knows would create an even bigger abyss between Steven and me.

I ran upstairs.

In the guest room, the box was in the drawer, still carefully wrapped in the sheet, with the pearls resting inside. I sat down on the bed. Tried to achieve homeostasis. Maybe Steven and Luke were right. Maybe I was losing it. Imagining things that weren't really what they seemed.

A creak came from out in the hall. Goosebumps rippled up my arms and down my legs. My heart was in my throat. Diesel? No, I hadn't let him out of his crate. A hall clock ticked. Each click was like a little detonation, sending a shock to the middle of my chest. There was nothing in the room to use for defense. My phone was downstairs.

I poked my head outside the door frame.

No one was at the stairs, but the air felt thick, like someone was watching. I crept down the hall. The smell of soap drifted out from the laundry room. The stack of clothes on the ironing board was exactly as I left it that morning. The guest bathroom was dark, and the door nearly closed. I put my fingertips on it. Pushed just enough that it inched open, slowly letting light in from the hallway. The shower curtain had been pulled back and, at its edge, there was an arm, a shoulder, a figure taller than me. I heard a disembodied scream and realized it was coming from me. The figure didn't move. My heart slowed and eyes adjusted. It was Steven's suit coat, on a hanger suspended from the shower rod. He must've decided to leave it behind.

My light blue suit pants were still in a ball on the closet floor. The bed was a mess, like I left it. Everything else was in order – except for Diesel's crate. The door was open. A folded piece of paper was propped on top. I ran over and grabbed it.

'*You don't listen very well.*' It looked as though it had been scribbled by an eight-year-old.

There, in a black ball, in the corner of his crate, was Diesel with a yellow scarf tied around his neck. The same one that had been hanging on the back of the lab door for months.

"Diesel!"

His nose was tucked under his back leg. He didn't

move, didn't even glance up. The image of three hanging rats flashed in front of my eyes. "Oh please, no!"

I pulled him out of the corner. He was warm. Thank God he was warm. But motionless. I laid him on his side and tried to unknot the scarf. His eyelids flickered. The knot was too tight for me to get my fingers in. I ran to the bathroom and grabbed a pair of scissors. I could barely get them between his fur and the scarf. I squeezed the scissor loops until finally the blades made a slice. The scarf popped away. He didn't move. I shook him, screamed at him to wake up. His limbs went rigid and he gasped, then jumped up and took off out of the crate. He stopped and coughed, then shook his head in a sneeze. After a few moments of quiet contemplation, Diesel laid down at the foot of the bed. I sat on the floor beside him. He put his head on my lap and nosed me until I scratched his ears.

The yellow scarf lay crumpled beside the crate. I had to take action and knew exactly what I was going to do. But not at that moment, not when Diesel was alive and close to me.

Chapter 34

ARMSTRONG ARMOR

Anne's flower shovel was speared into the dirt beside an azalea bush. She must've left it there yesterday after she saw me. I walked up her steps and rang the doorbell. It chimed a melody of eight bells. She opened the door and, when she saw me, leaned out. Her brow was knitted.

"Was everything okay yesterday?" she asked.

"Yes, just fine. But I really need to know who was at my house."

"Wasn't it your niece?"

"If I show you a picture, do you think you'd recognize the woman you saw?"

"Sure."

Anne frowned while she scanned each person on the group photo from the gala. Her eyes moved steadily across the picture, from left to right, until she was almost at the end; they flicked back a notch and opened wide.

"That's her – the one in the red dress."

"Advantage Security. How may we help you?" a man's voice asked.

"Hi. My name is Mackenzie Smith, and I've a home security account with you."

"What can we do for you today, ma'am?"

"Would you be able to tell me how many codes exist on my account?"

"Do you mean access codes?"

"Yes."

"I'll need your password."

"It's Diesel."

"Yes it is. And what's your birth date?"

I told him.

"Okay…," he said, long and drawn out. His computer keys clicked in the background. "It looks like you have two access codes. A primary and a contractor code."

"That's a mistake. The contractor code should've been taken off back in December, or sometime around then."

"Let's see." There was a long pause. "Hmmm…well, there was one code put on for a week at the end of last year. Yup. It was taken off in December."

"And the current contractor code?"

"Looks like it was put on just over a month ago."

"So you're saying we now have two access codes?"

"Yes, ma'am. Your primary code, which recently was

changed, and a contractor code."

"Can a contractor code only be added on the keypad?"

"No. You'll be pleased to know that we added a call in option as a service to our customers. That way, if you are far from home, you can give someone access without giving away your own passcode. All we need from you is the account password and date of birth of the account holder to get it rolling."

Fennel had the account password, in case the alarm went off while she was dog sitting. It would identify her as a responsible party. We didn't feel bad about giving it to her, because we thought there was really nothing she could do with it once she didn't have a code. Problem was, I didn't realize how easy it would be for her to get a new code. All she had to do was say she was me, use the password, and rattle off my birth date. She'd known it from booking plane tickets to conferences for me.

My heart began to beat in my throat. I instructed him to take off all codes immediately and change the password. I also asked him to keep a record of all the old ones. He assured me that their system always kept track of when all codes were activated and deactivated. I suspected this would be important information for the person I was going to call next.

This time when Armstrong came in, Diesel didn't jump or bark. He sniffed his feet and followed him to the table. I set the note and the scarf in front of Armstrong and went into the kitchen. The cappuccino frother sank into the cup, swirling and hissing. I stopped it just before the crown of milk slipped over the rim. If only I'd recognized that point long ago in Fennel, before she cracked.

Back at the table, Armstrong was inspecting the note. He asked me to go over the story that I'd shared with him on the phone. This time in excruciating detail.

"So, you're saying that your student, who is likely sleeping with your husband, came and tried to strangle your dog with a scarf she'd previously left here, all because you failed her on a cadaver exam, for which she passed the course anyhow."

A flush ran up my cheeks. It did sound ridiculous, when he put it that way.

"And she might have strangled your rats to help out her *CAFÉ* friends, who are really trying to protect animals, not kill them."

"I know it sounds —"

"And that she was smart enough to frame you for research fraud in retribution."

"With help."

"There's one thing — well actually there's many, but that's beside the point — that still doesn't make sense. The first set of dead rats and the first threatening text. That happened when she wasn't even around."

"True. And when they found her, they were able to escalate their cause."

"Hmmm. This is a really jagged trail. I've learned not to trust those."

Armstrong sealed the note and scarf in a plastic bag. He pushed himself away from the table, thanked me for the information and told me to call if anything else came to light.

"Strangled? By who?" Steven asked. He'd barely dropped his suit case in the front entrance.

"Fennel, that's who."

He grabbed his head as if it was going to explode. "Jesus. Not this again."

"Anne identified her."

He shook his head. "She can't get into the house. I changed our code when you asked."

"Well she did."

"There's no way she'd hurt Diesel."

"You know her so well."

"Did you ever consider that maybe your perception of Fennel is distorted because of this crazy notion you have about her and me."

"Crazy notion? I'm crazy for being upset that you don't move away when she whispers in your ear? Or you touch her hand? Never mind the fact that you lied to me about that."

"I'm sorry, alright! I should've told you!" He sighed. "There's nothing going on. Nothing. And I'm not going to try to get any more information from her. It's not worth it."

My inner core wanted to believe him. The distance between us had been torture.

He sat down and sighed. Again. "So now what?"

"Armstrong is looking into it. He said it sounded suspicious but still circumstantial. Really, either you or I could've made the call to the security company – there was no proof it was her."

"Yeah, but Anne saw her."

"She didn't actually see her go in. They couldn't simply fingerprint to see if she was in the house, because she's been in here before."

Steven looked out the window. "And, if we prove it was her?"

"She could be charged with attempted aggravated cruel treatment of animals."

"I still really don't think it's her."

"Wow. What kind of spell has she cast on you? What more proof do you need?"

Steven glared and stomped away. Once again.

Chapter 35

THE INQUISITION

A Federal Express employee stood on the front step holding a glossy cardboard envelope. He handed it to me. The noon sun flashed off it and directly into my eyes. His foot tapped double time while he waited for my signature. He was completely oblivious to the impact that this particular delivery was about to have on my life. I closed the door as the truck pulled away and rested my hand on the knob before turning back into the house.

The plastic pull tab shredded through the envelope's edge. Inside was a document: *Smith Laboratory Investigation* and attached, a cover letter stating the meeting time and place for full disclosure of the report to the committee. On the next page was the synopsis. Key words, vaguely comprehendible, were scattered like trash. *Fraud. Fabrication. Misconduct. Animal cruelty.* There must've been a mistake, something I missed, something if re-read would offer new insight. But my eyes could no longer focus on the quivering pages. The document swirled through the air and hit the floor.

An hour, maybe two, later, my phone rang. It was Luke. We hadn't talked, since I'd accused him of sleeping with Fennel.

His voice was kind, soft. "I just heard."

"How?"

"They asked me to be on the committee. I said no. Too much of a conflict."

"What am I supposed to do?"

"You know the truth, Mack. You defend it at the meeting. I might not be there, but I'll be behind you every step of the way."

"Listen, Luke. I'm really sorry about –"

"Don't say another word. It's past. I told you before, no matter what, you're my friend. Always will be. That's just the way it is with us."

I hung up feeling like a small piece of me was resurrected.

Under an overcast morning sky, autumn leaves on the tree outside my bedroom window shivered on their branches. Inside, where everything should've been safe and secure, the bedroom ceiling hung over me like a great white suffocating expanse. In my internal darkness, an excessively long distance existed between the top of my head and my toes. A long blank hollow space. My gut was aching. I'd hardly eaten or slept over the past week. The bedroom was a self-imposed oubliette and the shower a long lost friend. Since the Federal Express package arrived at my door, time had passed with excruciating slowness. But, finally, the long awaited Friday morning had arrived.

The drive along Whyte Avenue with Steven was silent except for the occasional throat clear. I didn't trust myself to drive. We sailed along through several green lights, until we hit one that turned amber. Steven made a last-minute decision to stop. The seatbelt cut into my neck. I wasn't sure he was fit to drive, either. We sat and waited. Outside my window was the pink and blue awning of the store, *When Pigs Fly*. It seemed appropriate. If, five years previous, someone had shown me my life as we sat at that light, I'd never have believed it.

Steven and I continued the drive in silence, until we reached the administration building at the university. He wished me luck and told me to call him for a pickup when the meeting was over. I waited.

"You alright?" he asked.

"Fine." I tried my best to smile and stepped out of the car.

The administration building smelled like an old carpet. A short flight of marble steps rose to the second floor, where the wood-paneled wall was scuffed and chipped from years of traffic. In the reception area of the VP Research Office, a young secretary led me to an empty room, where I was to wait until the committee was ready to receive me. The room was freshly painted and had new light fixtures that cast a yellow glow, preserving a turn-of-the-century atmosphere.

Portraits of VPs from days past hung there, some life-like, others waxy. Most either had no smile or only a tight curling of their lips. They all watched, judged, while I contemplated where to sit. As I made my way around the table, Elizabeth's laugh came from outside the closed door.

After what seemed like an eternity, the secretary who had received me came into the room and told me that it was time. She led me to another room, where the committee members had been assembled and, I assumed, had been discussing their rights, obligations, and duties. The secretary showed me to my chair, which had been placed on the opposite side of the table from all the committee members. Elizabeth was directly across from me. She was seated beside a tall white-haired man with a meticulously-groomed beard and round wire-framed glasses. He was the at-arm's-length committee member whose name, according to the folded card set in front of him was Dr. Fred Parsons, professor in the Department of Biology. Next to him was an attractive man in a three-piece suit – Jake Lemieux, university legal counsel. An all-too-familiar face sat one chair over from him. Andrew Pickett, with his gleaming smile. At the head of the table was the VP Research, Dr. Zachary Tellrom.

With not a minute wasted, Dr. Tellrom started the meeting by thanking us for coming. In a calm voice, he stated the purpose of the meeting – a chance to ask questions, to get clarification if needed, and to provide me with an opportunity to address Pickett's findings. It was, he said, by no means meant to be a trial for me, nor was it any kind of appeal process. That may come in the future, if there was actually need for it. All heads nodded in agreement, except for mine and Pickett's. Nor was this, Tellrom said with eyes intent on me, a time for any defensive action, but simply an opportunity to tell each side of the story as a preliminary step in determining the next course of action. Considering the sensitive nature of the topic at hand, he said that they had wanted to keep the committee small. Pickett was to begin and, then, one by one, the others would get their chance to question him. I'd be able to present my case, only at the end.

When directed to proceed, Pickett nodded and put a pair of reading glasses on the end of his nose. "Let me begin with the issue that was initially raised as a concern. Dr. Smith's publication of rat data."

While Pickett spoke, Fred Parsons studied the bulky document in front of him and stroked his beard. Jake Lemieux rolled his pink and blue tie and stared at some vague point on the table. The only two people with their eyes on Pickett were the VP Research and Elizabeth.

"Now, it's usually desirable if the findings can be reviewed without revealing the complainant's identity. Unfortunately, in this case, it's vital that we all understand who lodged the accusations against Dr. Smith."

This unexpected news made my heart race.

"This information must be treated with great care, as the repercussions for the whistleblower in this case could be severe," Pickett warned.

The VP spoke up, "As I mentioned, this is not a trial for anyone and we are not a jury. All information shared in this room must be dealt with in the utmost confidence. If identities must be disclosed to make sense of all this, do so."

"My reason for disclosure will make sense, once you know who it is. Without further ado, then, the complainant was," Pickett paused and looked directly at me, "Ms. Fennel Gutterson."

The sound of her name pounded on my ear drums, like a jackhammer on concrete.

"What!" The whites of Elizabeth's eyes showed.

Pickett sat silent, hands folded on the table, eyes raised to the ceiling, as if he was a preacher about to say something profound. He broke his gaze with the ceiling and proclaimed, "For those of you who don't know, Fennel Gutterson is a graduate student who has been working with Dr. Smith. She lodged the complaint after what she said was much contemplation. As she would explain to me, Dr. Smith instructed her to fabricate the data. This happened after a large data loss in the lab that would have delayed submission of the paper."

"That's absolutely not true!" I said.

"Dr. Smith," Zachary Tellrom said in a firm voice, "no interruptions, please."

"If I may continue," Pickett looked over his reading glasses at me, "Ms. Gutterson indicated she was under the impression that Dr. Smith was worried about another group potentially submitting similar find-ings first."

I wanted to scream. There wasn't one single time when that was ever suggested or even hinted at.

"Ms. Gutterson told me that she was directed to

analyze twenty-five percent of the data. This would be checked by Dr. Smith for accuracy and, if all was well, Fennel would then continue to analyze the rest of the data. The first twenty-five percent checked out very well, indeed. It was after that time, however, that Dr. Smith realized the analysis was not happening fast enough. She then directed Fennel to fabricate the data."

"May I comment?" Elizabeth asked Dr. Tellrom.

"No. Not until Dr. Pickett has finished." He nodded towards Pickett to continue.

"In my interviews with Ms. Gutterson, she revealed that she was very conflicted about whistleblowing. She was afraid. Very afraid. Frightened about the rat deaths. Basically frightened for her life. She also felt that people wouldn't believe her claims of fraud and would, instead, assume that her revelation would be interpreted as a way to get back at Dr. Smith for accusing her of cheating on an anatomy exam."

Pickett flipped pages in the document in front of him, halted in the middle, and smoothed the paper. "In fact, the whole prospect of a jilted student crossed my mind, when I first heard about the cheating issue. But then, I considered the issue of the rats in Dr. Smith's lab."

An image of the three of them hanging in their cage flashed in my mind.

"There's no evidence that Dr. Smith had anything to do with their demise, but I find the timing of their death suspicious. It happened soon after she was notified of the fraud claim. The claim may have led her to act rashly, to destroy the rats so they wouldn't be available for replication studies."

"That's absolutely not true!" My voice came out loud and erratic.

"Please, let me finish." Pickett stared at me. "What I was going to add before I was interrupted was that the rat issue is, of course, circumstantial. It also would require a full investigation. However, you can see how a student might draw a conclusion about bad things happening to her, if she got in the way.

"Of course, I interviewed other key people from Ninsun, such as Dr. Luke Hesuvius. He confirmed that Fennel was distressed about being accused of cheating and that, in the end, there was no evidence found against her for doing so. He also acknowledged that Fennel confided in him about the stress she was under in Dr. Smith's lab.

"There were others, who are no longer part of the Ninsun group, but who presented important character information about Dr. Smith. For example, Dr. Herb Raucket. He was Mackenzie's PhD supervisor. I happened to run into him the night I arrived. He'd been in town for the Ninsun gala and was leaving the next day. Now, it might seem frivolous for me to bring him into this, but he revealed interesting details about Dr. Smith's carelessness with laboratory data as far back as when she was a PhD student. She a made a grievous error of which no one would have been the wiser, if it weren't for another graduate student."

Pickett closed his report. "I believe this is enough information for now. With that, I will close."

"Thank you, Dr. Pickett," Zachary Tellrom said. "I'll now open the floor. I'd like to remind you that we'll proceed in an orderly fashion, starting with Dr. Montgomery. Remember, you're to direct your questions to Dr. Pickett, not Dr. Smith."

Elizabeth looked at the notes she'd been scribbling. "I was aware that Dr. Smith had a loss of data in her lab. My question to Dr. Pickett is whether Fennel was asked to just make up any old numbers, or if she was given specific instructions?"

"Fennel confirmed that she was instructed to falsify the data in such a way as to show a novel outcome for Dr. Smith."

Elizabeth looked at Zachary Tellrom. "I do have a hard time believing that Dr. Smith would've told the student to do such a thing. But, then again, I know she instructed the student to complete the on-line manuscript submission with an unfair authorship order."

"Right," Pickett said. "I'd forgotten that important point. Could you explain for the rest of the committee?"

"Dr. Jerome Schlemmer conceptualized the study," Elizabeth said. "Therefore, he asked to be first author on the publication. Because the study *was* his intellectual property, he should've been recognized as a lead author, if not first, then last. That's convention in our field. He was sorely disappointed when Dr. Smith put her name first and him second. Second place is really no better than a student."

Zachary Tellrom asked if she had anything further to contribute. She smiled and said no.

"Okay then –" he said.

"No wait…actually – there *is* one more thing. I hope that some damage control can be done with respect to my other department members. Their reputation is at risk seeing as how they're also authors on the fraudulent paper."

"Suspected fraud," Zachary said. "You and I can talk more about this later." He motioned to Dr. Parsons, the unfamiliar professor sitting across from me.

With a look of confusion on his face, he began. "I don't understand why any student, in their right mind, would follow directions to be dishonest. Perhaps Dr. Pickett could explain that."

Pickett cleared his throat. "I'm sure this will be a little embarrassing for Dr. Smith. I know it was for the student." He waited a moment. "It seems that a relationship of the romantic sort may have started between Fennel and Dr. Smith's husband. So, it's quite simple, you see. She was worried that, if she didn't play along, Dr. Smith would expose her adulterous behavior to Fennel's very religious father."

The room was silent. My face was hot. I didn't know if anyone was looking at me, but it felt like they all were. Finally, Zachary Tellrom instructed the lawyer to take his turn.

"I have one question for Dr. Pickett."

Pickett cocked his head and squinted at Mr. Lemieux.

"Dr. Pickett, is there any reason that you would personally want to see Dr. Smith fail?"

"I take offense at that question," Pickett said, his British accent thicker than usual. "I've done nothing but present the facts to this committee. These were the facts that were passed on to me by the people I interviewed and that became apparent in the data I analyzed."

The room was so still I wondered whether any air was being exchanged.

"Hmmm…facts," Jake Lemieux said. "As legal counsel I'm here to advise the group on process, not to enter my opinion of Dr. Smith into the findings. It's important for me to remind you that a person's career is at stake here. As such, it will be prudent of you, as individuals and as a committee, to consider your conclusions carefully." Lemieux looked at each member around the table.

Pickett glared at him. Lemieux, not rattled in the least, continued. "Thus, I believe we should strike all speculation about the rats and their demise from the record. It's pure speculation, but it has the potential to influence your opinion of Dr. Smith in a negative manner. As does the irrelevant information about the potential affair. Professor Pickett never said that Dr. Smith actually told Fennel she'd expose her. That was the student's assumption. Furthermore, the issue with the paper comes down to the student's word versus Dr. Smith's. And what about the responsibility of the other authors whose names appear on the paper? Shouldn't they have –"

"So you're willing to overlook all this evidence?" Pickett asked as he picked up the thick document in front of him and slammed it back down on the table.

Jake Lemieux sat unfazed. "No – but, unlike the rest of you, I'm not here to make a judgment. I'm here to counsel process."

"Spoken like a true lawyer." Pickett shook his head.

"Okay gentlemen," Zachary said. "Let's stick to the

issue at hand. Dr. Smith, I think we need to hear from you, now."

My parched throat made my voice start with a crack. "I'd like to start by apologizing for my outburst earlier. As you might imagine, it's painfully difficult to listen to Dr. Pickett's findings. The accusations made against me are all false."

People rarely are aware of their breathing while they talk but, at that moment, I was painfully aware that I was near panting. I slowed down and took a deep breath. "First and foremost, I never told Fennel Gutterson to falsify any data. For any reason. If that's what happened, then she took it upon herself. Or someone else convinced her."

"Such as?" Pickett said.

"Dr. Pickett." Zachary said. "Please let Dr. Smith continue."

"That's okay," I said. "I'm happy to make a suggestion. The animal activist group, *CAFÉ*, has been wanting to see me fail for years. Fennel had found a friend within that group. Their connection would explain not only the paper, but also the rat deaths."

"They're animal activists! Not killers." Pickett sneered.

"Think about it," I said. "Is my lab functioning right now? No. Mission accomplished."

The biology professor scribbled something down.

I continued. "The only thing I can be rightly accused of is that I trusted someone when I shouldn't have. As supervisors in academic settings, I believe that we inherently trust our students. We set a path for them, and we trust that they will follow its course. Whether they participate in our labs by analyzing data for our next publication or participate by analyzing data for their own research projects – to which our names will be attached in some form – we trust them. We don't have time not to trust them. We can't possibly watch over their shoulder to see every data point that they record in an experimental protocol. We're too busy chasing down the next grant to support the next round of students and the next set of personnel in our labs."

The shake in my voice made me feel like an amateur. I reminded myself to breathe. "With respect to Fennel Gutterson, it's important for everyone to know that she is not a reliable source of information. She has a historically-poor academic record at our institution. She was failing classes and not handing in assignments – all of which she had a plethora of excuses for, including sick relatives. How she ended up getting this far, passing all her courses and such, should be what's investigated."

"Oh, please." Elizabeth snorted.

"Her father has made substantial contributions to the department," I said.

"Exactly what are you insinuating?" Elizabeth's face was crimson red.

"Dr. Smith," Zachary said, "that's truly conjecture."

"So is most of what's been said here today," I said. "I did not wish to keep Fennel in my lab."

Elizabeth cleared her throat.

"She had been causing much grief, not only for me, but also for others who work in my lab. However, I was instructed by Dr. Montgomery to do so because of the large ongoing donations from her father to the department."

Jake Lemieux jotted a note.

"Finally, I have to restate that I had no hand in the demise of my rats. I treated them humanely and always with respect."

I yearned to tell them to investigate Fennel's role in the rat killings, especially in light of Diesel. However, the committee had no idea about that and, the way things were going for me, Pickett would twist that event. He'd probably suggest that I strangled Diesel in order to frame Fennel.

"Very well," said Zachary. "Does anyone else have anything to add?"

Silence. No one dared to look up.

"I'd like to ask Dr. Pickett what his final impression is regarding his investigation," Zachary said. "Once we know this, we'll ask Dr. Smith to leave so the committee can meet *in camera* to discuss the findings. We'll inform Dr. Smith of our decision about next steps within a week."

My hands were clammy. Sweat rolled down my spine. Pickett stood up, leaned forward on the table with both hands, and looked up to the ceiling again, as if he was still contemplating my fate. His eyes buzzed down and locked gaze with the VP. "I believe that serious research fraud has been committed."

The warm room began to feel icy as the blood drained from my extremities. I don't remember being excused, but as I walked past the room where I first waited, the waxy faces hanging on the wall laughed. Out in the reception area, a woman in a bright yellow suit approached, briefcase slung over shoulder, notepad in hand. She was impossible to miss. She looked like a bee. I knew her, but the time and place escaped me. Then, she opened her mouth. It was Diedre Noshan, the news reporter that, not long ago, accosted me about my dead rats.

"Dr. Smith, I'd like to –"

"Not now." I walked toward the exit.

"Can you comment on the accusations of research fraud that have been levied against you?"

"No." My shoulder grazed hers as I started down the stairs. I hurried to the back of the building and hid behind a large ash tree. When I was certain she was nowhere in sight, I mined through my purse for my phone to call Steven.

Chapter 36

RUBEE COMES THROUGH

I spent five days sitting in an armchair in my home office. I left it to sleep and grab food, but otherwise, sat there and stared at the wall. Diesel sat by my feet the whole time. He followed me to the kitchen when I got food. I didn't have much else to do. Couldn't prepare for any meetings. Couldn't wait for any packages to be delivered. All I could do was wait for the committee's response to Pickett's recommendation. I suspected that, when I received the final word, I'd need a lawyer.

I watched my email, but there was little except for spam. Luke had sent one right after the meeting. He just said he was sorry. Elizabeth must've briefed him. I hadn't heard from him since, but I understood. He was busy with the clinic. I couldn't expect more.

I watched my phone, too. Didn't answer any unknown numbers, though, because most were either reporters or hang-ups. On that fifth day, however, a name popped up on my phone that made my heart leap. Anbu Mathew. And then I remembered. Anbu was dead, and Rubee and Emily had been back from India for months already.

Rubee barely said hi before saying that she needed to see me. It was extremely important she said. She was talking so fast, I could barely understand what she was saying. She sounded almost as panicked as the night she and Emily came home from the airport, after returning Anbu's body to India, to find her bedroom window smashed. A brick had been thrown through it with a note that said, *'Go home animal killers'*.

I interrupted and asked if she was in danger. She said no, and that she'd explain everything when I got there.

When I arrived at her home, Rubee greeted me with a smile. Her cheeks had filled out. Emily was toddling at speed. Anbu would've been proud. She invited me in. There were boxes everywhere and most of the furniture was gone.

"Bee, you're moving?"

"Yes, back to Kerala."

"I'm so sorry I haven't been in touch. Things have been –"

"You do not need to explain, Doctor Mackenzie. I have heard. I am so sorry. I cannot stand to stay in a place that has disgraced my Anbu and that has treated you so terribly."

A pot of tea was waiting on the kitchen table, with a plate of sugar cookies beside. We sat. Emily ran.

"I found something," she said. "When I saw it, I knew I had to call you." She sipped her tea. "I had to sell Anbu's desk. I advertised it on Kijiji. The men who came to get it nearly knocked a hole in the wall. They set the desk down on its side to get a better grip. That is when I noticed it."

Her face glowed. I don't think I'd ever seen her eyes open so wide.

"This was taped underneath the drawer." She slid a picture of Saint Therese across the table to me. There she was in her brown robe, holding a bouquet of flowers. I flipped the card over, and saw the words 'get down on your knees and pray' scribbled in Anbu's handwriting. My heart raced.

Rubee smiled. "This means something, doesn't it?"

I told her it would be helpful and asked if I could keep it. She said of course, as long as somehow it would clear Anbu's name.

Tears welled up in her eyes. "He did not deserve the smudge that the university left on him. And Emily surely does not need that legacy."

That night, I sat in my office chair and stared at the words scrawled on the back of the card. I now had two messages about getting down on my knees and praying. Anbu was a particularly spiritual man. Still, I couldn't imagine him ever telling me to turn to God, even though he may have hoped for it. One thing I knew for certain. He was trying to tell me something.

I slipped out of my chair, onto the floor beside Diesel. He stirred out of his sleep and rested his head on my bent knees. I stroked his ears. How should one pray? I didn't know anymore. The last time I'd thought about God, he was an old man with a white beard. I must've been sixteen at the time. Hadn't thought much about him since. So, there I was on my knees, not knowing what to do next. Anbu wanted me to pray, but I didn't know how.

I closed my eyes and sat there in the blankness. Anbu's coffin popped into my mind. My throat constricted. What kind of prayer was that? Then I remembered the priest at his funeral. Talking about how he'd been so happy to have seen Anbu in church every single day in the days before he died. As far as I knew, Anbu went to church on the weekends. Every single day seemed like a stretch, even for him.

I had a moment of illumination while Diesel snored on my lap. He jumped when I looked at my watch – 9:45 pm. Too late. It'd have to wait until morning.

What time did churches open? It seemed to me that people of religious persuasion would want to begin early in the morning, when everything was still and all you could hear were birds singing in the trees.

The smell of fallen leaves and damp earth mingled in the cool air. The odd leaf crunched under foot, while others swirled away before being crushed. Dried maple seeds flittered against one another in the trees, sounding like the fizz of a newly poured soda. One seed broke free from its stem and helicoptered in front of me. I caught it. In my fingers, it looked like a wing, plucked from an angel's back.

After two more blocks east, it appeared – the symbol that had remained unbent amidst years of storms and controversies – high upon a steeple. I walked around to the front entrance. The blemished wooden door was adorned in the middle with a heart, pierced by thorns and sprouting wings. The door groaned when it opened.

The smell of old wood, incense, and warm beeswax was oddly comforting. My footsteps echoed on the floor of the empty church, as I made my way to a pew near the altar. I sat and rested my arms on the wood of the bench in front, which had been worn smooth by folded hands. A flickering sanctuary candle, concealed in red glass and suspended by gold links, cast a dull glow on the tabernacle. Mary was in front of me and was still being protected by Joseph and baby Jesus. On the other side of the altar was St Therese, in her chocolate brown robe and cream-colored shawl, with a bouquet of pink and white roses resting in her arms. Below her, forty candles flickered like red fireflies; they'd been set aflame for a dollar and a prayer. She smiled knowingly. The same way she smiled at Anbu's funeral. The same way she smiled at me from the prayer card Anbu had left behind.

I knelt down, crouched really, and started what I came there to do. The underside of the pew was rough. A nail had popped out from the wood. It drew blood. I sucked my finger and continued with my other hand. There was nothing more than a few lumps of bubble gum. Down on all fours, I started on the second pew and nearly got to the end when I heard a familiar voice.

"Hello?" Fr. MacIntyre called out. His footsteps were rhythmic and heavy.

I stood and brushed off my knees.

"Well, if it isn't Mackenzie Smith." Fr. MacIntyre smiled, as if he'd just seen a long lost family member. "Dear Child, what are you doing down there? God's the other direction."

"Trying to remember how to pray, I guess."

"It's like riding a bike. Just get on and do it. God doesn't care how."

I smiled. He asked how I'd been since Anbu's death and reminded me how hard it must've been. I agreed and without warning my eyes welled with tears.

"Oh, my dear. Come. Sit over here with me." He led me to the other side of the church, close to St. Therese, and sat in the third pew. He cradled my hands in his and stared intently. Deep into my soul, it seemed. He then turned and nodded towards St. Therese. "I think Anbu had a real devotion to her. He always came and sat here."

He blessed me and left. His footsteps echoed as he retreated to the back of the church. When I couldn't hear them anymore, I looked over my shoulder, just to be sure. I fell to my knees and stuck my head under the pew. I scanned from one end to the other, but there was nothing. Nothing under the pew ahead either. I laid down on my side, aware of the grit on the floor that had been brought in by holy soles. I peered to the pew behind. There, at the far end, duct tape had been used to secure a manila envelope to the underside of the wood. I scrambled to my feet and across the kneeler one row back to the pew's edge. I slid underneath, as if doing an oil change, and used the light on my phone to get a better look. My name was on it, in Anbu's hand writing. I ripped it away, and stood and brushed myself off. An elderly woman who was praying in a pew across the aisle, glanced over at me from her folded hands. I smiled, tucked the envelope under my arm, and exited before Fr. MacIntyre could come back to give me a second blessing.

Diesel sniffed the yellow envelope pieces that had fallen to the ground between the front door and kitchen table. With all the pages from the envelope spread before me, my eyes didn't know where to settle first. There was an electrocardiogram for patient 7, Jacklyn Gardner, from a routine visit during the trial. Long before I saw her in the cafeteria. Several portions of the trace were circled with red pen. In one circle, there were several spikes in the trace that looked like they were happening three times as fast as the rest. In another circle, there were no spikes. Just a stretch of baseline. I wasn't an expert, but obviously, this was not normal. A post-it note was stuck to it. In Anbu's hand-writing was the question, 'Will 7 go to heaven?".

Three pages had been copied from the daily record notes of patient 20, Brenda Deswicki. On them, Schlemmer's hand writing. The notes suggested that the patient had been experiencing a racing heart. And then, one week later, an entry that an electrocardiogram showed some abnormalities. He requested that it be repeated. This, in itself, was strange. When Luke and I reviewed the tests in her file, there were no abnormal ones. I took particular note of her electrocardiograms, being that she had died of a heart problem. In the medical chart at Ninsun, Brenda Deswicki was a picture of complete health. I felt compelled to call her husband, but would wait.

There were also copied medical record notes from the file of patient 15. This was Agnes Bantle. But the notes in this envelope were nothing like the ones I copied. In fact, the last entry on the notes from Anbu's envelope stated that the patient was deceased. I wished I hadn't shredded the copy I'd made of her file.

All three patients were Schlemmer's.

Mixed in with all the medical pages was a white sheet of paper torn in half. On it, a scene filled with grass, trees and blue sky. Cartoonish, but drawn with an adult hand. It was entitled, "*May the Stars Align*". In the sky were five bubble clouds with one word printed inside each. *Contract. The. In. Is. Cloud.* Beneath the clouds was a tree with thick branches. Perched on a middle branch was an old obese woman with the face of a demon. Her frizzled hair had been colored red. It matched her eyes. A shiver went up my neck and prickled my scalp.

I scrutinized the picture. Looked at every detail, except for the old demon. I avoided making eye contact with her. Anbu often spoke in secret codes. I knew the title was one. I played with the words. *A line of stars. Star line.* I looked at the clouds. Five of them. Thought about stars. Five-points. Lines, stars, points. And that's when it hit me. *Line star.* Starting with the contract cloud, I drew a five-pointed star, without lifting my pen from the paper. *Contract is in the cloud.*

Perhaps Anbu had a premonition. He must have been aware of some kind of danger, maybe not mortal, but something. Otherwise, he wouldn't have been leaving things behind for me to find. But a contract? The old woman in the tree glared at me. Had Anbu made a deal with the devil? Or was there a devil after him? One who knew that Anbu had stumbled onto the truth?

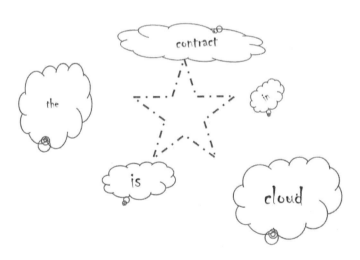

Chapter 37

SUSPECTING SCHLEMMER

It felt strange to dial Luke's number. It seemed so long since we last talked. I'd wondered if he would ever want to speak with me again. More deeply, I wondered if he believed the outcome of the review committee. Or perhaps he was embarrassed to know me. I had become one of the headstones on the *Retraction Watch* website. A decision had been made to retract my paper. And while the article on *Retraction Watch* was careful not to point any fingers directly at me, it was stated, with certainty, that while the responsible party had yet to be determined, there was no doubt that data from my lab had been fabricated. There was only one redeeming aspect to the story. They had found one of the worst pictures ever taken of me, from a glossy report at the university. It made me look eighty years old. Some said it looked like I had a black eye. When the picture was first published in the university's *New*

Trail magazine, I was horrified. Now, I considered it a blessing. Surely, if any *Retraction Watch* readers were to pass me on the street, they might think I was Mackenzie Smith's granddaughter.

Luke answered after seven rings. I knew on the eighth, it would go to voicemail. While his speech was friendly, his voice was distant and thin. It seemed to get even thinner after I said I needed to talk to him about the patients with missing consents.

"You need to let this go, Mack. Isn't your life complicated enough right now?"

I laughed. "My life is nothing right now. I'm not sure you can imagine, and I'm not asking you to. All I'm saying is that I have some new evidence, and it came from Anbu."

"Anbu?"

"It's a long story. I'd rather tell you in person. It could affect you. Badly."

"How so?"

"I don't want to talk about it over the phone. Please, can we meet? Somewhere discreet. And whatever you do, don't tell Schlemmer."

Truth was, I questioned my own sanity and conclusions. What I'd pieced together from Anbu's information was nothing short of multiple murders and a cover up.

I sat at a corner table in an out-of-the-way lounge in one of the oldest hotels on Gateway Boulevard. Luke's suggestion. It was a good one. I couldn't imagine anyone from the university spotting us there. I stood when Luke got near the table. I missed his friendship and wanted to hug him. But he stood behind his chair, hung his jacket off the back, and sat without moving towards me. My cheeks burned as I sat back down.

"So, don't keep me in suspense," he said.

"Like a drink?"

"Not thirsty."

"I need one." I waved over the waitress and ordered a rum and coke.

"I don't want to sound rude, but I'm on a tight schedule, Mack."

"Of course." I wiped my sweaty hands on my pants and began to tell Luke the whole story. He didn't take his eyes off me. I finally felt like I had his attention. Like in the past. After telling him about the church and what I found in the envelope, I reached down into my briefcase and pulled out the copies of the medical files. Luke's face went grey as he looked over them.

"Obviously," I said, "there's some dirty business going on, and Anbu knew about it."

Perspiration beads were collecting on Luke's forehead. He looked up from the documents. "You think I had something to do with this?"

"God, no! It's obviously Schlemmer. They're all his patients."

Luke's shoulders dropped. He unrolled a napkin from a knife and fork and wiped his forehead.

"But," I said, "you could get hurt by association. This needs to be reported."

His lips began to part, but before he could say

anything, his phone rang. He looked at the screen and excused himself, nearly knocking into the waitress who was almost at the table with my drink. I sipped on it while watching him pace back and forth behind the glass lobby doors. At one point, he stopped talking and just nodded his head. It looked like he hung up without saying goodbye, but I couldn't be sure. Back at the table, his expression was softer than before and color had returned to his cheeks.

"Everything okay?" I asked.

"Just the regular clinic issues." He placed his hand on the documents and froze. "But, maybe there is no such thing as regular. I can't believe this."

"I couldn't either. But it would explain a lot of things. Like Schlemmer's hostility whenever I brought up patient issues."

"But what does he have to gain?" Luke paused. "Never mind. That's a dumb question."

"Mmhmm. Imagine if they found out. Phase III would be shut down so quickly."

Luke's face blanched.

"Listen," I said, "I know this is your life we're talking about here, too."

"Yes, but if people are really being hurt, that…well, that just can't be. We need to handle this carefully. We can't tip off Schlemmer. I need to get some evidence together so that we're certain."

"What more do you need?"

"An iron clad case. We have to prove he did this beyond a doubt."

"Without access to patient files, there's not much

more I can do."

"You shouldn't be doing anything." Luke took in a deep breath and quietly said, "Leave it to me."

Chapter 38

CRACKING CODE

Conner and I sat at my kitchen table, me with a coffee and him with a glass of water. I showed him the prayer card that Rubee had found.

"Not Madonna, I guess," he said.

"No, definitely not." I pulled out the drawing that was in Anbu's envelope. Conner adjusted his glasses. His face had no expression as he studied it. I didn't say a word. It was his first time seeing it and I didn't want to rush him. His eyes paused on something and focused in. He smirked.

"Batibat." He pointed to the demon-woman in the tree and glanced at me. "It was in Anbu's search history at the hospital."

I faintly remembered. It seemed so long ago. He pulled out his phone, typed something, and handed it to me. There on the screen was a similar looking demon-faced woman, except without the red hair. I scrolled down:

"Batibat: a huge, old, demon woman who lives in trees; known for suffocating her victims to death at night by sitting on their chest."

And underneath that was a link to sleep apnea.

Death, chest, apnea.

Anbu hadn't made a deal with the devil. He had figured out who had. Patients were dying. Their hearts were stopping. And it was because of *Guarafit*. I was more convinced than ever that the picture had a clue buried in it. I was certain that, if only I could see it, Schlemmer would be sunk for good.

"What do you think about the clouds?" I asked.

"They're nice."

"No. I mean, what do you think Anbu meant by the contract being in the cloud?"

"Did he draw the star?"

"No, I did."

Conner stared at the picture for a bit. "Only one cloud I can think of."

He pulled out his laptop and began typing. "Anbu and I talked about cloud storage that morning. I asked why the hospital guy couldn't just put his video here." He turned his computer screen to me. On it was a cloud storage site called *Anvil*.

"Best cloud ever," he said. "Anbu used it, but not from work. Hospital firewall."

"Can you get into his account?"

"Probably. Username is easy. Don't know about the password."

In the username box, Conner typed in Anbu's email

address. Most people used that, he said. We tried several potential passwords, including the one that gave us access to his drive at the hospital. Nothing was working.

I stared at the picture that Anbu had drawn. There was a sun in the corner, opposite the batibat.

"Save the rays!" I said.

Conner jumped.

"The last thing Anbu said to me." I felt like I'd struck gold.

Conner typed it in, but nothing happened. He tried several different formats, every logical combination of caps, numbers, spacing. Still nothing. My heart sank. Even though it had nothing to do with the picture, I suggested that he try *'say a raise'*. Several versions of that also resulted in nothing. He started playing around with the word *'batibat'*, but we just kept getting the same error message that the password was incorrect.

An hour later, we were still sitting in front of the computer. Conner hadn't touched a key for at least half an hour. He just sat there silently, with his index finger on St. Therese's face, and his middle finger spinning her around and around. I got up to get a coffee for me and another glass of water for him. When I came back, he was sitting silently, staring at the prayer card.

"What did you say her name was?" he asked.

I told him. He started mumbling to himself. He flipped the card over and looked at a brief biography of her.

"Lisieux. She's from France," he said.

"Guess so." I sighed and sat down.

He pulled up another web page and typed in

'pronunciation of Therese'. In a North American accent, the computer said, "*Teresa*". He scrolled down and clicked on *French*. The woman's sultry voice said, "Therese", which sounded like 'tah-rays'.

"Oh my God!" I jumped off my chair and hopped around. "St. Therese! That's what he said!"

Conner was smiling. He typed in *sttherese*, *st.therese*, *StTherese*, *St.therese*, and *st. Therese*. All we got in response was *incorrect password*. He sat and thought, then typed in *St. Therese*. The screen went white. A small blue circle appeared in the middle. It spun for what seemed like an eternity until, finally, a page with several folders opened.

We were in.

Underneath all the folders, was the file, *HDL82much.mov*. Schlemmer didn't move it, Anbu did. He must've finally had success using the SecureID fob the morning of the car crash to get the video off the hospital system and transfer it to the cloud.

My hands started shaking. "Play it!"

Conner clicked the mouse and the movie loaded. There, in black and white, was my lab door shot from above. In the top left hand corner of the screen was a time stamp. It was marked with a date that I couldn't mistake – the night before Anbu discovered that the lab rats were dead. The time was 11 pm. After a couple of seconds of recording, a woman dressed in a lab coat approached the door, looked around, and punched in a code to let herself in. Her hair looked thick and blonde. Too thick. Like a wig. The door closed behind her. A few seconds went by and then the video jumped forward 15 minutes. It showed the same woman leaving.

She glanced up briefly to the ceiling, through a pair of square glasses, and hurried away. She had nothing in her hands going in and she had nothing coming out.

"Rewind to her face," I said.

The video frames were blurred. Still, Conner zoomed in and out on her face, frame by frame, studying each one carefully.

"It's her," he said.

"Who?"

"The Tim Hortons lady."

"Luke's resident?" I put my face up to the screen, but it certainly didn't look like any of Luke's students. No, she looked older than a student.

Conner advanced through several frames of her face. There was something about her expression that was familiar.

"Are you sure she's the person from Tim Hortons?"

"Pretty sure."

After studying every frame of her face, and not coming up with anything, we closed the video to look through Anbu's other files. The first folder was labeled 'Rubee'. It was filled with pictures of her and Emily. Underneath that folder was another called 'Contract'. I didn't have to tell Conner to open it. He was ahead of me. Inside was one file, a PDF that had been saved there a week before Anbu died. The first page was a scanned bank statement with a hefty starting balance. My heart skipped a beat when I saw the name at the top. Luke Hesuvius. Conner started scrolling through it.

"Wait," I said. There were several transactions. Mostly deposits and withdrawals that looked fairly insignificant.

Except for one.

"Whoa." Conner's eyes got twice as big as they had been all day when he saw the withdrawal for $250,000.00. "What do you think that was for?"

"His car probably."

"Must be nice." Conner scrolled to the next page. Another scanned bank statement, this time from a different bank. There was no name on it, just a numbered company. It showed a deposit for $250,000.00 and, on the next page, a withdrawal for $275,000.00.

"Must've added in a car starter," Conner said.

The final page was a shareholders agreement drafted by *Zirica*, the pharmaceutical company that was running the *Guarafit* trials. I couldn't believe my eyes when I saw who the agreement was with. Lucy Briggs. I had no idea, and Luke had never mentioned it. I could feel my chest start to fill with anger. How was it that she got her paws into everything?

I pushed myself away from the table, went to the bathroom and splashed water on my face. I tried to make sense of it all. What would Anbu have been doing with Luke's bank statements? And how did he find out about the shareholders agreement?

Back at the table, Conner was about two inches away from the screen. "That's her," he said when he saw me.

I went around the table to see what he was looking at. On the screen was an image of Lucy Briggs, with longer cinnamon hair.

"She's the Tim Hortons lady."

"Lucy?"

He nodded and flipped back to the movie. "That's

her there, too."

I'd been thrown off by the wig and glasses. When Conner pressed play, I could clearly see that it was her shifty eyes glancing up to the camera. Even through the blur.

I looked at the batibat in the picture that Anbu drew. The cinnamon-haired demon. I knew exactly who she was.

"Oh my God, Conner. Go back to the PDF." I scanned down to the withdrawal out of Luke's account and the deposit into the numbered company. It was done on the same date, long before he bought his car. It was long before Anbu died. It was, in fact, before Anbu even joined the research team. I needed to know if that numbered company was Luke's and there was only one person who could help.

Armstrong invited me in to his office. When I'd called him, he said he was too busy to meet. I insisted that this would change the story on Anbu. With some hesitation, he agreed. In his office, I handed him a USB stick and told him that everything he needed was there. He plugged it in and started by looking at the video of Lucy. I explained to him who she was and the scene that Conner had witnessed in Tim Hortons.

"So, you think she killed the rats? And Anbu figured it out and confronted her."

"Absolutely."

"Why would she kill your rats?"

"Besides her dislike for me? She never could stand that I got the lab at Ninsun and that she had to move to Ontario."

Armstrong opened the scanned bank statements. First Luke's and then the numbered company. He sat back in his chair and stroked his chin with his thumb and forefinger.

"Luke's company?" he asked.

I shrugged. Who else's would it be? "I just don't get why Anbu put it with these other files."

"Him and Luke like each other?"

"Like father and son. Luke took Anbu under his wing. Luke even delivered his eulogy."

Armstrong nodded, but his eyes were unblinking. A hundred and one knots slipped in my stomach.

Chapter 39

ONLY AN ORCHID

Armstrong handed me the orchid. He said it was ready to go. I looked carefully, but all I saw were deep purple flowers on two sprigs that emerged from a healthy set of leaves. Around the base of the greenery was thick moss.

"You okay?" he asked.

I nodded and balanced the orchid in my hands while he wrapped a plastic cover around it. He told me not to worry; it'd be hard to knock any of the components loose.

"Call me as soon as it has been delivered," he said.

"I'll do better than that. I'll be back here to give you a full report."

"We discussed this," he said.

"You may need my help interpreting. Nobody knows Luke like I do. Never mind Lucy."

"She may not even show today, Mack. Don't get your hopes up."

"You said she was booked to fly in this afternoon. She'll be over at Ninsun as soon as humanly possible."

"What is it about this guy?" Armstrong shook his head.

"That would take a while to explain."

"Just go before the flower dies."

When I got to the Ninsun reception desk, there were no patients in the waiting room. Genie looked at me expectantly, as if I was a patient there for an appointment.

"I'm here to see Luke," I said.

"Is he expecting you?"

"No, Genie, he is not expecting me. But this will only take a minute."

"Well, you know how busy he is."

"It's the end of the day. I know he has no patients. I just want to drop this thank you for him."

"I can give it to him."

"I'd rather deliver it."

Genie pursed her lips and spun round to her phone. She spoke quietly into the receiver, but not enough to camouflage my name.

She hung up and spun towards me. "He'll see you for a minute."

"That's so kind of him. Thank you."

There was a mild tremor in my hand as I made my way to his office. By the time I reached his door, my hands were slicked with sweat.

I knocked and waited.

Finally, the door opened.

"Mackenzie," his tone dropped off at the end. "Look at you! You look great."

"Thanks." I forced myself to smile and look him square in the eyes.

"This is unexpected." He avoided my gaze, but didn't budge from the doorway.

"I just wanted to give you this." The plastic covering shook as I handed him the orchid.

"What's this?"

"Open it."

He set it on his desk and pulled the plastic down.

"It's like the one you got me," I said.

He stared. Probably didn't remember.

"I just wanted to thank you, you know, for being there for me. During the hard stuff. And always."

"Not necessary."

"So, how you doing? Good?"

He turned from the desk and stood in front of me. "Really good."

"Any new news?" I lowered my voice. "If you know what I mean."

"Not yet. Soon." He flipped his arm and looked at his watch. "I wish I could talk more now, but I gotta get back to work."

"Oh, of course."

"Thanks for the really nice…flower."

I pictured the electronics below the moss. "You probably don't need to water it very much."

"I certainly won't."

I backed out of his doorway.

"Goodbye, Mackenzie." With a flat hand, he pushed on the door. It closed in my face.

"So?" I bolted into Armstrong's office and set my purse down.

He was staring at a computer monitor. "It's in the garbage."

"That asshole."

"It's a clean can." Armstrong smiled at me. "Don't worry. We've still got audio." He turned up the volume. "He's quite the obnoxious jerk." Armstrong looked at me. "Sorry. I know he was a friend or whatever."

I started babbling about how he was just a friend, and then downgraded it to how he was really just a colleague. Armstrong smiled. I felt completely adolescent.

There was a bang on the audio. Armstrong turned back to the monitor.

The picture transmitted from inside the can started to shake. "Oh you poor thing." It was a woman's voice.

"That's Genie," I said, feeling like I'd made my first substantial contribution.

In her hands, the orchid made a resurrection. She placed it on the shelf behind Luke's desk. "You look good here. He just doesn't realize it. Probably need some water, don'cha baby?"

"Shit," I said.

"Don't worry. She'll have to drown it before we have a problem."

The picture was skewed a bit; the camera must've gotten jarred. Didn't matter, we could still see what we needed to and more, including Genie's long fingernails. Not long after she left, Luke came into his office. He looked at the orchid and shook his head. He leaned out his office door. "Genie," he called.

She showed up soon after. "Yes, boss?"

"Did you do that?" He pointed to the orchid.

"Yes. You need some life in here. And it's just a poor plant. Who cares if she brought it?"

He laughed and asked Genie if she was leaving for the evening. After she confirmed, he asked her to make sure the doors were locked and told her to do something nice for herself. No after-hours work. She giggled and was gone. Luke closed his door and flipped his middle finger at the orchid.

"Think he's on to us?" I asked.

"No. He's just an idiot."

Luke checked his watch and sat in front of his computer. He turned on a song by Sister Sledge. It was so loud that Armstrong turned down the volume on our end.

Halfway through '*He's the Greatest Dancer*', Luke's phone rang. After a moment, he said, "The coast is clear," followed by some suggestive talk about being ready. He hung up, checked his hair in the mirror behind his door and sprayed himself with cologne that he kept in his filing cabinet. I could smell it.

His phone rang again. "Be right there." He left his office. A couple of minutes later he returned. Lucy followed him in. He closed the door and BAM! Lucy was pinned against it. She was moaning, he was groaning, and clothes were flying.

"I'm sorry," Armstrong said and turned the monitor away from me, "You can leave, but I need to listen. People say the darndest things in the heat of it."

"I'll stay. It won't take long."

Even though their rendezvous made me feel oddly betrayed, I was not going to miss a thing. It took only about two minutes before he pulled away and, as he did, she let out one last ear-piercing scream.

"She lies about a lot of things, doesn't she?" Armstrong said.

Lucy tried to hang onto Luke in an embrace. He pulled away, pulled up his underwear and pants, and straightened himself.

"You know," Lucy said, "at some point, it's gotta be more than a fast fuck in your office."

"Baby, you know that's the way it has to be for now. We've got bigger problems at the moment."

"Schlemmer?"

"No, he has no idea. He's so wrapped up in that stupid grant of his. It's Mack. I've been trying to keep her at bay. Telling her about all this 'investigating' I've been doing."

"Mack won't be a problem for much longer. Leave that to me."

"Don't –,"

Lucy reached across the desk and put her finger on Luke's lips.

"Besides," Lucy said, "the files look great. Her word against ours. She found medical documents in a church? Who's gonna believe that? Everyone thinks she's a lying cheat. God, that was a brilliant move, huh?" Lucy beamed.

"Something's off." Luke pointed over his shoulder with his thumb. "She brought me that flower."

Lucy's face turned stone grey. "Bet that made your day."

Luke mimicked Lucy's words.

She stood up to leave.

"Sit down."

Lucy plopped down into her chair and flicked her hair.

"We've got a bigger problem." Luke tapped his fingers on the desk. "Fennel."

"What about her?"

"She's gonna talk."

"So what? Everyone thinks she's a jilted dog-killing mistress."

"She'll spill everything to get her name cleared about that stupid dog."

"And who's gonna believe her?"

"Her rich daddy's lawyers. That's who."

Lucy waved it off. "You've still got the trump card, don't you? She's not going to want her daddy to see those. She'll never talk."

"Glad to see you're so certain of yourself."

"Why wouldn't I be?"

"Because there's also Steven," Luke said. "She confided in him."

"Call her. Make it clear that she needs to tell him she lied about the whole thing. Or else."

"Already tried. She hung up on me."

Lucy rolled her eyes and shook her head. "Up the ante then. Text her one of those precious photos and tell her the next stop is the internet if she doesn't do it."

Luke leaned back in his chair. His thick blonde hair took up more than half our monitor. It looked like he covered his face with his hands.

"Don't go getting all soft on me," she said.

He sat up. "Patients are dead. Or did you forget that little fact?"

"So what? Don't tell me *you* actually think there's a connection." Lucy blew a puff of air through her nose. "They were sick and going to die anyhow. Just remember *that* the next time you get all sentimental in that nice car of yours." She shook her head. "Four sickos. So what? There were a hundred healthy ones."

Armstrong looked at me. His brow was knitted. "Four?"

I shrugged. That's definitely what she said. But there were only three on Anbu's list.

"You're starting to sound like Mack," Lucy said.

Luke slammed his fist down. "Fuck you!"

Lucy jumped.

He leaned forward. "You know it's not about those patients."

There was a long silence.

"Well," she adjusted her sitting position, "you just need to let that go."

"Just like that, huh?"

"Yeah. Just like that."

"Like I didn't know him." Luke shook his head

in disgust.

"He was driving like an idiot."

"So you say."

"Why is this coming up now? We've been over this."

"Mmmm." Luke started clicking a pen furiously. "Let see. Because he left clues for Mack all over the place?"

"And that's exactly why what happened was, shall we say, a blessing."

"A blessing? Or a convenient outcome? If anyone found out that —"

"If you even think of saying anything," Lucy hissed, "I'll fuck you over so badly."

The pen clicking stopped. "You know, sometimes I hate you."

"Funny, I feel the same."

Luke spun in his chair. The side of his face was slicked with sweat. "I want out."

"Out? Of what?"

"What do you think?"

Lucy huffed. "Now I know you're crazy. No way."

"It's not your money."

"It is on paper." She flashed a big smile. "And I'm not ready to sell."

Luke's eyes narrowed. He got up, went to Lucy, and wrapped his hand around her throat, slowly, like a python. "I said, I want out."

Armstrong gripped the arms of his chair. His knuckles were white. "Shit," he said under his breath.

Lucy slapped Luke's hand away and stood to leave. He came at her. She kneed him in the groin and, while Luke was writhing, she bolted.

Armstrong and I watched, while Luke sat down and caught his breath. He didn't move. After ten minutes, he got up, shut the lights and left.

Armstrong rewound the file to a frame with Lucy's face. Her eyes were rolled back in her head. When he clicked play, she said, *"He was driving like an idiot"*. The wind was knocked out of me again, like when I heard her say it the first time. Armstrong played it over again, and as he did, all I could think of was Conner at the funeral, telling me about the argument he witnessed in Tim Hortons.

Armstrong looked at me, stunned.

"Anbu's voice. On the phone. That morning. He was frantic."

"Stay put." Armstrong loped from his office.

I rewound, hit play, and let her words slither into my ears. I rewound again, just a bit further. *Four sickos*, she said. Four. Jacklyn Gardner, Brenda Deswicki, Agnes Bantle. Who else?

Armstrong burst back into his office with a file. He sat down and flung it open. Pictures of Anbu's car in the ditch fanned across his desk. "After I was at your house, the day your dog nearly mauled me, I got to thinking about what you said. I came back here and pulled photos from the accident." He was out of breath, but still didn't wait for me to answer. "Something about them always bothered me. I knew he drove a rattle trap, but there was something weird about…" He focused on one picture. His eyes darted back and forth across it. He flopped back in his chair and exhaled.

"What?" I said.

"Here's what." He pointed to a scrape by the front bumper. Rust bubbled out from it.

What did that have to do with anything?

"You don't see it do you?" he asked.

I shook my head.

He moved his finger to the tail end of the same side of the car. There was another scrape. It was fresh. Not a speck of rust.

He asked me if I might know what kind of car she drove. I reminded him that she didn't even live in Edmonton. Likely rented vehicles when she came to town. He jotted down a note: *rental places re: accident.*

When I saw the word accident, a switch flipped. "Number four."

"What?"

"The fourth patient. Angela Ashbury. Luke told me she died in a car accident."

Armstrong pulled up a program on his computer. After scrolling through multiple files, he shook his head no. "Frankly, my dear, I think he lied to you."

Chapter 40

KERALA

I boarded the flight to India with excitement in my heart. I thought about the times that Anbu would've boarded the very same flight and how he must've felt about leaving behind the cold and snow for the coconut trees and backwaters of Kerala. He always talked about those trips back home and how they grounded him. You could see it in his eyes and in the way his smile lit the room when he talked about it. Then again, he said he loved Canada. It had become his home, and he felt that the people around him were his brothers and sisters. Respectable people, he said. How disappointed he must've been to learn differently. And Rubee. Her dream of returning home to Kerala came at a high price. I knew my visit would stir memories, but Anbu deserved redemption. Rubee had written to me. She told me how people who used to be friends would not look at her when she passed them on the street. And Anbu's brother, who'd previously held public office for years, lost in the latest round of elections. No one ever spoke of these things as being related to Anbu, but deep in Rubee's heart, she understood.

At the Cochin airport, the taxi driver greeted me politely and suggested that the ride would take a while. When we finally reached Kottayam, I imagined a young Anbu running along the red gravel that lined the skinny roads. Gangly arms and legs, agile and quick. I liked to think of him hopping onto the trunk of a coconut palm and scampering to the top to get its fruit. The car crossed a bridge over the lush backwaters and turned onto an even skinnier street, where we narrowly missed an auto rickshaw and a group of women in saris. Horns were honking everywhere, but the women didn't even flinch. We turned again and entered a residential area that was spotted with both mansions and modest homes painted in pinks, lilacs and orange. Children, dressed in clothes that were just as bright, smiled and waved from their front porch. I waved back. We passed many churches, including one that was decorated with thousands of colored lights. It was the church's inaugural celebration, the driver said. He beamed when he told me that, if I liked the outside of the church, I'd love the inside and that there were many beautiful churches in Kottayam. I told him I'd be sure to visit one. Really, I thought, as a way to connect with Anbu more than anything else. To see where his faith and goodness had been planted.

The driver studied me for a moment through his rear view mirror. Quietly, he asked if he may know what was the purpose of my visit. He said it wasn't often someone with white skin and hair like fire came to their town without an escort.

"I'm here to see Rubee Mathew. I knew her husband, Anbu."

His voice lit with cheer, "Anbu!"

"You knew him?"

"Yes, Madame." He shook his head. "So sad. So very very sad."

I nodded and tried to swallow the constriction in my throat.

"I knew Anbu since the time he was a boy," the driver said. "My own son played with him. Oh, and what a man Anbu's father was. A very good man. Military man." He looked out his side window. "You know, Madame, I do not say this of just anyone, but that man, his father, had a heart of gold." His eyes met mine through the mirror. They were glassy. "He saved my boy."

"In the military?"

He laughed. "Oh no, Madame. My Jayan was just a boy. Anbu's father gave me money for medicine." He shook his head and looked out his side window again. "I wish I could have saved his son. I don't believe a word of what they say about him." He didn't look in the mirror after that, but shook his head repeatedly as he talked about poor Rubee, a widow at such a young age. And Emily. Such a beautiful child.

The taxi came to a stop in front of a small yellow bungalow with two coconut trees, one on each side of the walk; they leaned toward each other. It was the home of Rubee's father, the driver said. She'd been staying there since her return. While I paid him, he told me how nice it was to meet someone from Anbu's life in Canada. How, before everything, they had heard great stories about his research and had even seen a video of a rat jumping through a hoop.

He smiled and said, "We certainly were not surprised to see such a thing."

"Why is that?"

"When he was just a boy, he had a pet weasel. He taught him to run a whole obstacle course. People from all around would come, just to see this. People didn't believe it was possible to tame a weasel. And when other people tried, they always got bit. No one could ever figure out his secret."

I knew what it was, but I didn't necessarily understand it, and wasn't sure that if I shared it with the taxi driver, he would understand it either. Anbu had always said that he simply spoke to the animals with his heart. That if you spoke to anything with your heart, it would listen and respond in kind.

"Enjoy Kottayam," the driver said as I exited the car.

I thanked him and ensured him that I would. As I walked towards the house, a child in a bright purple dress appeared in the open doorway. Black curls fell to her shoulders. She squealed and ran back in. A moment later, Rubee appeared with the child in her arms. She smiled widely and shouted welcome while she walked towards me. The sleeves of her salwar fluttered in the breeze. I embraced her and Emily at once.

"It's so good to see you, Bee. You look beautiful."

She smiled, and dropped her eyes. "Thank you. It is good to see you as well."

"And look at Emily. She's just like her mom."

The little girl buried her face in the nape of Rubee's neck.

Rubee led me inside. The front room was painted apple green and was filled with sunlight. Several flowering plants were bent over with the weight of their blossoms.

"It is small," Rubee said.

"It's beautiful."

A man with grey hair came in through the back door and greeted me with a smile. Rubee's father. He set down a level that he'd been using to build a planter in the backyard and insisted on taking my luggage to the guest room. From the kitchen came a woman who was, quite simply, an older version of Rubee. Her mother clasped both my hands and welcomed me into the kitchen for a lime soda. While we drank, she smiled and politely tried not to look at my hair.

Later that evening, after a feast of chicken biriyani and vegetable korma, a small crowd began to gather in their home. There was tea with milk and sugar and lively conversation. Emily ran between the adults, hugging the doll I brought her.

"Come, please," Rubee's father announced. "Come everyone and sit."

One by one, each person sat at a chair around a large wooden table. Rubee's mother and father sat on one side of me and Rubee on the other. Anbu's mother, two sisters and two brothers sat across from me, and his aunts and uncles filled all remaining spaces, except for one. In that chair sat a reporter who was an acquaintance of Anbu's brother.

Rubee's father continued. "Our honored guest, Dr. Mackenzie, has come to deliver news about our Anbu. We thank her and wish for her to begin."

The only sound in the room came from Emily, who was squealing while she ran around a plant in the living room.

Their eyes felt heavy upon me, and I didn't want to keep them waiting any longer. "First, may I say how nice it is to meet the people who loved Anbu and to see the city where he grew up. He was one of the most honorable men I have ever met. And he loved you all. Especially you, Bee."

Rubee's eyes sparkled with tears.

I took a deep breath and continued. "Anbu was the best associate I ever had in my lab. He treated the animals with respect, and they loved him back. We passed all our audits with flying colors because of the good work he did."

All heads nodded in agreement.

"He didn't deserve what happened to him."

They all nodded again. The reporter's eyes were intent on me.

I continued. "You probably all saw the newspapers after Anbu's death. I want you to see this now."

I asked Rubee to pass me my bag. I pulled out a newspaper clipping and spread it open in front of Rubee. In bold letters, the title of the article was 'Real rats exposed: Guarafit trial shut down in wake of patient deaths'. It was written by Diedre Noshan. Rubee pulled the paper close and focused on the picture in the middle of the page. It was of Anbu, Rubee and Emily posing together at a work picnic. I'd given Diedre my story in exchange for her agreeing to print the picture and a caption that I provided.

"What does it say?" Anbu's sister asked.

Rubee cleared her throat. "Anbu Mathew, pictured here with wife Rubee and daughter Emily, was cleared of all wrong-doing."

Rubee put her hand over her mouth and raised her eyes to me. The others around the table leaned in to see the picture. While they were commenting how wonderful this was and passing around the paper, Rubee put her hand on my shoulder and whispered thank you.

When everyone quieted, Anbu's brother asked how this all came about.

The reporter scribbled notes, while I explained how Anbu started to see problems with the patients and that he confronted Luke about it.

I stopped until the reporter's pen stopped. When he looked up and smiled, I continued. "Dr. Hesuvius – I'll just call him Luke – told Anbu to be quiet. But, as you know, that's not the kind of person Anbu was. He started collecting more information and snooping around. He figured out that Luke had invested a lot of money in in the pharmaceutical company that was running the drug trial."

"Anbu never told me what was going on," Rubee said. "But he did say near the end that Luke was not necessarily a good man."

"He was right. But none of us knew it."

Once I explained, it wasn't hard for them to see the conflict of interest that existed with Luke having a stake in *Zirica*. Because of the way he set it up through Lucy, under a numbered company, he never had to disclose it to the patients or the university.

"People were losing weight. The word got out. And Luke and Lucy were set to get very wealthy. On top of that, *Zirica* was paying Luke a consultant fee for every patient he enrolled. So, when Anbu went to Luke about the patients who were having problems, he poked a tiger."

I explained how Anbu got blamed for the rat deaths, like Lucy had schemed, simply to get him off the project. But he kept digging day and night to clear his name before the meeting with the animal ethics board. Luke must've sensed it and made sure that Anbu wouldn't be able to attend the meeting that morning. And he certainly found more than Luke and Lucy expected. None of us figured out how he came across the monetary arrangement between them. It didn't matter, though. What was important was that he did and that he was smart enough to leave clues behind for me to solve.

"That is just like him," Anbu's mother said. "He loved solving games when he was a boy. He would sit for hours, when he was only six years old, trying to undo little metal puzzles."

His sister smiled. "He was a weird boy."

They all laughed.

I did, too, and then said, "He still played with them in my lab, when he was trying to figure out something else. He said that there was no greater pleasure than to disentangle something without force."

"How did he figure out it was Lucy who killed the rats?" Rubee asked.

I told them about the video and how Anbu had waved his phone in front of Lucy the morning in Tim Hortons. "She followed him onto the highway," I said.

"Did she run him off the road?" the reporter asked.

Anbu's mother gasped.

"The police are still investigating. They found the rental car she was driving, but there was no damage when she returned it."

"Someone else could have fixed it," the reporter said.

"Yes. They're looking into that. Especially since the Ontario police found Anbu's phone in her apartment after she was arrested. That puts her at the crime scene."

"Did you actually see the video?" the reporter asked.

"Yes, Anbu had stored some documents in his cloud for me to see. We think he uploaded them and then tried to tell me just before the accident."

Anbu's mother started weeping. "He knew he was going to die."

"He was very scared," I said. "But he was so smart." I touched her hand. "He knew enough to leave clues in safe places for me. And Conner also helped."

"Who was Conner?" the reporter asked.

Rubee explained that Conner worked with Anbu at the *Superstore*. "Anbu made only enough money to rent a basement room, when he first arrived in Edmonton. You cannot imagine, but it gets so cold." Rubee rubbed her arms. "He was sleeping on the cement floor covered only with newspaper."

"My boy?" Anbu's mother asked.

Rubee reached across the table and patted her mother-in-law's hand. "He did not want to worry you, Amma."

After a moment, Rubee smiled and looked at the reporter. "Anbu had been laying on that floor when he got bit by something. The bite stung and the skin around it seemed to be swelling. He didn't know Conner very well, but he needed to talk to someone. Poor Anbu. He didn't know what had bitten him. He thought it might be poisonous and that he might die. When he described the creature to Conner, he found out it was only a centipede."

Anbu's siblings laughed. Rubee giggled as well and explained how, after Conner heard the story, he went to help Anbu exterminate. That's when he saw his living quarters. Without saying a word, Conner and his brother, who owned a furniture store, showed up the next day with a bed and quilt and pots and pans.

All the while Rubee spoke, the reporter was frowning. He looked at me. "They also came after you, Miss Mackenzie?"

It took me a moment to realize he was not talking about centipedes. I explained how, like Anbu, I started asking too many questions. I also told them of the situation with Fennel and more rat killings. Turned out that Lucy was wearing evening gloves that matched her dress at the gala for a good reason.

"They were trying to ruin me," I said.

"And did they?" the reporter asked.

"Nearly." I explained how I could have my position back, if I wanted it, but that the university had not made any formal announcement about me or Anbu. They'd had enough bad press and were trying to keep the story about Luke as quiet as possible. My redemption was the story on the website *Retraction Watch*. They presented the facts so thoroughly that there was no doubt about my innocence.

"The best part," I said, "is that *Zirica* is essentially worthless."

The room broke out into applause and jubilance.

We sat in our circle the rest of the evening sharing stories about Anbu, of his quirky sense of humor, his deep faith in God, and his love for animals. Rubee pulled out pictures of him with his pet weasel and its obstacle course. Anbu had the same smile on his face as when he was in the lab with Huey, Dewey and Luey. Even in death, he filled a room with warmth and grace. When I turned into bed that evening, I knew he could finally rest in peace.

The next morning I woke to the sound of birds in the mango tree outside my window and the smell of coffee. When I made my way to the kitchen, Rubee was in front of the stove. She was making breakfast, she said, like they used to have in Canada. Her mother had taken Emily to play with her cousins, and her father was at work. She served me fried eggs with toast, and sat across from me with the same on her plate.

She smiled and quietly said, "Doctor Mackenzie, is it true about your dog?"

I wondered how she might have heard about Diesel. Then again, there had been so many stories flying around Edmonton. Any one of her and Bu's associates could've heard about it and passed it along.

"Yes, Bee. Unfortunately it is."

"And was it that Fennel?"

"Yes, Lucy ordered Fennel to hurt my dog as a warning to me. But, I've learned that nothing is as simple as it seems."

"Oh?"

I looked at Bee's innocent eyes. I wasn't sure she'd understand how Luke got compromising pictures of Fennel. "Lucy threatened to send something to Fennel's father that would not be good to see."

"Oh."

"Fennel couldn't go through with hurting Diesel. Not completely, anyhow. She told the police she kept the scarf lose enough so he could breathe."

"How did she get in?"

"Dog sitting. She copied a key for a guest she had invited to stay with her for the weekend." I didn't think Bee needed to know it was Luke and that the pictures were taken on my bed.

A bright yellow finch landed on the window sill. It was a perfect opportunity to change the subject. Bee and I spent the rest of our breakfast talking about the different kinds of birds in Kerala. After clearing the dishes, Bee insisted that there was a place she needed to show me. It was very special to Bu, she said.

We hopped onto her scooter and wound around several roads lined with fruit stands and small shops. We passed a bus only to have a car and another scooter come straight for us. I held my breath and squeezed shut my eyes while everyone honked. Somehow, miraculously, we came out on the other side. We climbed a hill and, suddenly, Rubee turned and shouted, "There it is!"

When she pointed to the church, the scooter wobbled. She pulled up the drive and parked in front of an arch.

"This is Vimalagiri," she said. "We married here."

Outside, the spires soared up to the sky, and inside, the pointed ceiling arches seemed to reach as high. We settled into a pew underneath them.

I put my hand on Bee's. "I bet you were a beautiful bride."

She smiled brightly. "Yes, Bu said so." She sighed and looked up. "He was my sun, my moon, and my stars. I miss him."

"Me too."

"Will you go back to work there?"

"Yes. When I return home. I'll be working with Dr. Schlemmer."

"What?"

"He had no idea," I said.

"He was not an investor?"

"No. He was just paid to run the trial."

Somehow, in that church, I felt like I needed to confess how wrongly I'd judged him. In all the mess that followed Luke and Lucy's exposure, it became clear that Schlemmer had nothing to do with it, even though they were all his patients. Luke had changed records and promised to call patients, when he had no intention of ever doing so. Schlemmer was none the wiser. There was no way he could keep track of details on each patient in such a big trial. Of course, after the story about Luke broke, every paper that Schlemmer published was being scrutinized.

The suspicion Schlemmer endured took its toll. He took a leave of absence for two months, which led him to realize that the whole thing was, perhaps, the best thing that could've happened. In order to get through the stress, he started playing the harp again. In one of our first friendly conversations ever, I asked him why he stopped in the first place. That's when he told me about Kathryn, the woman in the picture in his desk. They were to be married after they finished their music degrees. One cold, snowy night, he had missed a phone call from her. She was stranded after her car broke down. He only found the message on his machine the next day. Tragically, they found her frozen body in a ditch, halfway between a payphone and her car. Schlemmer didn't play the harp again after that. Nor did he marry. He buried himself in anything other than music, including medical school and put her out of his mind as best he could. Until he met me. Her doppelgänger. He told me that he wished I would just disappear most days.

"I always wondered about him," Bee said. "I thought Luke was the good one."

"Me too."

"I'm so sorry, Doctor Mackenzie. I know you regarded Luke as a good friend."

"One of my best."

"Such deceit."

I nodded and had to swallow hard before continuing. "You'll be happy to know that Dr. Schlemmer and I are bringing back all the trial patients." I turned to Bee and took both her hands in mine. "If it weren't for Bu, so many more patients could've died."

"He is a hero then."

"Yes, he is."

She knelt down, folded her hands on the pew in front of her, and began to pray. I wanted to give her some space, so I walked to the other side of the church. That's when I saw it. On the right side of the altar, there she stood, in her brown robe with a bouquet of roses in her arms. It was St. Therese. I stopped and caught my breath for a moment.

"No way," I said quietly.

I began to walk towards her, and if someone would've told me to stop and walk no further at that moment, I couldn't have. I went right to her. She was surrounded by fresh roses, whose scent wrapped around me. I felt as if my heart would burst with the joy I was feeling. I had closed the circle and knew, without a doubt, that Anbu was at peace.

In the taxi to the Cochin airport, I imagined Anbu as a young man, driving the same route on his first journey to Edmonton. He had little idea how much his life would change when he stepped off that plane in Canada, deep in February, thinking the ground was covered with white sand. While I watched the coconut trees whiz past my window, I felt lucky to be returning to Steven and Diesel. Steven turned out to be my hero. Even though he said he wasn't going to, he kept working to gain Fennel's confidence until she spilled everything, including the story of her tryst with Luke and mistake of letting him take X-rated photos of her in our home. Steven convinced Fennel to go to Corporal Armstrong and to tell him everything she knew about Luke and Lucy. In return, Steven promised that we would not press charges against her for assault on Diesel.

I looked over to the seat beside me and the bag that Rubee had passed through the taxi window. Plantains to keep me from getting hungry, she had said. I peeked inside. Underneath the fruit, wrapped in gold foil, was a gift. I pulled it out and opened it. Inside was a blue leather bound book with its title in gold. *A Course in Miracles*. On the inside cover was a familiar signature scrolled in blue ink. Anbu Mathew. A small piece of paper fluttered out. On it was a note.

> *Dear Doctor Mackenzie,*
>
> *You and my dear Anbu received many lessons in deception. May this book restore your faith in goodness and miracles, as you have restored mine.*
>
> *Lovingly,*
> *Rubee*

Afterword:

A Course in Deception beautifully details, through a provocative story, the challenges of academic life when greed supersedes the scientific process and deception settles in. While the plot is set on a university campus, the revelation of facts relates to us all. *A Course in Deception* is built on symbols and actions that have very different meanings on a deeper level. This is similar to stories told through the ancient art of Kathakali – a form of classical dance that originated in Kerala, South India, where the loveable Anbu Mathew was born. Kathakali performers, robed in elaborate costumes, enact myths and legends from ancient Sanskrit literature. Perhaps the most striking thing about Kathakali is the performers' colorful make-up, which symbolizes the three *gunas* or categories of personal qualities – *sattva* (goodness), *rajas* (ambition), and *tamas* (darkness). The different combinations of green, red, and black in the painted-on masks help to tell the stories of deeply complex characters. Kathakali performers use hand gestures called mudras to express dialogue, and facial expressions to tell the emotional content of the story. Every step that a dancer takes is towards a purpose, but how truthful is it? Sometimes, spectators view the performance without fully understanding the deception in disguise. Only when the audience remains patient and watches the whole performance, do they understand the total deception.

At the beginning of *A Course in Deception*, we meet Anbu, a man with *sattva* nature. Anbu moved to Canada from Kerala, India when he was only eighteen. His dream was to pursue an education in North America, find a good job, marry a nice wife and raise a happy family. Indeed, Anbu turned into a hard-working, devoted husband and new father who found his dream job working as a research associate in a university laboratory. Unbeknownst to him, however, there were researchers in the academic world around him who wore the dark mask of the *tamas* guna. These researchers were driven by greed and viciousness that led to Anbu's demise, as well as to that of patients who were entrusted to their care. Not everyone in Anbu's world embodied the *tamas* guna and it is only at the conclusion of the story that we come to this appreciation.

For many readers, association of the dark *tamas* guna with science will seem to be a paradox. Society has long viewed the scientific world as a place that systematically reveals the truths about life through rigor, precision, virtue and honesty – all those things associated with the *sattva* guna. There is a steadfast belief that science equals truth despite the fact that it is completed by people with frailties – people who may have a disproportionate amount of the characteristics of the *rajas* and *tamas* gunas, and who may be driven by *ego*. Now, when people hear the word ego, they often think of someone who is boastful or conceited. However, an ego also can be understood or explained by the fear of showing vulnerability, which would mean losing the egotistical mask.

So what can fuel the ego in the world of research? Scientists are being cultured to believe that they must publish or perish. In order to generate the number of publications that will be seen as respectable by their peers, researchers need to run productive laboratories. This isn't as easy as it may seem. A successful laboratory requires funding, often in the form of government grants. But these grants are hard to attain. Researchers not only need a good scientific plan, but also need to show that they have been productive. How do they do this? By proof of previous funding, publications, and presentations, especially keynotes. Thus, the race to publish, and not perish, can become a vicious cycle. If any link in that cycle gets broken, there is potential for career damage. When personal financial benefits become part of the business of science, the situation gets even more complicated. It can become the perfect breeding ground for aspects of the ego, such as competition and selfishness, to emerge.

Professional rivalry and greed within academia can become motivations for the weak to abandon the pledge *Primum non nocere – First, do no harm*. The drive for fame and fortune in the scientific world has been brought to light more recently through media such as the website

Retraction Watch. There, it is not uncommon to find reports of academic misconduct and research fraud tied to researchers who were driven to be the first to report ground-breaking research, even though it was false, or who were fabricating findings and publications to keep their funding. While the majority of science *is* driven by those with virtue and other characteristics of the *sattva* nature, unfortunately, not all scientists are upright.

A Course in Deception weaves a tapestry of characters and events on a journey through academia, from illusion to redemption. *Magna est veritas et praevalet — Great is truth, and mighty above all things* (1 Esdras 4:41).

Joviyah

Acknowledgements:

There are innumerable friends and family members who were instrumental in my writing journey. Some with writing advice and others who simply lent an ear and didn't give up asking how the book was coming along. Like my father, Chris, who never let a visit pass, even after seven years, without inquiring about the book. Thanks, Dad. I love you.

When I stepped out of academic writing to begin this story, I felt a sense of liberation. Along with that excitement, however, there was also a sense of apprehension and unease. The creative writing world was unfamiliar and filled with uncertainty. During that time, the encouragement I received from early (and friendly) readers of my work was instrumental in continuing the writing journey. There are several special people who were there from the start, including Michelle Andrade, Joan Rieger, Charlene Shinkewski, Lisa Cameron, Carol Boliek, Tracy Heron Beck and Sue Chanyi. Your kind advice, words of encouragement, and support in those early days, and all along the way, have meant more to me than any of you can imagine. I'm filled with gratitude for your love and friendship.

As I undertook my more 'formal' creative writing education, there were some notable writing groups and experiences for which I am grateful. First, the Alberta Branch of the Canadian Authors Association welcomed me with open arms. They were instrumental in providing great writing workshops and connecting me with other writers and opportunities that would be vital in my journey. Through them, I was introduced to my Edmonton writing group where early ideas for this novel were formed and characters were shaped. I'd like to thank the authors in that group, including Dennis Lee, Anton Capri, Michael Dean, Sandra Konrad, Juanita Krause, Diane Wishart, Jeananne Kirwin and Christine Forth. Thank you, also, to Jeanne Wood, whom I met through that group, for your thoughtful commentary on the manuscript over many coffees and teas.

I was fortunate enough to attend some wonderful writing retreats, including Banff's Centre for the Arts Writing with Style and the Sage Hill Summer Program. In these retreats, I had the privilege of working with such notable authors as Lisa Moore, Helen Humphreys and Lawrence Hill. Lisa – thank you for encouraging me to persevere in those early days. Helen – your reading of my whole manuscript (when I was only expecting feedback on one chapter) was like an early Christmas present. Lawrence – your honest, detailed and kind feedback changed the landscape of the story and made it better. At those retreats, I also had the good fortune of meeting two other writers whom

I'm grateful for. I'd like to thank Michelle Read from British Columbia for her feedback on an early draft of this manuscript after we met at the Banff retreat, and Ruth Asher, a kindred spirit from Sage Hill, for her views on Fennel and for her friendship in writing and life with dogs.

As this manuscript neared the finish line, my academic career and creative writing endeavors came together. This was made possible through Dr. Paul Hagler, a mentor, colleague and friend from the University of Alberta. Thank you for your supreme editing skills of the final manuscript and the time you took to educate me about Mustangs. I am grateful for your friendship over the years.

Other friends who were always there to provide encouragement and to ask when they might *finally* get a copy of the book included John Wolfaardt, Gabriela Constantinescu, Raj Casey, Al Black, Wade Armstrong, Brian Maraj, Tammy Hopper, Rosa Scarsellone, Bill Mahon, and Sandra Demchuk. Thank you for your friendship and patience. Thank you, as well, to the Floden family for their early encouragement and support.

Much gratitude also to my family – brothers and sisters, their spouses, and my nieces and nephews – whose support was always there during the writing process, as it has been throughout my life.

Max B. Telzerow – thanks for the awesome author pic!

Max (the one with four legs) – thank you for always being by my side and my feet. You were the best company a writer could ask for.

Finally, my sincerest thanks to Toviyah John, who I know is grateful to his mentors, Dr. Colin Wilkinson and Dr. Bala Rao. Toviyah, you inspired the beginning and the end, and brought another level to the story throughout. Without you, there would be no Anbu. I appreciate all the times that you went out of your way to help with this project. Thank you for keeping me and this story foremost in your thoughts, for always being there to listen, always having my back, and always giving good counsel. You have been my rock.